One Wonderful Night

Louis Tracy

FRANCIS X. BUSHMAN AS JOHN D. CURTIS.
BEVERLY BAYNE AS LADY HERMIONE.

ONE WONDERFUL NIGHT

A ROMANCE OF NEW YORK

BY

LOUIS TRACY

AUTHOR OF
MIRABEL'S ISLAND, THE WINGS OF THE MORNING, ETC.

1912

A FOREWORD

Moving picture enthusiasts who reveled in the romantic mysteries that tangled the plot of ONE WONDERFUL NIGHT will find even more pleasure in reading this fascinating story.

"THE LADIES' WORLD" contest—the greatest in the history of motion pictures—has just come to a close. Under the auspices of the "Ladies' World" with its million circulation monthly, moving picture lovers all over the United States have been voting for the actor to impersonate the heroic part of John Delancy Curtis in the photo-play of ONE WONDERFUL NIGHT—probably the most interesting and absorbing presentation ever made on the screen.

Five million, four hundred and forty-thousand, seven-hundred and sixty votes were cast. Francis Bushman won the prize. With a vote of 1,806,630 he was chosen the typical American hero. In the Essanay Company's elaborate production of ONE WONDERFUL NIGHT, Mr. Bushman is supported by a strong cast, including beautiful Beverly Bayne as Lady Hermione.

Those who have witnessed the photo-play production will find the book even more intensely interesting. The hero, John Delancy Curtis, drops in from Pekin, China, for a brief rest from strenuous engineering work, and on his first night in New York finds a marriage license in the pocket of a murdered man's coat, rushes off in a taxi to the address of the woman named therein, marries her, punches a frantic rival on the nose, flouts her father (an English baronet), takes the fair one to a hotel, holds a banquet at which the Chief of Police of New York is an honored guest, and sits down to gaze contentedly into the future of bliss that a half a million a year will bring.

We bespeak for the reader pleasure, entertainment and diversion in this absorbing and unusual story.

CONTENTS

ILLUSTRATIONS

CHAPTER I

DUSK

"There, sonny—behold the city of your dreams! Good old New York, as per schedule.... Gee! Ain't she great?"

The slim, self-possessed youth of twenty hardly seemed to expect an answer; but the man addressed in this pert manner, though the senior of the pair by six years, felt that the emotion throbbing in his heart must be allowed to bubble forth lest he became hysterical.

"Old New York, do you call it?" he asked quietly. The tense restraint in his voice would perhaps have betrayed his mood to a more delicately tuned ear than his companion's, but young Howard Devar, heir of the Devar millions—son of "Vancouver" Devar, the Devar who fed multitudes on canned salmon, and was suspected of having cornered wheat at least once, thus woefully misapplying the parable of the loaves and fishes—had the wit to appreciate the significance of the question, deaf as he was to its note of longing, of adulation, of vibrant sentiment.

"*Coelum non animum mutat*, which, in good American, means that it is the same old city on the level, and only changes its sky-line," he chortled. "Bet you a five-spot to a nickel I'll walk blindfolded along Twenty-third Street from the Hoboken Ferry any time of the day, and take the correct turn into Broadway, bar being run over by a taxi or street-car at the crossings."

"I'll take the same odds and do that myself. How could any normal human being miss the rattle of the Sixth Avenue Elevated?"

Devar's forehead wrinkled with surprise.

"Hello, there! Hold on! How often have you told me that you had never seen New York since you were a baby?" he cried.

"Nor have I. Ten years ago, almost to a day, I sailed from Boston to Europe with my people, and I had never revisited New York after leaving it in infancy, though both my father and mother hailed from the Bronx."

"There's a cog missing somewhere, or my mental gear-box is out of shape."

"Not a bit of it. One may learn heaps of things from maps and books."

"Start right in, then, and take an honors course, for behold in me a map and a book and a high-grade society index for the whole blessed little island of Manhattan."

"Thank you. What is that slender, column-like structure to the left of the Singer Building?"

Devar gazed hard at the graceful tower indicated by his friend; then he laughed.

"Oh, you're uncanny, that's what you are," he said. "You've lived so long in the East that you've imbibed its tricks of occultism and necromancy. I suppose you have discovered in some way that that mushroom has sprung up since the old man sent me to Heidelberg?"

"I guessed it, I admit. It does not figure among the down-town sky-scrapers in the latest drawing available in London."

"And d'ye mean to tell me that you can pick out any of these top-notchers merely by studying a picture?"

"Yes. Probably you could do the same if you, like me, felt yourself a returned exile."

Young Devar awoke at last to the fact that his companion was brimming over with subdued excitement. Whether this arose from the intense nationalism of an expatriated American, or from some more subtle personal cause, he could not determine, but, being young, he was cynical. He looked at the strong, set face, the well-knit, sinewy figure, the purposeful hands gripping the fore rail of the promenade deck; then he growled, with just the least spice of humorous envy:

"Say, Curtis, old man, you ought to have a hell of a good time in New York!"

"At any rate, I shall not suffer from lack of enthusiasm," came the quick retort.

Devar felt the spur, and his restless, bird-like eyes condescended to dwell for a few seconds in silence on the splendid panorama in front. The *Lusitania* had passed through the Narrows before the two young men had strolled along the upper deck of the great steamship to the 'vantage point of a gangway which made a half-circle around the commander's quarters. Already the Statue of Liberty loomed majestically over the port bow, and the wide expanse of the Hudson River was framed by the wooded slopes of Staten Island, the low shores of New Jersey, and the heights of the Palisades. Somewhat to the right rose the imperial outlines of newest New York, that wonderful city which, even in the memory of children, has raised itself hundreds of feet nearer the sky. A thin, blue haze gave glamour to a delightful scene, glowing in the declining rays of a November sun. The gigantic strands of the Brooklyn Bridge showed through it like some aerial path to a fabulous land, while, merging fast in the shadows, other dim specters told of even greater engineering marvels higher up the East River. A fleet of bustling vessels, for the most part ferry-boats and tugs of every possible size and shape, scudded across the spacious waterways, and lent to the picture exactly that semblance of vitality, of energetic purpose, of relentless effort to be up and doing—whether the New Yorker was going home from his office, or his wife was coming into town for dinner and a theater—which one, at least, of the city's uncounted sons had confidently expected to find in it.

So John Delancy Curtis drew a deep breath that sounded almost like a sigh, but a pleasant smile illumined his somewhat stern face as he turned to Devar and said:

"I am giving myself fourteen days' free run of the town before I go West to visit some relatives. They live in Indiana, I believe. Bloomington, Monroe County, is the latest address I possess. Don't forget to ring me up to-morrow. You remember the hotel, the Central, in West 27th Street."

"Oh, forget it!" cried the other vexedly. "Why in the world are you burying yourself in that pre-historic shanty? Man alive, the Holland House is only a block away, and there are 'steen hotels of the right sort strung out along Fifth Avenue, 'way up to Central Park— —"

"It's just a whim," broke in Curtis, who did not feel like explaining at the moment that he was choosing a quiet old inn in a side street because he had been born there! Nevertheless, his words held that ring of decision, of finality in judgment, which invariably forms part of the equipment of men who have lived in wild lands and lorded it over inferior races. Devar was vaguely conscious, and perhaps slightly resentful, of this compelling quality in his new-found crony. Oft-times it had quelled him for an instant during some stubbornly contested argument, though he raged at himself just as often for yielding to it, as if, forsooth, he were one of those patient, animal-like, Chinese coolies of whose courage and endurance Curtis spoke so admiringly. Yet he was drawn to the man, and clung to his friendship.

"Right-o! I s'pose the place owns a telephone," he snickered, and then hurried away to finish packing. Curtis, whose belongings were locked and strapped hours ago, remained on deck, and watched the preparations for bringing the great liner alongside the Cunard pier. When her engines were stopped in mid-stream a number of fussy little tugs began nosing her round to starboard. It seemed a matter of sheer impossibility that these puny creatures should move such a monster; but faith can move mountains, and in half an hour, or less, the tugs had moved the *Lusitania* to her allotted berth.

4

Meanwhile, in each wide arch of the Customs shed, parterres of joyous faces grew momentarily more distinct. It was easy to discern the very instant when one or other eager group on shore recognized the features of relatives and friends on the ship. A frenzied waving of handkerchiefs, small flags, or umbrellas, an occasional wild whoop, a college cry or a rebel yell, would evoke similar demonstrations from the packed lines of onlookers fringing the lower decks. One fact was dominant—to the vast majority of the passengers, this was home.

Suddenly, Curtis found that he was the sole tenant of the open promenade. Everyone on board had hurried to the less exalted levels, the many to hail their loved ones, the few to watch that first unique demonstration of welcome to a new land which New York gives so generously. Somehow, he had never felt himself more alone—not even by night in the solemn plains of Manchuria—and he threw off the feeling, almost with contempt. Was not this city his very own? Had he not a birthright in every stone of it, from pavement to loftiest pinnacle? This was *his* home-coming, too, more real, more literally complete, than in the case of any but the few born New Yorkers who might figure among the two thousand passengers carried by the *Lusitania*.

Insistently claiming his share of recognition, he turned abruptly, and made his way to the third deck. There he met a lady, a young bride, who was returning to the States with her husband after a prolonged tour through Europe. Her pretty face was wrung with emotion, but a second glance revealed that her distress was due to the pleasant pain of happiness.

"Have you seen your father and mother?" he asked sympathetically, knowing that she had looked forward to this great hour with so much longing.

"Y-yes," she sobbed. "They are there—somewhere. B-but, oh dear! I cannot see them now for my tears."

Someone dug a joyful thumb into Curtis's ribs. It was the girl's husband.

"Gee, it's fine to be home again!" he said huskily. "Your leaning towers of Pisa are all right by way of a change, but deal me the Metropolitan for keeps, an' I've just spotted my old dad grinning at me like a Cheshire cat from the middle of a crowd wedged so tight that it would take a panic to squeeze in an extra walking-stick."

So the knowledge was borne in on Curtis that one could feel quite as lonely on C Deck as on A, and, case-hardened wanderer that he was, he badly wanted someone to yell at gleefully among the waiting multitude.

Now the gangways were out, and West folded East in her willing arms. The stolid masses of steamship and Customs shed obliterated the orange and crimson sky still gleaming over the Jersey shore, and pallid electric lights revealed but vaguely the ever-changing groups beyond the gangways.

To an experienced traveler like Curtis all Custom-houses were alike, dingy, nerve-racking, superfluous clogs on free movement. Taking his time, for he had none to embrace or greet with outstretched hand, he strolled quietly off the ship, collected his baggage, which was piled with other people's belongings under a big "C," and nodded to Devar, similarly engaged at "D."

The boy ran to him for an instant.

"I may look you up to-night," he said. "Dad is in Chicago, and won't be here till the morning. You remember we passed the *Switzerland* after breakfast, and she signaled that she was steaming with the port engine only?"

"Yes."

"Well, her trouble was known by wireless, and there is a man on board whom dad has to meet. This chap is important. I am not."

"My dear fellow, don't think of leaving your friends on my account this evening," and Curtis, without looking around, showed that he had noticed the befurred elderly lady and two very pretty daughters who were taking Howard Devar under their elegant wings.

"Oh, that's my aunt, and two of my cousins. I have dozens of 'em, dozens of cousins, that is. Anyhow, old sport, don't wait in after 7.30; just leave word where you may be about eleven."

No further protest by Curtis was possible, because Devar's present behavior was of the whirlwind order. He seemed to own as many trunks as cousins, and a lantern-jawed Customs official was gloating over them already. Perhaps Curtis felt a faint whiff of surprise that his young friend had not introduced him to his relatives, but it vanished instantly. Steamer acquaintance is a nebulous thing at the best; in that respect, the land is more unstable than the sea.

At last, the stranger in his own country was consigned to a porter, his two steamer trunks, a kit-bag, a suit-case, and a bundle of worn golf clubs were placed on a taxi, and a breath of clean, cold air blew in on his face as the vehicle hurried along West Street, that broad and exceedingly useful thoroughfare which New York has finally wrested from its waterside slums.

The chief city of America is fortunate in the fact that a noble harbor presents her in full regalia to the voyager from Europe. That favorable first impression, unattainable by the majority of the world's capitals, is never lost, and now it enabled Curtis to disregard the garish ugliness of the avenues and streets glimpsed during a quick run to the center of the town. For one thing, he realized how the mere propinquity of docks and wharves infects entire districts with the happy-go-lucky carelessness of Jack ashore; for another, he knew what was coming.

Or he fancied that he knew, a state of mind which, particularly in New York, produces brain storms. His first shock came when the taxi drew up in front of a narrow-fronted, exceedingly tall building, equipped with revolving doors, while a hall-porter, dressed like an archduke, peered through the window and inquired severely:

"Have you reserved a room, sir?"

Yes, this was the Central Hotel, rebuilt, gone skyward, in full cry after its more pretentious *à la carte* neighbors, and the hall-porter was pained by the mere suspicion that the fact was not accepted of all the world of travel.

Although the newcomer confessed that he had not made any reservation of rooms, the Archduke graciously permitted him to alight—indeed, quelled an incipient rebellion on Curtis's part by ordering a couple of negroes to disappear with most of the baggage. So Curtis announced meekly to a super-clerk that he wanted a room with a bathroom, and was allowed to register. As in a dream, he signed "John D. Curtis, Pekin," and was promptly annoyed at finding what he had written, because, being a citizen of New York, he had meant to claim the distinction, and ignore his long years in Cathay.

"You'll find 605 a comfortable, quiet room, Mr. Curtis," said the clerk. "Going to make a long stay, may I ask?"

"A few days—perhaps a fortnight. I cannot say offhand."

"Well, sir, I can't fix you better than in 605."

From some points of view, the clerk had never uttered a truer word. It was wholly impossible that he or Curtis should guess how an apparently empty and really excellent apartment in the Central Hotel should be full to the ceiling that evening with that dynamite in human affairs called chance. If the slightest inkling of the forthcoming explosion could have been vouchsafed to both men, there is no telling what Curtis might have done, for he was a true adventurer, of the D'Artagnan genus, but the clerk would certainly have used all his persuasiveness to induce the guest to occupy some other part of the house. In later periods of unruffled calm, he was wont to date from that moment the genesis of gray hairs among his once raven-hued locks.

But chance, like dynamite, not only gives no warning of its explosive properties but resembles that agent of disruption in following a curiously wayward path. Curtis was piloted into an elevator by an affable negro, was conducted to 605, which, of course, lay on the sixth floor, and was plunged forthwith into the prosaic business of consigning a good deal of soiled linen to the laundry.

The room was insufferably hot, so he directed the negro attendant to shut off the radiator, and himself threw open the window. Glancing out, he discovered that he was located in a corner which commanded a distant glimpse of Broadway. Directly before his eyes, in the topmost story of a comparatively low building, a lady who had forgotten to draw the blinds of her flat was apparently indulging in calisthenic exercises, so Curtis, being a modest man, drew the blind in his own room, and busied himself with a partial unpacking of his baggage. The door faced the bed, at a distance of some six feet. A wardrobe occupied the recess, and the negro, while unstrapping a steel trunk at the foot of the bed, balanced the bag of golf clubs against the front of the wardrobe—an action simple enough in itself, but comparable in its after effects to the setting of a clock attached to a bomb.

Soon afterwards, Curtis dismissed the man, and noticed casually that the opening of the door caused a pleasant draught of cool air. He wrote a few letters, dressed, electing for a Tuxedo and black tie, filled a cigar-case, donned a green Homburg hat, threw an overcoat over his left arm, picked up the letters, extinguished the lights, and went out. Again there came that rush of air from the window, and, just as the lock snapped, a crash from the interior announced the falling of the golf clubs, probably owing to a swaying of the wardrobe door. Simultaneously, Curtis realized that he had left the key on the dressing-table.

It was hardly worth while searching the floor for a chamber-maid: he decided to inform the civil-spoken clerk, and have the key brought to the office, at which sapient resolve Puck, who was surely abroad in New York that night, must have chuckled delightedly. Unhappily, there were other spirits brooding in the city, spirits before whose deathly scowls the prime mischief-maker would have fled in terror, and Curtis, all unwitting, brushed against one of them in the hall. His only acquaintance, the clerk, was momentarily absent, so he turned to a bookstall and cigar counter, and bought some stamps. A man who had been seated in a sort of café, which the news-stand and a flower-stall partially screened from the main hall, rose hurriedly when he saw Curtis, and purchased a cigar. In doing so, he touched the young man's shoulder, and said: "Pardon!"

Curtis turned, and looked into the singularly unprepossessing face of a swarthy foreigner, a powerfully-built, ungainly person of about his own age.

"That's all right," said he, licking a stamp.

"I jostled you by accident, monsieur," said the other, in correct French, though with a quaint accent which Curtis, himself no mean linguist, put down to a Polish or Czech nationality.

"*Ca ne fait rien,*" he replied civilly, and the stamping of the letters being completed, he took them to the letter-box.

The stranger, who seemed to be rather puzzled, if somewhat reassured, dawdled over the lighting of the cigar, and watched Curtis enter the dining-room. Then he went back to his chair in the café. So much, and no more, did the youth in charge of the counter observe—not a great deal, but it went a long way before midnight.

A clock in the hall showed that the hour was five minutes to seven. Half hoping that Devar might actually put in an appearance a little later, Curtis gave his hat and coat to a negro, and decided to dine in the hotel. Evidently, the place still retained its old-time repute as a family and commercial resort. The family element was in evidence at some of the tables, while, in the case of solitary diners, each man could have been labeled Pittsburg, Chicago, or Philadelphia, almost without error, by those acquainted with the industrial life of the United States.

He ate well, if simply, and treated himself to a small bottle of a noted champagne. At half-past seven, meaning to give Devar ten minutes' grace, he ordered coffee and a glass of green Chartreuse. As a time-killer, there is no liqueur more potent, but, regarded in the light of subsequent occurrences, it would be hard to say exactly how far the cunning monkish decoction helped in determining his wayward actions. Undoubtedly, some fantastic influence carried him beyond those bounds of calm self-possession within which everyone who knew John Delancy Curtis would have expected to find him. His subsequent light-headedness, his placid acceptance of a mad romance as the one thing that was inevitable, his ready yielding to impulse, his no less stubborn refusal to return to the beaten path of common sense—these unlikely traits in a character gifted with the New England dourness of purpose can only be explained, if at all, as arising from some unsuspected hereditary streak of knight-errantry brought into sudden and exotic life by the good wines of France.

Be that as it may, at twenty minutes to eight he paid what he owed, lighted a cigar, donned his hat, and, still carrying the overcoat, was walking to the office to leave word about the key, when his attention was attracted by the peculiar behavior of the man who had pushed against him at the cigar counter.

This person, apparently obeying a signal from another man of his own type who had just emerged from the elevator, hastened from the café, and the two ran to the door. Now, the weather had been mild during the afternoon, and the revolving shutters of the doorway were folded back to allow of the overheated hall being cooled. A porter stood there, and it was ascertained afterwards that, noticing a certain air of flurry and confusion about the foreigners, he asked if they wanted a taxi. They gave no heed, but continued to gaze up and down the street, as though they awaited someone. Equally did they seem to expect, or dread, an apparition from the hotel. It would have been hard to pick out, at that instant, two persons more singularly ill at ease in all New York.

Curtis saw that the clerk, now at his desk, was engaged with a lady, so he strolled to the door, being rather interested in the excited antics of the pair on the sidewalk. He had just passed through the door when an automobile dashed up, and he fancied, though he could not be quite sure in the half-light, that the chauffeur nodded to the waiting men. The porter opened the door of the automobile, and a young man in evening dress, and carrying an overcoat, leaped out. Obviously, he was in a desperate hurry, and Curtis heard him say in French:

"Don't stop the engine, Anatole. I shall be but one moment."

At that instant the two foreigners sprang at him. One, swinging the porter off his feet, seized the newcomer's right arm, and, helped by his comrade, endeavored to force him back into the vehicle. The effort failed, however, so the second desperado drew a knife and plunged it deliberately into the unfortunate man's neck. It was a fearsome stroke, intended both to silence and to kill, and, with a gurgling cry, its victim collapsed in the grip of his assailants.

Curtis, though almost stupefied by the suddenness of the crime, did not hesitate a second when he caught the venomous gleam of the knife. Throwing aside his coat, he rushed forward, but he had to cross the whole width of the pavement, and the murderers, realizing that the capture of one or both was imminent, thrust the inert body in his way. The chauffeur, who must have seen all that happened, had already started the car, the two men scrambled into it, and all that Curtis could do was to run after it and shout frantically to the driver of a taxi coming in the opposite direction to turn his vehicle and block the roadway.

The man understood, but was naturally slow to risk a sharp collision merely at the order of an excited gentleman in evening dress. He stopped quickly enough, but, by the time his help was available, pursuit was hopeless; the one thing Curtis could do he had done — while running up the street he had deciphered the number of the car, X24-305.

Before Curtis rejoined the dazed hall-porter a small crowd had gathered, and it was difficult to get near the body lying on the curb. A man picked up an overcoat, and Curtis, cool and clear-headed now, took it, and appealed to him, if he knew where the nearest doctor lived, to run thither at top speed. The man obeyed him instantly.

"Meanwhile, let me see to the poor fellow," he said. "I am not a doctor, but I know enough about wounds to say whether those scoundrels have killed him or not."

The throng yielded to an authoritative voice, and some of the more sensible bystanders formed a ring, thus securing a semblance of light and air around the prostrate man. Curtis struck a match, and it needed no second glance to learn that the stranger's lung had been pierced by an almost vertical thrust; indeed, he was already dying. The poor lips, from which blood and froth were bubbling, strove vainly to articulate words which, in the prevalent hubbub of alarm and excitement, it was impossible to distinguish. A policeman came, and, as a traffic station for the precinct happened to lie within a couple of doors, the moribund form was carried in, and placed on a stretcher kept there for use in emergency.

A doctor was soon on the spot, but he arrived just in time to record the last flicker of life in the tortured eyes. Then, as one in a dream, Curtis gave the policeman the details of the crime, the name of the chauffeur, and the number of the car, his testimony being borne out to some extent by the hall-porter, and, so far as the car was concerned, by the sharp-eyed driver of the taxi. His own name and address were taken, and a police captain and a couple of detectives, called to the scene by telephone, thanked him for his alertness in securing valuable clews, not only in regard to the car and chauffeur but also in describing the features, figure, and dress of one of the criminals.

Finally, he was warned to hold himself in readiness to attend the opening of an inquest on the following morning, and the police intimated that they did not desire the presence of witnesses while the dead man's clothing was being scrutinized.

So Curtis went out into the street, and, with no other purpose than to avoid the publicity and questioning of the crowd gathered in and around the hotel, sauntered into Broadway. At the corner he halted for a moment to put on the overcoat. He had gone some few yards up the brilliantly illuminated thoroughfare when he fancied that his nervous system needed the tonic of a cigar, and he searched in the pockets of the overcoat for a box of matches he had placed there before leaving his bedroom. The box had gone, but in the right-hand pocket his fingers closed on a long, narrow envelope, made of stiff linen paper, which somehow seemed unfamiliar. He drew it out, and examined it, standing in front of a well-lighted shop window.

Then he whistled with sheer amazement, as well he might. The envelope held a marriage license for two people named Jean de Courtois and Hermione Beauregard Grandison.... In a word, he was wearing the dead man's overcoat, and the fearsome conviction leaped to his brain that the dead man must be Jean de Courtois.

CHAPTER II

EIGHT O'CLOCK

From one aspect, Curtis's sense of dread and horror was merely altruistic, the natural welling forth of the springs of human sentiment. If the man now lying stark and lifeless in that dreary official bureau had in truth been hurrying on his way to a marriage feast, then, indeed, tragedy had assumed its grimmest aspect that night in New York. But, beyond an enforced personal contact with a ghastly crime, Curtis had no vital interest in its victim, and it should have occurred to him, as a law-abiding citizen, that his instant duty was to communicate this new discovery to the authorities. Nay more, such definite information would help the police materially in their pursuit of the murderers. It might lay bare a motive, put the bloodhounds of the law on a well-marked trail, and render impossible the escape of the guilty ones.

That was the sane, level-headed, man-of-the-world view, and, to one inured to deeds of violence in a land where the Foreign Devil oft-time holds his life as scarce worth an hour's purchase, no other solution of the problem should have presented itself. But, for all his strength of character, Curtis had been breathing an intoxicating atmosphere ever since he set foot on American soil. His home-coming had begun by producing in his soul a subtle exaltation which had survived a conspiracy of repression. Devar's careless acceptance of the city's grandeur had jarred; the exuberance of the joyous throng on the jetty had touched dormant chords of sad memories; even at the very portals of the hotel the building's newness had struck a bizarre note; and now, as though to emphasize the vile crime of which he had been an involuntary witness, came the stifling knowledge that somewhere in New York an expectant bride was chafing at delay—a delay caused by an assassin's dagger, while there was not lacking even the tormenting suspicion that somehow, had he been more wide-awake, he could have prevented that malignant thrust.

Yet, his head remained in the clouds. In common with most men whose lot is cast in climes far removed from civilization, Curtis worshiped an ideal of womanhood which was rather that of a poet than of the blasé, cynical town-dweller. He had seen death too often to be shocked by its harsh visage, and, perhaps in protest against the idle belief that the crime was preventable, his sympathies were absorbed now by the vision of some fair girl waiting vainly for the bridegroom who would never come. His analytical mind fastened instantly on the theory that murder had been done to prevent a marriage. He took it for granted that the Jean de Courtois of the marriage certificate was dead, and his heart grieved for the hapless young woman whose aristocratic name was blazoned on that same document. So, instead of retracing his steps, and warning the officers of the law, he bent his brows over the certificate, and, in acting thus, unconsciously committed himself to as fantastic a course as ever was followed by mortal man.

It is only fair to urge that had he known the truth, had the veil been lifted ever so slightly on other happenings in the Central Hotel that night, he would not have hesitated a moment about returning to the conclave of policemen and detectives. He acted impulsively, absurdly, almost insanely, it may be held, but he did honestly act in good faith, and that is the best and the worst that can be said of him, or for him.

And now to peer over his shoulder at the printed form and its written interlineations, which he was perusing with anxious, thoughtful eyes.

It was headed "State of New York, County of New York, City of New York," and bade all men know that any person authorized by law to perform marriage ceremonies within the State was thereby "authorized and empowered to solemnize the rites of matrimony between Jean de Courtois, a citizen of the French Republic, now residing in the Central Hotel, West 27th Street, New York, and Hermione Beauregard Grandison, a citizen of Great Britain, now residing at 1000 West 59th Street, New York."

It had been issued that very day, November 8th. Annexed to the license was the actual marriage certificate, with blanks for names and dates, to be filled in by the person performing the ceremony. A set of printed rules, reciting various duties, legal obligations, and penalties for infringing the same, was also inclosed; but Curtis was in no mood to master the provisions of "An Act to Amend the Domestic Relations Law, by providing for Marriage Licenses," for they must perforce be silent on the one topic wherein he needed guidance—the course to be pursued in the circumstances now facing him.

His thoughts were focussed on the name and address of the girl who had been so cruelly, so wantonly, bereft of her lover, and it seemed to him both fitting and charitable that someone other than a police sergeant or detective should interpose between the grim tragedy of 27th Street and the even more poignant horror which was fated to descend on some house in 59th Street. Apparently, fate had decreed that he should be the messenger charged with this sad errand, and, with a singular disregard of consequences, he accepted the mandate.

He did not act blindly. When all was said and done, the certificate had come into his possession by unavoidable chance. At the hapless bride's residence he would surely be able to meet someone who could accompany him to the police office, and give the details needed for a successful chase. Indeed, he argued that he was saving valuable time by his prompt action, and, reviewing the whole of the facts while being carried swiftly up Broadway in a taxi, he found, at first, no flaw in his judgment.

Though busy in mind with the extraordinary events of the past quarter of an hour, his alert eyes missed few features of the abounding life of the Great White Way. As it happened, a stranger in New York could not have entered the city's main thoroughfare at any point better calculated to bewilder and astound than the very corner where Curtis had picked up the cab. On both sides, from the level of the street to a height often measurable in hundreds of feet, nearly every building blazed with electric signs. Many of the devices seemed to be alive. Horses galloped, either in Roman stadium or modern polo-ground; a girl's skirts were fluttered by a rain-storm; a giant's hand, with unerring skill, bowled a ball at ten-pins in a bowling alley; the names of theaters, of hotels, of drugs, of patent foods, of every known variety of caterer for human needs and amusements, flickered, and winked, and stared, at the passer-by from ground floor to attic—while each and all—horses, skirts, rain-drops, hand, ball, pins, and names—glowed in every known shade of color from every known form of electric lamp.

The glare of this advertisers' paradise was so overpowering that even the marvel-surfeited citizens who crowded the sidewalks would gather in dense groups at a corner, thence to watch and take in the dazzling significance of some sign new to their vision. Curtis noticed many such assemblies before the taxi sped out of the magic area which ends at 42nd Street; but it was all novel to him; he could not discuss the contrast between last week's glorification of Somebody's Pickles and to-night's triumph of Everybody's Whisky, and he was almost bemused by the display, which provided such a bizarre anti-climax to the terrible drama he had just witnessed.

It was a positive relief, therefore, when the vehicle bowled swiftly into a quiet cross street, and he was vouchsafed only fleeting glimpses of broad avenues where fresh multitudes of lamps again bade defiance to the night.

In one place, an illuminated dial showed that the hour was eight o'clock, and the curiously simple fact of noting the time roused him to a perception of all that had happened since he strolled out of the dining-room of the Central Hotel. He smiled dourly when he remembered the mislaid key. Did it still repose in the bedroom? Or had a housemaid found it, and restored it to a numbered hook in the office? Had not that immaculately dressed clerk said he would find Number 605 "a comfortable, quiet room"? Well, it might be all that, yet Curtis could hardly help dwelling on the thought that had he been put in any other cell of the human beehive called the Central Hotel it was highly probable he would not now be flying across New York on a self-imposed mission so nebulous, so ill-defined, that already his orderly brain was beginning to doubt the logic which inspired it.

Was it too late to draw back? To this handy automobile city distances were negligible quantities, and he would rejoin the detectives before they could have any reason to suspect him even of carelessness in withholding from their ken the new and important fact revealed by the accidental change of overcoats.

And, yes—by Jove!—it would be assumed that *his* overcoat was the dead man's, though, indeed, certain papers in the pockets would soon show that there was a blunder somewhere, because the John D. Curtis mentioned therein necessarily figured as the chief witness in the case now being worked up against three unknown malefactors. Oddly enough, it was contemporaneous with this thought that the queer similarity of his own name to that of the unfortunate Frenchman first dawned on him. John D. Curtis and Jean de Courtois were, as names, particularly as the names of two men of different nationalities, sufficiently alike to invite comment. Well, that being so, there was all the more reason why the identity of poor Jean de Courtois should be established beyond doubt, and this reflection appealed so strongly that, when the cab stopped, Curtis was once more reconciled to the policy hurriedly arrived at while he was standing at the corner of Broadway and 27th Street.

He opened the door, alighted, glanced up at a rather imposing block of flats, and said to the driver:

"Is this 1000 West 59th Street?"

"Yes, sir. Quite a bunch of people live here," was the answer.

"I take it, then, that the lady I wish to see occupies one of the flats?"

The driver smiled broadly, for it seemed to him that the naïve statement sounded rather funny.

"I guess that's about the size of it," he said.

19

Curtis smiled, too. This needless blurting out of confidences to a cabman was the one folly essential to a complete restoration of his wits.

"Wait for me," he said. "I may be only a minute or two, and I shall want you to take me right back to the point I came from."

The man nodded, and turned to set the time index of the taximeter. A few steps led up to a spacious doorway, and Curtis passed through a revolving door. Halfway along a well-lighted passage he saw an elevator sign, and found an attendant sitting there.

"I believe that Miss Grandison lives here?" he said.

"Second floor—Number 10—take you up?" was the time-saving reply.

"Yes, but I am not anxious to see Miss Grandison herself. I would prefer to speak to some male relative."

The attendant looked puzzled; perhaps he was wishful to make smooth the way for a visitor who was obviously a gentleman, but the problem offered by Curtis's request presented difficulties, and he fell back on his official instructions.

"Sorry, but you must explain matters to the maid at Number 10," he said, quite civilly, and Curtis was soon pressing an electric bell at the door of the flat itself.

A neatly dressed girl appeared. Her out-of-doors costume suggested that she was either just going out or just returned, and Curtis, unaccustomed to the domestic problem as it exists in New York, fancied that she ranked above the level of a house-maid.

"Is Miss Grandison in?" he asked.

"I'll inquire, sir. What name shall I say?"

It was a noncommittal answer, so he changed ground in the next question.

"I would prefer not to meet Miss Grandison herself if it is in any way possible to interview a relative of hers, or a friend," he said.

This colorless statement, intended to be reassuring, seemed to have such an alarming effect on the girl that he hastened to add:

"I am here with reference to Monsieur Jean de Courtois."

His hearer smiled, and her manner changed from fright to friendliness. Indeed, if he had not been so wrapped up in the highly disagreeable task which lay before him, he could hardly have failed to notice that she welcomed, rather than resented, the visit of a smart looking young man to the establishment.

"Oh, come in, do," she said, glancing up at him with demure but very bright eyes. "Why didn't you say at once that you had been sent by Mr. de Courtois, without trying to scare me stiff by talking about relatives?"

He obeyed, and he closed the door.

"I really meant what I said," he persisted. "Something has happened to prevent Monsieur de Courtois coming here this evening — —"

"Not coming! Then there will be no wedding!"

Her voice was subdued, but she put such distress, such perplexity, into her words that at any other time Curtis would have marveled at the gamut of emotion which the feminine temperament was capable of. Still, he had to risk even a mild display of hysteria, so he went on quietly:

"You will understand now why I would rather meet some person other than Miss Grandison."

"But who is there to meet? She is alone. I do believe I am the only living being she knows in New York, except Mr. de Courtois.... Why can't he come? What is keeping him? Has he met with an accident?... Oh, I can see by your face that he is hurt — or he has been kidnapped! Yes, that's it, for sure! And that dear young lady will be trapped like a bird in a cage!... Miss Hermione! Miss Hermione! Here is someone come to tell you that Mr. de Courtois has been spirited away.... Oh dear, to think that this should be the end of all our planning and contriving!"

During this crescendo of excited and scarcely intelligible utterances the girl had first backed away from Curtis, and then turned, running to open, without knocking, a door on the right of the extreme end of a corridor which divided the suite into two sections.

Curtis did not attempt to stop her. Whatsoever the outcome, he was committed now to an undertaking from which there was no retreat. He half expected that the maid, whose disjointed outburst betokened, at least, that she was her mistress's trusted confidante, would reappear from the room into which she had vanished. But he was mistaken, doubly mistaken, since the mental picture he had formed of Hermione Beauregard Grandison was utterly falsified by the slight, elegant, girlish figure which presented itself before his astonished eyes. Somehow, those superfine Christian names and that aristocratic surname had prepared him for a rather magnificent person, young, probably, because the dead man might be of his own age within a year, but decidedly impressive. He had gone so far as to imagine her an actress, of the sinuous, well-rounded type, who would address him in a deep contralto, and, if and when she fainted, would sink gracefully on to a couch correctly placed for scenic effect.

The reality took his breath away.

He saw a girl, not a day older than twenty, dressed in a simple costume of brown cloth, and wearing a hat, veil, and gloves of harmonizing tints. The veil had been hurriedly lifted above the brim of the hat, and a pair of what seemed to be intensely dark violet eyes gazed at him from a small-featured, pallid face from which every vestige of color had fled.

"Is this thing true?" she said, halting timidly within a few feet of him. "Perhaps Marcelle has misunderstood you. Who sent you?— Monsieur de Courtois himself, I suppose?"

Her voice, so wistful, so pleading, perfect in cadence yet almost childlike in its evident anxiety to be reassured, reached uncharted depths in his soul. At once he began to ask himself why this mere girl should be exposed to the impish trick which fate had played on her, and, in the same breath, he was conscious of a fierce anger against the ghouls who had contrived it.

"Are you Miss Grandison?" he asked, rather to gain time than because of any doubt as to her personality.

"Yes. And you?"

"My name is Curtis—John D. Curtis. I only landed in New York three hours ago."

He added the explanatory sentence in order to clear the ground, as it were, for the strange and horrible story he had to tell, but its effect was curious in the extreme. The girl's white face blanched to that wan hue which personal fear lends to distress.

"Where have you come from?" she gasped.

"From Pekin."

"From Pekin!"

"Yes. I have been traveling without pause during the past eight weeks."

By this time he had ascertained two certain facts about Hermione Beauregard Grandison. In the first place, she was the prettiest and most graceful creature he had ever met; in the second, she had all the hall-marks of good breeding and high social caste. His brain was so busy over these discoveries that he disregarded the really remarkable way in which the object of his visit had been shelved for the moment. It might reasonably be expected that the disconsolate lady would be concerned mainly as to the fate of the missing bridegroom, but the mistress evidently shared the maid's disquietude about Curtis himself.

And, precisely as in the case of Marcelle, Miss Grandison's face showed relief when it became manifest that he was a complete stranger.

"Pray forgive me for questioning you in this manner," she said, with a rapid reversion to a conventional air that disconcerted her hearer in a way she little imagined. "Will you come in here, and be seated?… Now, please tell me just why you have called, Mr. Curtis."

She had preceded him into a prettily furnished dining-room, and the notion leaped up in his troubled mind that she was not so deeply moved by the malfortune of Monsieur Jean de Courtois as might be expected from the man's prospective bride.

Still, he tried bravely to accommodate himself to conditions which left his brain in a whirl.

"I had better begin by saying that your marriage cannot take place — to-night — —" he added, flinching from the necessity of bringing that look of dismay into those charming eyes. "That is why I asked your maid if there was no other person whom I could take into my confidence. You see, it is a terribly hard thing to be compelled to discuss such a matter with one so closely bound up with—with Monsieur de Courtois."

"But there is no one else. Marcelle and I live here quite alone."

More than ever did Curtis feel uncomfortable, but he had deliberately elected for this miserable job, and he meant to go through with it.

"So I gathered from Mademoiselle Marcelle herself," he said. "Well, then, Miss Grandison, I have no option but to inform you, with all the sympathy any man must feel for a woman in your position, that Monsieur de Courtois has met with an accident."

"Oh, how terrible! Is he badly hurt?"

"Yes."

"Yet it may be possible for the ceremony to be performed. Monsieur de Courtois has proved himself such a true friend, he has always been so anxious to help me, that I am sure he would be glad if I brought the minister to the hospital, or to his apartments in the hotel if he has been taken there, and the marriage would be solemnized without causing him the slightest inconvenience or worry, no matter how ill he may be, so long as he is conscious."

Curtis thought he had never before heard the English language twisted into such enigmas as these few simple words presented. It was an outrage to credit this well-mannered and delightful girl with the cold-blooded callousness which seemed to reveal itself in every syllable. That she was blithely unaware of this element in her excited utterances was shown by her eager face and animated attitude. She had risen from the chair in which she had seated herself when they entered the room, and obviously expected him to lose no time in conducting her to the bedside of Jean de Courtois.

"Pray sit down again, Miss Grandison," said Curtis, and his voice assumed a sterner, more commanding note, though he, too, stood up, and approached nearer, lest she might collapse in a faint and fall before he could save her. "I fear I have blundered woefully in assuming a role for which I am ill-fitted, but I must make you realize somehow that your marriage is irrevocably—postponed."

"Why?"

A slight color tinged her cheeks; she was actually becoming annoyed with him!

"I will tell you when you are seated."

"What nonsense! One can hear as well standing."

Nevertheless, she obeyed. People generally did obey when Curtis spoke in that insistent manner.

Now he was quite near her, and his tone grew gentle again.

"The accident from which Monsieur de Courtois suffered was fatal," he said.

She looked at him, wide-eyed, alarmed, but assuredly not with the soul-sickened terror of a woman who loves when she hears that her lover is dead.

"Do you mean that he has been killed?" she whispered.

"Yes."

"Oh, poor fellow. I have lost my only friend, and now, indeed, I am the most wretched girl in all the world."

Flinging her clasped arms on the table, she hid her face in them, and sobbed as though her heart would break. Curtis placed a hand on her shoulder, and strove to calm her with such commonplace phrases as his dazed brain could dictate, but she wept bitterly, just as a child might weep if disappointed about the non-fulfillment of some object on which its heart was set.

"It sounds horrid—I know—" she murmured brokenly, "that I should—seem to be thinking—only of myself. But—Monsieur de Courtois—was the one man—who could save me. Now—I don't know—what will become of me. How cruel is fate! If only—we could have been married yesterday—perhaps this dreadful thing would not have happened."

Curtis, who had never been so mystified in his life, followed up those last disjointed words as a man lost in a forest might cling to a path in the certainty that it would lead somewhere. He rejected all else, since the wild vagaries of events during the past few minutes were beyond his comprehension. He waited, therefore, until the vehemence of her grief had somewhat subsided, and then, with another friendly pressure on her shoulder, he spoke with as much firmness as he thought the situation demanded.

"Now, Miss Grandison, you must endeavor to regain self-control," he said. "Monsieur de Courtois has been killed, and your—your friendship for him—no less than the interests of justice—demand that those responsible for his death should be discovered and punished."

At that, she raised her head, and lifted her swimming eyes to his, and Curtis saw that they were blue, not violet, and that their hue changed as the light irradiated their profound depths.

"He met with no accident, then, but was murdered?" she cried.

"Yes."

"And for my sake?"

"I gather from what you have said that that is possible."

"But what have I said?"

"Well, you seemed to hint that your marriage might have prevented this crime."

"Why?"

No more exasperating monosyllable can fall from a woman's lips than that one word "why," and Curtis felt its full force then and there.

"That is what I am asking you," he said, a trifle brusquely.

"But how can I tell you?" she cried.

"I am only striving vainly to pierce the fog which seems to envelop us. Let me begin again. I, a mere stranger in New York, just three hours landed from the *Lusitania*, witnessed a murderous attack on a young man who was alighting from a cab in front of my hotel, the Central, in West 27th Street. I saw him stabbed so seriously that he died within a couple of minutes, and his assailants made off in an automobile, the very vehicle, in fact, in which he arrived. I managed to note its number, and I gathered, from instructions the victim himself had given, that the chauffeur's Christian name was Anatole. The two men who actually committed the murder—though the chauffeur was in league with them—seemed to me to be Czechs or Hungarians— —"

"Ah, I thought so," broke in the girl.

"And now may I ask why you did think so?"

"I may tell you later, perhaps. Please forgive me. I am quite unnerved, and oh, so unhappy. Why have you come here?"

"That is due to one of those fantastic chances which occur occasionally. In the effort to save Monsieur de Courtois, or rather to seize his slayers, because I was too far away to interfere when the blow was struck, I dropped the overcoat I was carrying. A crowd gathered, and someone gave me a coat which I took as my own. It was not until I had quitted the police and doctor, who arrived almost immediately, and I had gone into Broadway to avoid the clamor in the hotel, that I discovered I was wearing the dead man's overcoat, and in one of the pockets I found a marriage license. Here it is. By that means I learnt your address, and I came here quickly, hoping to save you some of the agony which the appearance of a policeman or detective would have caused. Unfortunately, I have proved but a sorry substitute for an official messenger."

"Oh, no, no, Mr. Curtis. You have been most kind, most considerate. If anyone is to blame, it is I."

"Will you pardon me, then, if I remind you that time is pressing? Even a half-hour gained to-night by the authorities may be invaluable. If you are able to supply any clew, the least hint of motive, the most shadowy of guesses at a personality behind this beastly crime, you will be rendering a great service."

"Please, please, give me time to think. I am not heartless—indeed I am not.… If I could do anything to save Monsieur de Courtois' life I would make the sacrifice—you will believe that, won't you?… But he is dead, you say, and I might blurt out something in my distress which would cause endless mischief. Perhaps I have thought too much of my own troubles. Now I must begin to endure for the sake of others. That is the woman's lot in life, I fear.… Have you a wife or a sister, Mr. Curtis, or is there some woman whom you love? For her sake, have pity on me, and do not drag me into the horrible arena of courts and newspapers."

Her pleading, her attitude, her pathetic gestures, gave extraordinary force to an appeal which, by contrast with her extreme agitation, was almost grotesquely inconsequent. Curtis was at his wits' end to find the line of reasoning calculated to convince this beautiful creature that she might, indeed, begin enduring "for the sake of others" by expressing her determination to give the police all possible assistance.

"There is no urgency for a few minutes," was the best reply he could frame on the spur of the moment. "Shall I leave you alone for a little while? Perhaps you would like to consult your maid? Indeed, her services might meet all the requirements of the case. The police would be the first to recognize that a woman who had lost her affianced husband under such terrible— —"

"Ah, but that is the wretched difficulty I am in. Poor Monsieur de Courtois was nothing to me."

"Nothing to you!"

Probably Curtis's brain did not reel, but it assuredly felt like reeling, and it is quite certain that his eyes blazed down on the half-hysterical girl with an intensity that magnetized her into a broken excuse.

"It is—quite—true," she stammered, with the diffidence of a child explaining some lapse which, it was hoped, might not be regarded as a real fault. "I never dreamed of marriage—in the sense—that people mean—when they intend to live happily together.... Monsieur de Courtois was to be my husband—only in name. I—I paid him for that.... I—I gave him a thousand dollars—and—and—— Don't look at me in that way or I shall scream!... I have done nothing wrong.... I was trying to protect myself.... Oh, if you are a man you will want to help me, rather than push me into the living tomb which threatens to engulf me before to-morrow morning!"

Even in their agitation, they both heard the jar of a bell. The girl sprang upright. There was something splendid in her courage, in the way she threw back her proud head and clenched her tiny hands.

"Ah me!" she sighed. "Perhaps it is already too late!"

CHAPTER III

EIGHT-THIRTY

They stood in silence, listening to the footsteps of Marcelle on the parquet floor of the passage. The outer door was opened, and a murmur of voices reached them indistinctly.

"I have had the honor of knowing you not much longer than ten minutes, Miss Grandison," said Curtis, and the strong, vibrant note in his voice might well have won any woman's confidence, "but if you feel that you can trust me, and my help is of value, please command me, that is, if your enemies are men."

She rewarded him with one swift look of gratitude.

"If it is my father, both you and I are powerless," she whispered. "And the other would not dare come without him."

A discreet tap on the door heralded Marcelle. That sprightly young person, despite her Parisian name, was unquestionably American in every inch of her self-possessed neatness; she smiled at Curtis while giving him a message.

"The driver of your taxi has sent up the hall-porter to ask if you wish him to wait any longer," she said.

Not often, even in comedy, has the mountain heaved and brought forth such a ridiculous mouse. Curtis did actually laugh; even his distraught companion tittered in sheer nervous reaction.

"Please tell him to wait, and not to worry about the fare," said Curtis. "I suppose," he added, turning to Miss Grandison, "the man put me down as a newcomer, and, taught by previous experience, thought it best to warn me how the register mounts."

The effort to restore their rather strained relations to a sedate level was well meant, but the girl's downcast eyes and tremulous lips revealed a state of piteous uncertainty and confusion that was more distressing to Curtis than anything which had gone before. Nevertheless, reminding himself that precious time was being wasted, he determined to seek a full explanation of circumstances which at present savored of Bedlam.

"Now that the fears of the taxi-driver have been stilled," he said cheerfully, "suppose you and I sit down and discuss matters like sensible people. I am an American, Miss Grandison, and, although long an exile from my own country, I appreciate the national characteristic of plain speech. Let me explain that I am not married, that I have no ties which prevent free action on my part, and that nothing on earth will stop me from helping a woman who pins her faith to me. With that preamble, as the lawyers say, I purpose taking off this heavy overcoat, and listening in comfort to anything you may wish to tell. Or, if you are afraid of being disturbed, what do you say if we go to some restaurant, where, perhaps, we may eat, and, at any rate, talk without fear of interference?"

"I think we had better remain here," said the girl sadly, though it was plain that Curtis's offer of protection during the alarm created by the hall-porter's errand had advanced him a long way in her esteem. "There are only two persons living who dare pretend to exercise control over my actions, and if they have arrived in New York this evening I have good reason to believe that I cannot escape them."

"Are they coming here from Europe?" asked Curtis quickly, for his active mind was already groping toward certain dimly defined conclusions.

"Yes."

"Could they have been fellow-passengers of mine on the *Lusitania*?"

"No, they are on board the *Switzerland*."

He smiled, and discarded that fateful overcoat.

"Then set your mind at rest," he said, with the nonchalance of a man who has shelved a major difficulty. "The *Switzerland* has broken down. We passed her early to-day. She is staggering into port with engines partly disabled and she cannot possibly reach New York before to-morrow morning."

"Are you quite sure?" came the eager demand.

"Well, there is nothing so uncertain as the sea but a young friend of mine said that those facts were signaled by wireless, and, to some extent, they governed his own movements. I myself can assure you that the *Switzerland* was limping along like a lame duck at 8 A.M. to-day."

"Ah, thank Heaven for that small mercy!" murmured the girl. For a few seconds she busied herself with gloves, veil, and hat-pins, and Curtis happened to glance at the overcoat, which he had placed over the back of a chair. To his dismay, he noticed that one of the sleeves, the left, was bespattered with blood, but he contrived to refold the garment so as to conceal this grewsome record of a tragedy before his hostess had divested herself of hat and gloves.

Then they seemed to survey each other with a new interest, for Curtis was a good figure of a man in evening dress, and Hermione Grandison became, if possible, more attractive to the male eye because of the wealth of brown hair which crowned her smooth forehead, almost hid her tiny ears, and clustered low at the back of her slender, well-shaped neck. Where the rays of light caught the coiled tresses they had the sheen of burnished gold. In the shadow they commingled those voluptuous tints by which the magic of Rubens has immortalized one fair woman, Isabella Brant, in every gallery of note throughout the world.

Hermione it was, now, who first broke the silence which had reigned in the room for a minute or more. Seating herself on the opposite side of a square table, and resting her elbows thereon, she propped her pretty chin on her small, clenched fists, and gazed fearlessly at Curtis.

"You must think me a very extraordinary person," she began.

"Let that pass," said he, with a smile, wise in the knowledge that the present was no hour for compliments.

"But I am, and I know it, not because I differ so greatly from other girls of my own age, but owing to the misery which has been my portion. The one man in the world who should wish to secure my happiness has become my persecutor. I am here to-night because I have run away from my father, and I have used every lawful means to get married—under conditions framed by myself, of course—in order to escape from a hateful marriage which he has planned."

She hesitated, for a reflective frown was deepening on Curtis's face.

"Now you recognize my name!" she cried. "Have you seen anything about me in the newspapers?"

"You are Lady Hermione Grandison?" he said, meeting her watchful eyes frankly.

"Yes."

"Daughter of the Earl of Valletort?"

"Yes."

"And about a month ago you were reported missing from some apartment in the Rue de Rivoli, on the eve of your marriage with— with some Hungarian prince?"

"Yes, Count Ladislas Vassilan."

"So you came here—with Monsieur Jean de Courtois?"

"I brought him here, and paid him for his services. I have no desire to minimize his friendly aid, but I was buying the security of his name as my husband, and he had given me his guarantee that, when it suited my purposes, he would help me to dissolve the marriage."

Curtis disregarded a perceptible coldness in her tone. He was too busy sweeping away the mists.

"What sort of guarantee?" he asked.

"His promise, his word of honor."

"Was he—a gentleman?"

"Not socially, but in every other sense. He was my music-master in Paris."

Curtis put his next question hurriedly. He was anxious to avoid the least suspicion on the girl's part that he might be crediting Jean de Courtois with motives which would not pass muster before a jury of cool-headed men so readily as they seemed to have satisfied an impetuous and frightened girl.

"How did your father ascertain that you were in New York?" he said.

"Oh, it seems that a certain period of residence was necessary before a marriage license could be obtained, and it was unavoidable that my name should be found out by those whom he hired to track me."

"But why were you not married under an assumed name?"

"Monsieur de Courtois assured me that such a thing would render the marriage invalid."

"He was wrong," said Curtis dryly. "It subjected you to some small legal penalty, but you would be just as effectually married if you called yourself Jane Smith."

"I really think you are mistaken. Monsieur de Courtois made the most exhaustive inquiries."

"Were you not leaving the ceremony to the latest possible hour?" went on Curtis, divided now between the fear of shocking her and the paramount importance of learning the truth about the curiously scrupulous Jean de Courtois.

"We were to have been married two days ago, but the license was stolen."

"So it is rather by accident than otherwise that Lord Valletort and Count Vassilan, who, I take it, is with your father on board the *Switzerland*, have not arrived in time to prevent the marriage—that is, if they were able to prevent it?"

"No, I think not. Poor Monsieur de Courtois was here this afternoon, and he was jubilant because we had plenty of time, provided we were married this evening."

"Where was the ceremony to take place?"

"I—I don't know. I left everything in the hands of Monsieur de Courtois."

A very real and active doubt of the Frenchman's good faith was beginning to peep up in Curtis's mind. Rather to account for the thoughtful lines on his forehead than for any reason connected with the license, he took that document from the table, where it had lain since he produced it, and affected to examine it judiciously. Therefore, he was really surprised when he found an endorsement on the back which read;—"Issued in duplicate. This license is not available if the original has been used."

"Oh!" he said, and the monosyllable might mean much or little.

"What have you discovered there?" said the girl, rising and coming nearer, to stoop over the table and scrutinize the paper with him.

"The original license certainly seems to have disappeared," said Curtis, who had suddenly become aware that the propinquity of a charming woman was one of the subtle joys of life.

"Ah me!" sighed Lady Hermione, straightening her supple form, and turning slightly aside.

There was a little pause. Curtis, whose enunciation was usually distinguished by its ease and clearness, found some slight difficulty in resuming the conversation. He resolved firmly that, in future, he would eschew liqueurs after champagne.

"I hate to act the role of inquisitor, Lady Hermione," he said, rather huskily as to the first few words, "but would you mind telling me why you are so opposed to Count Ladislas Vassilan as a husband?"

"First, because I do not want to marry any man; secondly, because Count Vassilan is a vile person, both in appearance and repute; and thirdly, because my father is only urging this match to serve his own ends. Our unhappy history is so widely known that there is no harm in telling you that my mother and he were separated during many years, and when mamma died three years ago she left all her money to me, absolutely under my control. I was young, only seventeen, but I managed to retain it, though goodness only knows how, and this horrid Hungarian prince wants it—to help him to regain a throne, he says—but I don't believe him."

"You could not be forced into matrimony," said Curtis, with a slow gravity that was lost on his dejected hearer.

"You cannot have lived in France, or you would not say that," was the bitter answer. "Everyone, everything, was opposed to me. I was a minor, and one against many. The laws seemed to conspire with my relatives to force me into the power of a beast.... Yes, it sounds horrid on my lips, but the man is really a beast," and she stamped an emphatic foot on the floor; Curtis could see the white circles over the tiny knuckles as her hands clenched in protest. They were such pretty hands, too. He had often smiled at the notion of a man kissing a woman's hand, but it did not strike him now as a specially foolish act.

"Let us forget him," he agreed.

"But how can I forget him? He will be here to-morrow. Once my father and he have found me, what am I to do? Die, I suppose!... I would rather die than marry Count Vassilan, and again I would rather die than figure in a vulgar brawl, such as the newspapers would take a delight in. My father is well aware of that, and will play on my weakness.... B-but—I may—be able—to defeat them—in another way."

Curtis stood up. The sound of her grief maddened him, and he threw prudence to the winds.

"The first reason you gave was the most convincing one, so far as you personally are concerned, Lady Hermione," he said, making the effort of his life to speak calmly. "You said you did not want to marry any man."

"Y-yes, it is true. I d-don't."

"Still, there is only one way out of your trouble. You must marry me—to-night."

The girl whirled round on him; her eyes were glistening with tears, but her face was radiant.

"Do you really mean that?" she cried.

"I do."

"Then never let anyone tell me that the age of chivalry has passed."

"I fancy it has just begun," he said, though the jest nearly choked him.

"But why should you do this kind and gracious thing for a girl you have been acquainted with only a brief half-hour? You see, I understand that you are a gentleman—I realize that, although I have plenty of money, I cannot offer to recompense you as I did that poor Jean de Courtois."

"No," he agreed grimly.

"Don't you grasp what this one-sided bargain implies? You are merely to pose as my husband until Count Vassilan leaves me in peace?"

"Yes."

"And then we are to obtain a divorce?"

"You are, not I."

"Isn't that a distinction without a difference?"

"Perhaps. The fact remains that I shall agree to all your terms save one—you, of course, can divorce me at your own pleasure. The procedure is simple in some States of the Union."

For no obvious reason, Lady Hermione blushed. For an instant, indeed, she was somewhat disconcerted, and the vivacity fled from her mobile face.

"Perhaps, Mr. Curtis, I have no right to let you make this sacrifice," she said, a trifle coldly. "It would be different if I could repay you in some way. Surely, although you may be a wealthy man, there will be expenses—you will, at least, lose a good deal of time, which you could occupy to better purpose?"

"I have given myself twelve months' respite from railway construction in China. I really don't see how I could pass a part of my holiday better than as your husband."

"In idle make-believe?"

"Every decent man has the heart of a child, and make-believe is reality to some children."

"But, even though in my need I take you at your word, how can a marriage become possible?"

"Here is the license. For the purposes of the ceremony I become Jean de Courtois. By singular chance, the change of name is not such a wrench as it might be if I didn't happen to be called John D. Curtis."

Still she hesitated. Somehow, becoming Mrs. John D. Curtis impressed her as a far more serious undertaking than purchasing the right to pose as Madame de Courtois.

"We don't even know where to get married," she faltered.

"Given a license and a comparatively small sum of money, New York abounds with facilities."

"Are you sure the ceremony will be legal if you appear under a false name?"

"Quite positive."

"Can you be punished if it is found out?"

"I'll run the risk."

After a fateful pause, which would have been considerably curtailed had Lady Hermione Grandison been vouchsafed the least premonition of events in which the night was still rich, she held out her hand.

"I can only thank you from the depths of my heart, Mr. Curtis," she said. "I must trust someone, and I do trust you most implicitly."

"You will never regret it, Lady Hermione," he said reverently. He wondered whether or not this was an occasion on which hand-kissing was permissible, but contented himself with returning the friendly pressure of the girl's fingers—retaining them, in fact, for a second or two.

"I have your word of honor that you will regard the ceremony as a formal compact between us two?" she murmured, unaccountably shy, and seemingly half-afraid that he meant to clasp her in his arms then and there.

"You have," he said, relinquishing her hand. Perhaps, at that instant, Puck sighed, and wondered what would have happened had this husband only in name strained to his heart the bride whom he had vowed not to embrace. But Curtis did nothing of the sort. His tone became intensely practical and businesslike, and he glanced at his watch.

"It is half-past eight," he said. "How soon will you be ready to come with me and hunt up a minister?"

"Now—I am ready now. Marcelle and I were waiting for—for that unhappy Monsieur de Courtois when you arrived. It sounds rather dreadful, Mr. Curtis, to talk of marriage, even as a mere means of cheating the law, at a moment when a man is already lying dead for my sake. Please don't consider me, but draw back, if you want to, before it is too late."

"My grandfather commanded the Fifth Cavalry during the Civil War, Lady Hermione."

"Pray, how does that interesting fact affect us?"

"It is well-known that the Fifth never retreat, and the habit has become a family tradition."

He pocketed the license, and picked up the overcoat, meaning to put it on in the hall while her ladyship was rearranging her hat. But Marcelle was waiting there, hatted, and gloved.

"Have you fixed things?" she whispered breathlessly.

"We have," said Curtis.

"Goodness me! But I guessed it. Nobody can resist her, can they?"

"I didn't try," said Curtis, wriggling into the coat sideways.

"Poor *dear*. She has had a time. What a piece of luck I met her the day she landed."

Curtis had no opportunity to inquire just what Marcelle meant, for Lady Hermione had joined them. Sedulously keeping that tell-tale sleeve out of sight, Curtis took the lead, and opened the door, which Marcelle closed and locked.

While they were waiting for the elevator, Curtis fathomed Marcelle's stock of information as to the addresses of neighboring ministers of the Protestant Episcopal Church. It was nil. He appealed to the attendant when the elevator came up, but that worthy thoughtfully tickled his scalp under his cap, and suggested a consultation with the taxi-driver. Indeed, to further the quest, he went with them to the door, and, while Lady Hermione and Marcelle seated themselves in the cab, the three men discussed the religious problem on the sidewalk.

"Ministers don't use taxis much in N' York, sir," commented the driver. "Fact is, they mostly can't afford 'em, but I do happen to know where one old gentleman lives, an' he's sure to be home, because he's crippled something cruel with the rheumatiz."

"Is it far?" demanded Curtis.

"Three blocks away, in 56th Street, near Seventh Avenue. Lives next door to the church, he does."

"Take us there," and Curtis entered the vehicle, which whirled out of sight in the peculiarly downright fashion of the automobile.

The elevator man looked after it, and tickled another section of his scalp.

"I'd a notion she was going to marry that Frenchman," he said to himself. "Of course, it's her business, an' not mine, but of the two I'd take a chance with this new fellar. An' it's odd, too, that they shouldn't know where to go, unless they mean to pick up Froggy on the road. Well, wimmen is queer creetures, they are, sure, an' the English ones are just as queer as the Americans. Not that Miss Grandison ain't a peach wherever she comes from, an' I hope she'll be happy, night an' day till the time comes when she don't care if it snows."

He glanced up at the sky, rolled a cigarette, and, before returning indoors, sniffed a keen wind which was rustling the last crisp leaves in Central Park. The street was quiet, and no one was stirring in the mansion.

"I'm not likely to be wanted for another minnit or two," he said, "so I'll just give the furnace a shake-out. Unless I'm mistaken, there's a frost coming."

Had he prophesied a hurricane he would not have been far wrong, but it was entirely in keeping with the other remarkable developments of a night already noteworthy for its strange happenings that the elevator attendant at No. 1000 59th Street should have chosen the next few minutes to attend to the steam-heating arrangements in the basement.

There is little to be gained, however, from speculation as to the probable outcome of conditions which did not obtain, and the trivial space of time which was demanded for the shaking-out and recoaling of a furnace was largely responsible for John D. Curtis and Hermione Beauregard Grandison being made man and wife.

Curiously enough, the tying of this particular knot was facilitated by the fact that the clergyman was hale mentally but decrepit physically, and, as might be expected, resented the conclusion, long ago arrived at by his friends, that he was unfitted for work. He burgeoned with delight when a servant announced that two young people wanting to get married were waiting in the vestibule; he hobbled out of the library, where he was poring over an essay on the Sixtine text of the Septuagint, and ushered them into a parlor. The room was not well-lighted, because of some defect in the electric installation, but the old gentleman—"Rev. Thomas J. Hughes" was the legend on the door-plate—bustled about in the liveliest way, and talked most cheerfully.

"Ah, young folk—as usual, leaving things to the last moment, and then in a desperate hurry," he chirped. "Got the license—yes? Complied with all the formalities? Of course, of course. Where's the ring? You've *not* forgotten the ring?"

Curtis and Hermione looked at each other in blank dismay; even Marcelle's aplomb yielded under this unforeseen strain, and her agitation showed itself in a gasping murmur:

"Oh dear! What shall we do now?"

Mr. Hughes positively chortled over their discomfiture. He limped to a secretaire, and opened a drawer.

"See what it is to have a long experience in these affairs," he cried. "Do you fancy you are the first couple who failed to provide a ring? Ah me! When I was quite a boy in the cloth I learnt the necessity of keeping rings in stock, so a jeweler friend of mind replenishes my store, and, when I sell one, I apply a small profit to a favorite charity of mine. The wearing of a wedding ring has no legal significance, but it is a fine old custom, and should be preserved. Among the Romans the ring was a pledge, *pignus*, that the betrothal contract would be fulfilled. Pliny tells us that the ring, or circle, was of iron, but the ladies speedily determined that it should be of gold, and the Church went a step farther in recognizing it as a symbol of matrimony. Hence, perhaps, the Episcopal ring, and even the Ring of the Fisherman itself, though some authorities hold that signets—Ah, yes," for Curtis had intimated politely that the hour was growing late, "if the lady will say which of these rings fits; they are fifteen dollars each—cheaper, I believe, than you can buy them in Fifth Avenue.... Ah, *that* one? Very well. Now, as to the form of service?"

"The full marriage rite," said Curtis.

"Precisely, just what I would have suggested. I adhere to the time-honored formula. Now, let me examine the license—my eyes fail me a little, but I take the utmost pains to be accurate, because accuracy is of the greatest importance.... Yes, yes, State of New York—what are the names?"

"John D. Curtis and Hermione Beauregard Grandison," said Curtis. His tone was so calm and self-confident that even the prospective bride was deaf for a moment to the vital significance of the words. Then she whispered tremulously:

"Are you not making some mistake?"

"No," he replied, looking her straight in the eyes.

The minister, whose ears partook of the defects in his other faculties, caught the word "mistake."

"This is no place for mistakes, my dear young lady," he said, "A nice young couple like you should only require to be married once in your lives. Take my advice, and stick to one another in sunshine and in storm, and you shall be blessed even unto the fourth generation.... Now, all is in order.... Is this your witness?" and he nodded affably toward Marcelle. "Shall we have one other? William Jenkins, my factotum, has been privileged to assist on many such occasions.... Wil-li-am!"

He raised his voice, and a wizened little man appeared suddenly, having evidently waited outside the door until he was summoned.

Then, with due ritual, John Delancy Curtis and Hermione Beauregard Grandison were joined in the bonds of wedlock, and, by the time Mr. Hughes had completed the ceremony, he had pronounced their names so often, and was so accustomed to their form and sound, that when he filled in the certificate annexed to the license, "John D. Curtis" appeared therein in place of "Jean de Courtois."

Hermione was in a pitiable state of suppressed excitement before the ordeal was concluded. The solemnity and impressiveness of the vows she was taking disturbed the serenity with which she had schooled herself to regard the marriage as "make-believe." She was frightened at her own daring. A dread that the tie she was so lightly assuming might be harder to undo than she had contemplated was fluttering her heart and almost paralyzing her limbs. But Curtis was unemotional as an icicle; or, at any rate, he looked it, which was all that the half-hysterical girl by his side could ascertain by an occasional timid glance. The fact lent her a sort of courage to persevere to the end, and she signed her maiden name for the last time with a numb confidence in the man whom she had, so to speak, bargained for as a husband in an emergency.

Curtis did not fail to note that the aged clergyman's handwriting was crabbed and palsied as his bent frame. None could tell, for certain, whether he wrote "Jean" or "John," "Courtois" or "Curtis," though, indeed, the balance of probability inclined to the latter of the two names, Christian and surname, since those were indubitably what he meant to write.

Then, having stated his fee, and been paid for the ring, he handed Hermione a copy of the certificate.

"Treasure that during all your days, Mrs. Curtis," he said. "May it be a charter of lasting happiness and content!"

Mrs. Curtis! Another shock! Hermione felt that she would scream if there were many more such. And the pressure of the little gold ring on the third finger of her left hand was becoming intolerable. Iron, it used to be, said the minister, and a band of iron it seemed to have become since this man whom she had taken, so completely on trust had placed it there.

On the way out, Curtis tipped Jenkins, tipped him so lavishly that a queer little voice squeaked from a queer little face:

"Thank you, sir. Fair weather to both you and your wife, and a safe berth when you drop anchor!"

So Jenkins had been a sailor, for none but a shell-back would put his good wishes in such nautical lingo.

"I have just finished one long voyage, but seem to have begun another," said Curtis to his "wife." He accompanied the words with a laugh, and was really talking for the sake of breaking an awkward silence. They were descending a few steps from the door, and he noticed that a private automobile was speeding down the street from the same direction as the taxi had taken. It swung close to the curb, and was pulled up barely a yard short of the waiting cab, whose engine the driver was starting with the crank.

A shout came from the interior, and a man leaped out. The street was rather dark in that part, but Hermione recognized the stranger instantly.

"Count Vassilan!" she cried, and the fear in her voice thrilled Curtis to the core.

Almost as quickly, the man now running along the sidewalk knew that a long chase had ended, or he fancied that it had ended, which is not always the same thing.

"Here we are, Valletort!" he shouted. "Got 'em, by ——! You see after Hermione! I'll attend to this d—d Frenchman!"

Curtis gently disengaged the clasp of a tiny hand on his arm, a clasp which was eloquent of a woman's sore need and complete trust. He stepped forward to meet the Count, a stoutly built, heavy man, who had reckoned on closing with an undersized Frenchman. There was no time to rectify mistakes. Curtis met his rival's onset with a beautiful half-arm jab on the nose. Scientifically, it was perfect, since the blow was delivered at the back of the Count's head with complete disregard of intervening tissues, and its recipient went down like one of those pins which succumbed so regularly to the ball bowled by a colossal fist in the Broadway electric sign. The only difference was that the pin fell noiselessly, whereas Count Vassilan roared like a bull in anguish.

In the next instant Curtis, who, for a mild-mannered person, appeared to possess a singularly close acquaintance with the ethics of a street row, sprang at the automobile, pushed back a man who was getting out, slammed the door, seized the speed levers, and bent them hopelessly with a violent tug.

A swearing chauffeur fumbled in the seat, but was in no real hurry to alight, because he had noted the Count's *débâcle*, and Curtis ran to the two cowering women.

"In with you!" he said cheerily, adding, with a grin at the driver:

"Fifty for you if we win clear. Now, be a sport!"

Of course, the driver of a taxi would be a sport. In five minutes he pulled up somewhere in Madison Avenue, and, leaning back and twisting his neck, bawled:

"Where to *now*, sir?"

CHAPTER IV

AN INTERLUDE

The appearance on the scene of the Earl of Valletort and Count Ladislas Vassilan at a moment which, though undeniably critical, might be described as either opportune or inopportune—the choice of an adjective depending solely on the varying points of view of the one who gave and the one who received that powerful thump on the nose—was due to no feat of skill on the part of the engine-room staff of the *Switzerland*, but to a judicious combination of wireless telegraphy, money, and influence.

When it became evident, very early in the morning, that the vessel might, with luck, crawl up to the quarantine station about midnight, urgent messages were sent to two consulates and the Port Authorities of New York. In the result, a fast steam-yacht drew up alongside the vessel when she took the pilot on board, and the two magnates and their baggage were transferred from the disabled liner to the deck of the trim yacht.

She made praiseworthy efforts to reach a quay and a batch of Customs officers before eight o'clock, but failed by five minutes. Consequently, some slight delay was experienced, and, with the best of good will on the part of the officials, the two fuming passengers could not fling themselves into a waiting automobile until nearly twenty minutes past the hour.

Then, however, they made up for lost time. Intrusting their belongings to a porter and a taxi, with instructions to proceed to the Waldorf-Astoria Hotel, they bade the chauffeur travel at top speed to No. 1000 59th Street. Many times were they sworn at en route by endangered pedestrians and enraged drivers of horsed vehicles; the growing torrent of ill wishes thus engendered may have exercised some unrecognized form of telepathy at No. 1000, because a regulating valve in the steam-heat apparatus, which had never proved intractable before, suddenly took it into its metallic head to go wrong. Thus, the elevator man was not aware of a good deal of ringing of electric bells and hammering on the locked door of flat Number 10.

Ultimately, the valve resumed its normal functions, for no cause that a hot and oily human being could perceive other than the occasional "cussedness" which inanimate objects can be capable of; while surveying it wrathfully, he awoke to the racket in the upper regions.

Behold him, then, angry and perspiring, vowing by all his gods that he had other duties to perform than eternally watching the comings and goings of the mansion's occupants; being a free-born American of Irish ancestry, name of Rafferty, he would certainly have bandied contumely with Count Ladislas Vassilan had not the Earl intervened. The Hungarian had addressed Rafferty as though he were a dog: the Englishman, more certain of his social predominance, treated him as a person endowed with reason.

"Now, listen to me, my good man," he said, calmly but emphatically, "I am the Earl of Valletort, and the lady you know as Miss Grandison is the Lady Hermione Grandison, my daughter. She has come to New York in order to marry a wretched little French adventurer named Jean de Courtois, and it is absolutely essential, for her own welfare, not to mention other considerations, that the wedding, which is to take place to-night, shall be prevented. Two European consuls and several important men in your own city have helped me to land this evening from a vessel which will not disembark her passengers till the morning. Therefore, it is fairly obvious that you run several sorts of risk by refusing to help me in finding my daughter, and I can hardly believe that you know nothing about her movements.... Come, my man, don't be both a fool and a knave, but speak!"

Rafferty, who had calmed down during this impressive harangue, took thought, and did speak.

"If yer friend had said half as much, my lord, I'd have made him wise straight away," he answered. "Miss Grandison went off at 8.30

in a taxi with her maid, Marcelle Leroux, and a strange gentleman who certainly wasn't Mr. de Courtois, my lord. They wanted to find out where a clergyman lived, an' I couldn't tell them—not about the Protestant Episcopal, I mean, my lord—but the driver of the taxi remembered that there was a minister of that persuasion living in 56th Street, near 7th Avenue, an' next door to a church. So they made a bee-line that-a-way, my lord, an' I went to see to the furnace, an' that's all there is to it, my lord."

"You say the man was not de Courtois?" queried the Earl impatiently.

"I'm sure he wasn't the man who has passed under that name hereabouts nearly every day for a month, my lord," said Rafferty.

"Oh, some fellow of his own kidney he has hired to assist him," put in Vassilan, who held fast to that theory, in part, even after he had been painfully disillusioned as to other parts of it. "Come quickly now, you, and tell our chauffeur where to take us."

If Rafferty had dared, he would have given the chauffeur directions likely to lead to further bickering, but the presence of the Earl restrained him, for Valletort, though thin and hawk-nosed, was an aristocrat in every inch, whereas Count Ladislas Vassilan wore the stage aspect of a successful pork-butcher. So he explained matters to the chauffeur, yet smiled grimly when the automobile wheeled away almost in the very tracks of Curtis's taxi.

"Who sez there's no such thing as luck?" he chuckled. "That valve knew what it was about when it stuck, an' my name ain't what it is if that wedding isn't over and done with by this time. An' I gev him 'my lord' for it, too! Played the high-tone society act for all it was worth, eh, what?"

The next scene in the drama began for the Hungarian when he sat upon the sidewalk in 56th Street, and tried to pacify certain outraged blood-vessels in the nasal region. Of course, the curtain had been up some time, but, so far as he was concerned, the incidents which

51

followed his precipitate descent from the automobile were merely catastrophic. He had seen a vivid, violet-colored star close to his eyes, had felt a crushing blow, had heard his own voice vaguely; and then he awoke to a singular sense of personal dis-ease, and to the fact that the noble Earl had nearly lost his temper.

"It was entirely your fault, Vassilan," his lordship was saying. "You gain nothing but lose everything by your bullying tactics. Dash it all, the fellow downed you like a prize-fighter. Who was he? Not Jean de Courtois, I'll swear, so where has de Courtois gone? Can't you stand up? It's damn silly to sit there, nursing your nose. Our motor-car is out of action. We had better interview this clergyman, and learn exactly what has happened."

Vassilan rose. He was neither a coward nor a weakling, but he felt sore in mind as in body.

"What's wrog with the car?" he demanded. "Ad cad you led me ad hadkerchief?"

"That rascal who was with Hermione nearly pulled the gear levers out by the roots," said the Earl testily. "He pushed me back into the limousine—with some degree of force, too, confound him! Who can he be?"

"Suppose we idquire," growled Vassilan, and, mopping his nose with the Earl's handkerchief, he tugged viciously at the old-fashioned bell-pull which served the needs of visitors to the Rev. Thomas J. Hughes.

The maid-servant who took the names of the two men was surprised, and showed it, but her democratic respect for titles yielded to suspicion when she observed Count Vassilan's villainous guise.

"Wil-li-am!" she cried, and, when the ex-sailor appeared from the depths, she asked him to "look after the gentlemen" while she summoned Mr. Hughes.

"Cad you take me somewhere, ad supply me with a towel ad pledty of cold water?" said the Hungarian, addressing the wizened one.

Now, Jenkins was verger and pew-opener in the church as well as trusted assistant to the aged minister, but the ways and language of the fo'c's'l came back to him with irresistible force when he gazed on the Hungarian's damaged organ.

"Lord love a duck, you've had it handed to you all right," he gasped. "How did you get it? Did you foul a lamp-post, or bump a rock, or what?"

"It is edough that I have met with ad accided," snarled the Count. "Cad't you see that I wadt some water? Is there do place where I cad wash?"

"What you reely want is a tap," said Jenkins sympathetically. "An' I shouldn't be surprised if a slab of raw beefsteak across yer lamps wouldn't be a bully good notion, too, or you'll have a lovely pair of mice in the morning."

Then, hearing Mr. Hughes's voice from the library, he suddenly recollected the habits of later years.

"Come with me, sir," he said, leading the way to the basement. "I'll do my best for you."

Perhaps it was fortunate for the success of his mission that the Earl of Valletort was left free to deal with the clergyman. The Count's hectoring methods would certainly have stiffened the worthy old gentleman's back, whereas he yielded readily to the Earl's skillful handling. He was much pained at hearing that a peer's daughter should have fallen into the hands of an adventurer.

"Dear me! Dear me!" he wheezed. "This is very sad. The man looked quite a gentleman, I assure you. And he had not the least semblance to a foreigner. His name, too—John D. Curtis—is your lordship really certain of the facts?"

Now, "John" and "Jean" are sufficiently alike in sound to pass muster with the average man, who also connotes no difference between "D" and "de," but the Earl was moved to say quickly:

"Perhaps you are not accustomed to French names, Mr. Hughes?"

"No, I admit it. But, here is an unimpeachable witness," and the minister produced the license from a drawer in the writing-desk.

Lord Valletort glanced at it, and a peculiarly unpleasant scowl convulsed his aristocratic features. Hitherto, a stranger might have believed that Hermione's unfavorable picture of her father had been tinged by a high-spirited girl's hatred of the marriage which he was forcing upon her; but that fleeting expression spoke volumes. If Count Vassilan was of the bovine order, the Earl of Valletort savored of the tiger.

He contrived to smile, however, and the effort to figure wholly as a disconsolate parent cost him far more than he dreamed, since he examined neither the actual certificate nor the register, though both would have been submitted to his scrutiny by the bewildered Mr. Hughes.

"Thank you," he said. "I fully appreciate the position. The scoundrel has learnt how to give an English sound to his name. Probably my daughter taught him. Hard though it is for a father to say such a thing, she is the real brain behind this sordid story of intrigue and wrong-doing."

"Dear me!" gasped Mr. Hughes again. He felt that he must, indeed, be growing old. He had married many hundreds of couples during his ministerial career, and had, in many instances, compared the subsequent lives of his matrimonial clients with the impressions formed during the ceremony, yet never had he been so gravely at fault as in his summing-up of the characteristics of John D. Curtis and Hermione Beauregard Grandison.

Vassilan emerged from the kitchen, dripping but less gory, and the two visitors disappeared, whereupon Mr. Hughes confided his mystification to Jenkins.

But Wil-li-am shook his cadaverous head.

"Mebbe the Earl was right, an' mebbe he was wrong," he said decisively. "I didn't size up the Earl, so I let it go at that, but I did see the other guy—beg pardon, sir, I mean the other gentleman—an' he'll be lucky if he gets to bed to-night without being clubbed by a policeman. Someone has been at him already—hard at him—an' I'm not surprised, for his langwidge reminded me of my best days at sea."

"William!"

"What, sir? Oh, I meant my young days, of course. Now, I wonder——"

It had just occurred to Jenkins that Mr. Curtis and his bride could hardly have got clear away from 56th Street before the Earl and his companion turned up.

"Gee!" he cackled. "I wish I hadn't closed the door so damn quick!"

Mr. Hughes raised hands of horrified protest, and Jenkins wilted.

"Sorry, sir," he stammered. "I must have got a bit wound up when I saw the foreign gentleman's nose. When I went a-whalin' on the *Star of the Sea* we had a first mate who could man-handle anybody, but even he would have had to use a belayin' pin to stamp his trade-mark in *that* shape. Now, the question is—*could* it have been this here Mr. Curtis? It reely is a pity I was so—so spry on the door."

Outside, the chauffeur had announced that he had straightened the levers sufficiently to render them serviceable, and he was directed to make for the Central Hotel, 27th Street, but he had not reached Broadway before the Earl bade him return to Mr. Hughes's residence. What had happened was this—Lord Valletort's recollection of the physique and manner of Jean de Courtois fitted in so ill with the knock-down blow delivered to a portly individual like Ladislas Vassilan that he began to compare the remarks of the elevator man at 1000 59th Street with the confusion in the clergyman's mind on the question of names. Then, though the light had been dim, and his mind was given more to the recognition of his daughter than of the person accompanying her, he was conscious of a growing conviction that the French music-master was a being of an altogether different species. Vassilan, too, having regained some degree of self-control, confirmed him in the belief that there must be some error in their reckoning, and agreed that they might save time by interviewing Mr. Hughes again.

But when the mild eyes of the minister rested on the Count's truculent visage, and noted his water-soaked and blood-stained clothing, there was a distinct drying up in the fount of information.

"No," he said stiffly, in reply to the Earl's request that the marriage license should be produced again, "I regret that I cannot reopen that matter to-night. To-morrow, if you have any cause for complaint, you should consult the proper authorities."

"But you must allow me to emphasize the fact that the license is made out for the marriage of a man with a French name, whereas admittedly you have married my daughter to a man with an English or American name," said the Earl.

"I express no opinion on the point. Your lordship may be assuming facts which are not facts."

"I am making a statement which can be verified quite easily. The name I saw on the license was that of Jean de Courtois, an undersized Frenchman whom I know by sight, whereas my unfortunate friend is a living witness to the presence here of a man who must be of powerful build and exceptional strength."

Mr. Hughes surveyed Vassilan's battered face again, and a doubt, born of a vague memory, began to intrude into his own mind. Moreover, he was an eminently reasonable old gentleman.

"Ah, yes," he said. "My man, Jenkins, said something about a first mate and a belaying pin, whatever that may be—I fancy it is an instrument connected with the flaying of whales—and the bridegroom could certainly not be described as 'an undersized Frenchman' by anyone who paid due regard to the truth.... Well, the whole proceeding is highly irregular, but the circumstances are quite exceptional, so——"

In a word, the Earl and Count Vassilan were soon gorged with astonished wrath, for, no matter what discrepancies might exist between license and certificate, there could be no dispute as to the bold signature "John D. Curtis" in the register, while Hermione's handwriting compelled Lord Valletort to believe that he was not the victim of hallucination.

It is easy to see, therefore, how the chase after John D. Curtis became hot thenceforth, but cooled off perceptibly on the trail of Jean de Courtois. The hunters, of course, credited Hermione with a talent for craft and duplicity which she certainly did not possess; being rogues, or of the essence of rogues, they suspected her of roguery, and, in so doing, dug a deep pit for themselves.

On arriving at the Central Hotel they were plunged into a denser fog than ever, and by means so ludicrously simple that even a budding dramatist would hesitate to avail himself of such a crude device. The police had searched the dead man's clothing without finding any positive clew to his name. His linen was marked H. R. H., and certain laundry marks might serve to establish his identity after long and patient inquiry, but the detective who had charge of the case felt that it was becoming unusually complex when the victim's overcoat was produced and the pockets were found to contain letters, a *Lusitania* wine bill, and a Marconigram—all pointing to the clear fact that the owner of the coat was John D. Curtis.

The detective, Steingall by name, was one of the shrewdest men in the New York police, and his extraordinary faculty of observing minute facts which had escaped others while investigating a crime had earned him the repute of being "the man with a microscopic eye." But he owned to being mystified by this juggling with names.

"Why," he said to the police captain of the precinct, "this fellow Curtis is the man who witnessed the murder, and who will be our most reliable witness if we lay hands on the scoundrels who committed it."

"He *said* his name was Curtis," commented the other.

The implied doubt seemed to be justified, but Steingall stroked his chin reflectively.

"These papers bear out his story. Look at the dates on the telegram and the bill, and the postmarks on the letters. Can he, by some queer chance, have changed overcoats with the dead man?"

"A most unlikely thing, I should say."

"Something of the sort must have happened. Anyhow, let us get hold of him, and sift this matter thoroughly."

An ambulance came just then, to take the body to the mortuary, and, when it had departed, the two men quitted the traffic bureau where they had been talking, and entered the hotel. Here, excitement was still at fever heat. The press had heard of the murder, and a number of reporters were interviewing everybody in sight, while photographers were adding to the confusion by taking flash-light pictures.

The super-clerk was already showing tokens of the strain. He glared wildly at Steingall when the latter asked if Mr. Curtis was in.

"You're the hundred and first man to whom I have answered 'No' in the last quarter of an hour," he said.

"The first hundred didn't count, anyway," was the dry response. "Pull yourself together, and read that card slowly and collectedly."

"Well," he went on, seeing that the clerk had apparently mastered the copper-plate script, "you see I am not here for amusement. Now, about Curtis, are you sure he is not in his room?"

"His key has not been given up, but I have sent to 605, and we can't get in."

"What do you mean? Is the door locked?"

"We can open every lock in the hotel. It is bolted."

"Have you knocked?"

"We've done everything, short of breaking open the door."

Steingall looked perplexed, but the police captain was confident.

"He has buncoed us, for sure," he said with a smile, though the smile boded evil for John D. Curtis at their next meeting.

"Did you notice him particularly when he registered?" demanded the detective, after a pause.

"Yes. Came to-night by the *Lusitania*. Here is his signature."

The three men gazed at the register, and Steingall produced a card, on which Curtis had written the name of the hotel.

"Same handwriting!" he murmured. "By the way," he continued, addressing the clerk, "were you here when the murder took place?"

"Yes."

"Did you see anything of it?"

"Not a scratch. I was busy with a lady, who was worrying me about a train to Montclair. She was five minutes making up her mind whether to take the Jersey tunnel or the 23rd Street ferry."

"The only other person, beside Curtis, who saw the whole affair was the hall-porter?"

"I guess that's so."

"Call him into the office."

Questioned anew, the hall-porter was positive about everything except Curtis's connection with the attack. The reporters had scalped him, metaphorically speaking, and his brain was seething. He said "No" when he meant "Yes," and "Yes" for "No," and contradicted himself in each fresh version of the cataclasm which had seared his sky with lightning.

Steingall ultimately gave him up as hopeless that night. Perhaps, next morning, when he had slept and eaten, he might become sane again.

"It's an odd thing that Curtis should have wandered away in this fashion, wearing a strange overcoat," mused the detective aloud.

"He must know it," said the police captain meaningly.

"I rather think we must force that door," said Steingall.

The clerk did not understand the reference to the overcoat, but he was ready enough to adopt the detective's suggestion.

"Shall I send for the engineer, and tell him to bring tools?" he asked.

"There is nothing else for it," admitted Steingall with a shrug. Be it remembered he had seen Curtis, and heard his story. If such a man had committed the most daring crime recorded in New York during a decade, and had flouted the police with such cool effrontery, he (Steingall) would never again trust impressions.

The policemen, the clerk, and a strong-armed artificer went up in the elevator, and, after an imperative knock and a loud-voiced summons to open had been met with blank silence from the interior of No. 605, the workman got busy. The door was stout, and offered a stubborn resistance. It had to be forced off its upper hinge; then it yielded so suddenly that it fell into the room, with the engineer sprawling on top of it. The man yelled, thinking he was being plunged headlong into tragedy, but Steingall switched on the lights, and four pairs of eager eyes peered at nothing in particular. They found the golf clubs, which partially explained the blocking of the door, though it did not occur to any of them at once that the open window might have caused the bag to fall. They rummaged Curtis's portmanteaux and steamer trunks, and came upon evidence in plenty to prove that he was no mere masquerader in another man's name. But that was all. They could form no theory to account for his disappearance, until Steingall noticed the key, lying on the dressing-table, which, with its odds and ends of small articles, was the last place to invite scrutiny. He was gazing at it when the blind flapped, and the door of the wardrobe creaked.

"Confound it!" he cried. "The bedroom door was fastened by accident! The man forgot his key. Look here! I'll show you just how it came about."

He illustrated the slipping of the clubs, and his theory was borne out subsequently by the negro porter who had brought Curtis's belongings upstairs. But an atmosphere of suspicion, of non-comprehension, had been created around the missing man, and it was not to be dispelled, even in Steingall's acute mind, by whittling away the mystery of the blocked door to a minor incident which might occur in any hotel any day.

Leaving the mechanic and the negro to patch the shattered door sufficiently to serve its purpose until it was replaced by another in the morning, the clerk escorted the representatives of the law downstairs. Of course, their departure from the hall and their prolonged absence had been noted by the phalanx of reporters, and they were surrounded instantly. Searching questions were fired at them, but Steingall, who knew how to use the press for his own ends, countered by asking genially:

"In your hunt for copy, have any of you boys come across Mr. John D. Curtis?"

"The man who really saw the riot? I guess not. We want him badly."

An approving grin from his colleagues vouched for the speaker's accuracy.

"Who was killed, anyhow, Steingall?" demanded the journalist who had answered the detective.

"We don't know, yet."

"Does Curtis know?"

"He said he didn't, but I'll tell you something—I shan't be happy till I've had another chat with him."

"Can anyone say who 'John D. Curtis, of Pekin,' really is?" went on the reporter.

"That is the man we are looking for. If there are police officers present, I want them to understand that Curtis should be arrested at sight."

Everyone turned at the sound of the authoritative English voice which had intervened so unexpectedly in the conclave. They saw an elderly man, well dressed, and bearing the unmistakable tokens of good social standing. With him was a foreigner, a most truculent looking person, whose collar, shirt, and waistcoat carried other signs, quite as obvious, but curiously ominous in view of the cause of this gathering in the hall of the hotel.

"May I ask who you are, sir?" said Steingall.

"I am the Earl of Valletort," said the stranger, "and this is Count Ladislas Vassilan."

"Ah! Count Vassilan is not an Englishman?"

"No, but——"

"Is he, by any chance, a Hungarian?"

"Count Vassilan is a Hungarian prince. But the nationality of either of us is unimportant. Are you connected with the New York police?"

"Yes," said Steingall. He answered the Earl, but kept that microscopic eye of his fixed on the Count.

"Very well, then. I repeat that John D. Curtis must be found and arrested—to-night."

"Why?"

"Because he is a dangerous adventurer. I——"

"That's a lie, first sizz out of the syphon," broke in another voice. "I have the honor to be a friend of John D. Curtis. My name is Howard Devar, and I'll stand for John D. all the time against the noble Earl and any God's quantity of blue-blooded, full-blooded Hungarians."

Each member of the animated group was gazing at Devar's boyish, self-possessed, well-chiseled face, when another interruption held them agog. A stout, middle-aged man, followed by a stouter matron, bustled into the circle. The newcomers were just as clearly Americans as the Earl was English, and the man cried angrily:

"Who says that John D. Curtis is a tough? I'm his uncle."

"And I'm his aunt," chimed in the lady.

"Of Bloomington, Monroe County, Indiana," said the man.

"Mr. and Mrs. Horace P. Curtis," announced the lady.

"Shake!" said Devar. "I heard about you to-day on board the *Lusitania*.... Now, my lord, we are three to two. What charge do you bring against John D. Curtis?"

CHAPTER V

NINE O'CLOCK

A new note had crept into the voice of the taxi-cab driver when he stopped his vehicle in Madison Avenue and sought Curtis's further commands. No longer did he address his patron with a species of good-humored tolerance, almost of sarcasm; his mental attitude had now become one of respect, even of hero-worship. A little later, while smoking a thoughtful pipe in his own cozy flat somewhere near Second Avenue, he tried to explain this curious development to his wife.

"You see, my dear," he said, "I picked up a fare in Broadway, an' took him where he said he wanted to go. When he got out, he didn't seem to be quite sure whether he wanted to be there or not, an' you can bet I smiled when he said that he supposed the lady he was callin' on lived somewhere around. Anyhow, after hesitatin' a bit, an' tellin' me he wouldn't keep me a minnit, in he dives, an' kep' me coolin' my heels a good quarter of an hour. I grew uneasy, because fares do get so nasty about waitin' charges, so I signals the elevator man, name o' Rafferty, to ask if it was O.K. When Rafferty comes back, we had a chat, an' he tells me that this Miss Grandison—a mighty smart piece she is, too,—was goin' to marry a little Frenchman right away—she was expectin' him to call at eight o'clock an' take her to the minister's place—so it gev' both Rafferty an' me a jar when my dude turns up with the girl an' pipes us for any old address where people could get married. Well, I remembers the number of a shovel hat in 56th Street, an' away we hike, man, girl, an' lady's maid, with never a sign of any Frenchman anywheres. An', by Jove, in they skipped to the parsonage, an' were spliced."

"No, George!" exclaimed his highly interested hearer.

"Fact. True as I'm sittin' here. When they were comin' out, a queer lookin' specimen who opened the door wished 'em happiness. 'Fair weather to you an' your wife, sir,' he said; an' Mr. Curtis—that's my fare's name, I asked him—said something about havin' finished one long voyage an' beginnin' another. Then the fun began. I was just startin' the machine when a private auto dashes up, an' out jumps a foreign-lookin' swell. The girl spots him, an' screams his name—Count Vaseline it sounded like—an' he shouts, 'Here we are, Valtaw'—p'raps that was his way of sayin' Walter—'Got 'em, by—You see after Hermione. I'll fix this—Frenchman?'"

"Don't swear, George," remonstrated the driver's better half.

"I'm not swearin'. Ain't I tellin' you what he said?"

The point was waived.

"And the lady's name was Hermione, was it? It's a pretty name."

"You haven't got it quite right. It was more like the way I said it."

And, indeed, the correction was justified, since it is a regrettable fact that the taxi-cab driver's wife made "Hermione" rhyme with "bone," and laid no stress on the second syllable. Strong in her superior knowledge, for she was an omnivorous reader of fiction—and Greek names were fashionable last November—she passed that point also.

"Well?" she demanded breathlessly.

"Ha, ha!" The narrator laughed joyfully. "The Dago Count went for Curtis as if he was on to a sure thing, but before you could say 'knife' he was on his back on the sidewalk. I've never seen a man put down so quick. I couldn't have floored him so beautifully if I'd hit him with a spanner. But that was only part of the entertainment. Curtis—mind you, before that I'd been treatin' him as an ordinary dude in evenin' dress—acted like an injarubber man filled with chain lightning. He shoved 'Valtaw' back into the auto, grabs the brake an' gear lever, an' puts 'em both out of action, sweeps the two girls into my cab, and——"

Here the taxi-driver bethought himself, and grinned vacuously.

"Well—an' here I am," he concluded.

"I suppose he handed out a good fare," said his wife.

"Yes, he was quite decent about it. Tipped me a couple of dollars over an' above the register."

"I should have thought it would have been more. Men are usually generous when they are getting married."

"He was takin' on a rather expensive bit of stuff, unless I am much mistaken, an' p'raps he was just rememberin' it."

In this ingenuous fashion was a poor woman neatly headed off the scent of a fifty-dollar bill. She rang the knell of a new hat by her next question.

"What was the young lady really like—how was she dressed?" she cried....

Hardly a word was said within the taxi until the corner was turned out of 56th Street into Seventh Avenue. Curtis, who was sitting with his back to the driver, rose, apologized for the disturbance, and looked through the tiny rear window.

"That's all right," he said. "That car won't be able to move for several minutes; but we must leave nothing to chance," so he sank back into a seat, and permitted the driver to take them whither he listed.

Hermione's first words were not exactly those of a fair maid in utmost distress.

"Oh, how splendid it must be to feel sure that you are able to hit a wretch like Count Vassilan and knock him flat!" she cried.

Curtis was surprised. He could not see her kindling eyes, her parted lips, the color which was suffusing forehead and cheeks, and he rather expected to hear subdued sobbing.

"I should hate to have you dislike me as thoroughly as you dislike that fellow," he said.

"I never could. It cannot be in your nature to treat women as he treats them. I do hope you have hurt him."

"I am certain of that, at any rate," laughed Curtis. "He impressed me as weighing a hundred and ninety pounds or thereabouts, and, if it will afford you the slightest gratification, I'll take the first opportunity to work out the approximate force required to drive back a moving body of that weight while traveling forward, say, fifteen miles an hour. There are angles of resistance to be calculated, too, so it offers a decent problem. Meanwhile, the vital question is — where are we going?"

Hermione was easily chaffed out of her bellicose mood. He could picture the droop in the corners of her mouth as she said forlornly:

"I do not know."

"It is evident," he went on, "that they procured the minister's address from the elevator man at your dwelling."

"Ah, that Rafferty! Wait till I see him," broke in Marcelle.

"Please do not scarify Rafferty, if that is his name. I am much more to be blamed than he, because I assured your mistress that the Earl and Count Vassilan were safe on board the *Switzerland* till the morning. I see now that they telegraphed for a tug, and it is best to assume that they have been kept informed by wireless of nearly every move in the game.... You agree with me, I suppose, Lady Hermione, that your return to 1000 59th Street is out of the question?"

"It is, if this mock marriage is to serve any real purpose," she said.

"But pray remember that it is not a mock marriage. You and I are as firmly bound together by the law as if—well, as if we meant it."

She leaned forward a little; her face was etched in Rembrandt lights by the glare from some shop windows.

"Mr. Curtis," she said earnestly, "it is neither just nor reasonable that you should plunge yourself into difficulties for the sake of a girl whom you met to-night for the first time. Why not go out of my life now—this instant?... Marcelle and I can find refuge somewhere. The hour is early.... Why should you take all the risk?"

He was ready for some such appeal on her part.

"I was taught in school if I did a thing at all to do it thoroughly," he said, "and my experience of life has given the adage a halo. It would be worse than useless to desert you now, Lady Hermione. Whatever penalties I may have incurred in the eyes of the law are committed beyond hope of redemption. If I am sought for, the police know exactly where to lay hands on me, and my crime would become monstrous if it were proved that I ran away from my wife on the night of our marriage. No; we must face the music boldly, and together. We must go to some well-known hotel, register openly, secure rooms, and conduct ourselves on the orthodox lines of all runaway couples, who are presumably head over heels in love with each other. Moreover, in the morning, or whenever we are run to earth, you should allow me to face your father and play the part of the indignant husband. It is essential that your marriage should appear real, or you go back to bondage and I to prison."

"To prison!" The girl's horrified accents showed that she had hardly given a thought to the bald consequences of her escapade.

"Yes. I am not trying to frighten you; but what sort of mercy would a judge show to the craven who absconded before the battle began? If, on the other hand, I am, so to speak, torn from your arms—if a plausible lawyer can depict you tearful and inconsolable—if——"

"You make out a fairly strong case, Mr. Curtis. I have told you that I trust you, and I can only repeat my words of gratitude.... Marcelle, you will not leave me?"

"Never, miss, ma'am—that is, your ladyship."

Thus it befell that Curtis was ready with the name of a prominent hotel in Fifth Avenue when the driver halted in Madison Avenue. He made his choice almost at random, but selected one of the newest uptown caravanserais, merely because it lay a considerable distance from 27th Street. Otherwise, his object in picking a large hotel being to avoid notice among a fashionable throng, he might easily have taken his "wife" to the Waldorf-Astoria, in which event certain complications even then hot in the making would not have followed their intricate course, while Hermione's future must have been affected most powerfully.

"I suppose you are prepared to submit to certain conditions which govern this new venture?" said Curtis, when the cab was once more speeding onward to a definite goal.

"What are they?"

It would be scarcely fair to describe Hermione's tone as suspicious, for she was a loyal soul, and was wondering in her heart of hearts what manner of man this knight errant could be; but his very self-possession fluttered her; she had been so accustomed to think and act in her own defense that she experienced a subtle fear of this calm, cool-headed, masterful person whom she must learn to regard as her husband.

"Well,"—Curtis's speech was so unemotional that he might have been describing one of his Manchurian railway schemes—"we must treat each other with a certain familiarity—even use little endearments—in public—and address each other by pet names—mine is Chow."

SCENES FROM THE PHOTO-DRAMA.

71

Despite her troubles, the girl laughed, and Curtis recalled the tinkle of silver bells in a temple at evening on the banks of the far-away Wei-ho.

"But that is the name of a dog!" she tittered.

"Yes. In my case, it denoted some unpleasant personal characteristics when a stupid mandarin put obstacles in my way. I never gave any warning, but rushed in and bit him, not actually, of course, but in his illicit commissions, which annoyed him more than a real bite."

"I don't like Chow," she said. "Your name is John. Won't Jack do?"

"Fine." It was lucky she could not see the smile that flitted across his face. "And yours?"

"Mamma always used my full name, and I have never had anyone else to give me a pet name, unless it was 'Tatters' at school."

"We might bracket Tatters with Chow, and dismiss both," he said lightly. "And I like the sound of Hermione so well that it is pat on my lips already.... Now, you, Marcelle—remember that her ladyship has become Lady Hermione Curtis."

"Oh, not Mrs. Curtis?"

"No. An earl's daughter retains her courtesy title after marriage."

"All right, sir. I shan't forget." Indeed, Marcelle was jubilant. She had been "dying" to use her mistress's title, once she became aware of it, but it was taboo at 59th Street.

Curtis had covered a good deal of ground during that brief discussion in the cab, but Hermione was not quite prepared for its logical sequel in the hotel.

Naturally, they attracted no unusual attention when they entered the hotel. Other people merely noticed the passing of a distinguished looking young man in evening dress—for Curtis had promptly whipped off that ominous overcoat—and a slender, veiled lady, of elegant carriage, who walked up to the bureau, followed by a smartly dressed girl who gazed about her with bright, all-seeing eyes.

"My wife and I have been detained in New York this evening unexpectedly," explained Curtis to the hotel clerk. "We want a suite of rooms, a sitting-room, three bedrooms with baths—you would like Marcelle's room to communicate with yours, wouldn't you, dear?" and he turned suddenly to Hermione.

"Y-yes," she faltered, for the attack took her unaware.

"What floor, sir? We have a nice suite on the tenth."

"Not so high, please," said Hermione. Then she sprung a mine on her own account. "I know it is stupid, Jack, darling, but I am so afraid of fire."

"This hotel is absolutely fireproof, madam," put in the clerk, stating a fact implicitly believed by every hotel proprietor in New York in so far as his own building is concerned, "but we can accommodate you on the second floor, Suite F., fifty dollars a day."

"Thank you. That will be just right," said Curtis quickly, for he meant to live like a prince during one night at least, let the morrow bring its own cares. "Now, you understand that we are here without baggage, though my wife's maid will procure some necessaries while we eat, and I mean to get some clothes later, but, if you would like a deposit of, say, a hundred dollars——?"

He felt for his pocketbook, but, to the credit of the clerk be it said, the suggestion was negatived with a smile.

"No need at all for any deposit, sir," was the answer. "I wouldn't be on to my job it I didn't know how and when to discriminate in matters of that sort. Will you register?"

Curtis took a pen and wrote:

"Mr. and Lady Hermione Curtis, and maid." Some imp of adventure moved him to inscribe "Pekin" in the column for visitors' home addresses. But the clerk was obviously impressed by Hermione's title, no less than the singularly remote locality the couple hailed from. He leant back, and took a key from its hook.

"Page!" he said. "Show Mr. Curtis and her ladyship to Suite F." Then he added, as an afterthought: "Would you like dinner served in your sitting-room, sir?"

"I think so," said Curtis, "but my wife shall decide a little later."

Hermione kept silent until they were safely behind the closed door of a well-furnished and delightfully spacious apartment.

"Of course, I bear all expenses," she said firmly.

"What—are we quarreling already?" he asked.

"No, but——"

"You think I am being wildly extravagant. Why, bless your ladyship's dear little heart, this hotel doesn't begin to know how to charge like a taxi. Now, no argument till to-morrow. An American millionaire can really be quite a decent sort of fellow at times, and, if we may assume that this is one of the times, please let me play at being a millionaire—for once."

She raised her veil, and looked at him, straight in the eyes.

"Why are you so different from other men? Why have I never before spoken to a man like you?" she asked.

"But I am not different, and there are plenty of men like me; the other poor chaps haven't had my glorious chance of serving you—that is all. Now, won't you go and see if your room is comfortable, and whether or not Marcelle's quarters are just right? Then come back here, and we'll discuss menus, for which purpose I shall ring for a waiter *ek dum.*"

"Is that Chinese?"

"No, Hindustani. It means 'at once,' but every hotel-wala east of Suez understands it."

Still she lingered.

"Have you any sisters—a mother living?" she said.

"No. I'm the sole survivor of my own family. But I mean to give myself the pleasure of a full introduction while we dine, or sup. Do say you are hungry."

"I have not eaten a morsel since luncheon," she confessed.

"Oh, joy! I must interview the head waiter. No common serf will suffice. Please hurry."

She left him, not without an impulsive movement as though she meant to utter some further words of thanks, but checked her intent on the very threshold of speech. As the lock of the bedroom door clicked, and he was alone, he essayed a review of the amazing sequence of events which had befallen since he strolled out of the dining-room of the Central Hotel. He stood there, motionless, with hands plunged deep in his pockets, but, at the outset of a reverie in which judgment and prudence might have helped in the council, he happened to catch sight of himself in an oblong mirror over the mantelpiece, for the apartment, redolent of New York's later architecture, contained an open grate, and was furnished with the chaste beauty of the Chippendale period. In his present position the reflection in the mirror was oddly reminiscent of a half-length portrait of his grandfather, the warrior who rode at the head of the Fifth Cavalry in '61.

Then Curtis laughed, with the pleasant conviction of a man whose mind has been made up for him by circumstances beyond his control.

"It's bred in the bone—a clear case of Mendelism," he murmured softly, because he had just remembered how Colonel Curtis, before ever the war was ended and its bitterness assuaged, had decided a Southern girl's conflict between love and duty by galloping fifty miles across Confederate South Carolina and carrying off the lady.

Grandfather and grandson alike were men of action. Curtis seldom used a gesture, and never cried over spilt milk. Now he merely turned, peered into his own bedroom, assured himself that Hermione would find its prototype to her fancy, and then summoned a waiter.

Behind the closed door of the other room a girl was similarly engaged in taking stock of the situation; but she had feminine assistance, so there was bound to be talk.

"Oh, your ladyship, isn't this just the dandiest bit out of a novel you ever read?" cried Marcelle when she entered her mistress's room through a communicating door.

"It might be more thrilling if it were not a page out of my own life," said Hermione sadly. She, too, was gazing in a mirror, though, being a woman, the oppressive thought bobbed up through a sea of troubles that her hair must be untidy, and she owned neither comb nor brush.

"But, what luck, miss, your ladyship, to have found a gentleman like Mr. Curtis at the right moment. Talk about life buoys for drowning men and rich uncles from California in plays—who ever heard of anyone wanting a nice husband and getting him in such a way!"

Marcelle's eyes were positively glistening. And these two now were not mistress and maid, but a pair of highly strung women, and young ones at that.

"You have lost your wits in this night's excitement, Marcelle," said Hermione. "Don't you realize that I am only married under mere pretense. Mr. Curtis is nothing to me, nor I to him. He has been kind and gallant, and I am under an obligation which I can never discharge—but that is not marriage."

"It's awful like it, your ladyship."

"No, no. Drive such nonsense from your head. When you marry, don't you hope to love the man of your choice, and will you not feel sure that he loves you?"

"Oh, yes, miladi."

"Then how is it possible for any relationship of that sort to exist between Mr. Curtis and me?"

"You've gone a long way already, ma'am," giggled Marcelle.

"Please don't call me ma'am. It—it irritates me."

"Sorry, miladi, but you will admit, at least, a marriage being necessary, that you were fortunate in finding Mr. Curtis?"

"Yes, doubly fortunate—it is that fact which makes things hard for me."

"Makes what things hard, your ladyship?"

"Oh, I don't know. I scarce recognize my own voice. Marcelle, if I seem distraught and unreasonable, promise me you will pay no heed. For pity's sake, don't leave me!"

Hermione's eyes filled with tears, and Marcelle was on the verge of hysteria.

"I—can't imagine—what there is—to cry about," she murmured brokenly. "Nothing on earth would induce me to go away now—but

I do hope—and pray—you will be happy—even though—you only met your husband—little more than an hour ago!... And I believe in my heart, Lady Hermione, that you will soon see how fortunate you were in escaping that mincing little Frenchman——"

"Marcelle, the poor man is dead."

"Then it is the best turn he has done you, miladi. I never fancied him. There was something underhanded and mean about him. I have seen his face when you were not looking, and I'm sure he was a hypocrite."

"Marcelle, you will drive me crazy. Don't you understand that I have never intended to marry anybody—really?"

A knock at the door opening into the sitting-room came to Hermione's relief.

"Yes?" she said.

"If you can spare Marcelle, I would recommend that she should go to your flat for any clothes you may need," said Curtis's voice.

Hermione threw open the door.

"A little while ago you told me that it was impossible to think of returning there," she said.

"For you, yes, but not for your maid. Who is to hinder? That man, Rafferty, looked a decent sort of fellow."

"I can manage Rafferty all right," put in Marcelle.

"Of course you can," smiled Curtis. "Just pack a trunk or a couple of bags with Lady Hermione's belongings—you know what to bring—and get Rafferty to call a taxi without attracting too much notice. If you think you are being followed, put your pursuers off the scent.

But my own view is that 1000 59th Street is the last place anyone will think of watching to-night."

"Shall I go at once, your ladyship?" said Marcelle, and Hermione said "Yes," with a meekness that was admirable in a wife.

Curtis looked at his pretty bride's hat.

"I have ordered a meal," he said. "It will be served in a few minutes."

"I shall be ready," she replied, beginning nervously to take off her gloves. The wedding ring was inclined to accompany the left hand glove, but, after a second's hesitation, she replaced it. When she appeared in the sitting-room she had discarded her jacket, a close-fitting one of a style that fastened *à la militaire*, high in the neck. Beneath it she had been wearing a white silk blouse, and the delicate pink of her arms and throat was revealed now through its diaphanous sheen. A string of pearls supported a diamond cross on her breast, and on her left wrist was a watch set in small diamonds and turquoises and carried by a bracelet of gold filigree. She wore only one ring—*the* ring—and even the slight glance which Curtis gave it brought a vivid blush to her cheeks.

"I am not a past master in the art of ordering banquets," he said cheerily, turning at once to draw her attention to the table, "but the head-waiter here is a gourmet. He suggested caviare, a white soup, a king-fish, a tourne-dos, and a grouse—does that appeal?"

"You take my breath away," she said, with valorous effort to seem at ease.

"Now—as to wine?"

"I seldom touch wine."

"To-night it will make you sleep. What do you say to a glass of Clos Vosgeot?"

"Is that a claret?"

"Yes."

"Well, as it happens, that is the one wine I take."

The dinner proceeded most pleasantly. To his own astonishment, Curtis worked up sufficient appetite to enjoy the meal, though he would have stuffed himself remorselessly to save his charming *vis-à-vis* from the slightest embarrassment. But he only sipped the wine, for a sixth sense warned him that he must keep a clear head that night.

By inference rather than plain statement, for a deft waiter was constantly coming in and out, he supplied Hermione with glimpses of his own career, and ascertained from her that she had secured Marcelle's services through the good offices of a lady who was a fellow-passenger on the ship.

"She comes from New Orleans, but, notwithstanding her name, she does not speak French," said Hermione. "I think that rather accounts for——"

She stopped, and Curtis did not press for an explanation, but she continued, after a second's pause:

"Marcelle did not like Monsieur de Courtois. I imagined she was annoyed because he always conversed with me in a language she did not understand."

"Then I shall avoid Chinese," he laughed.

"Marcelle——"

Again she hesitated. She was positively dismayed by consciousness of the imminent disclosure, yet too well-bred even to appear to be withholding confidences.

"You have won Marcelle's golden opinion already," she said. "But let us talk of something else."

For the moment they were alone, and she glanced at the watch on her wrist.

"Have you made any plans?" she inquired, and her voice was low, yet sufficiently composed.

"For the future?"

"Yes."

"When Marcelle arrives, I am going to my hotel for some baggage. You, I suggest, are going to bed."

"You will return?"

"Within the hour—if I am alive."

"And to-morrow?"

"To-morrow, may it please your ladyship, we breakfast together at nine o'clock."

"Your plan, then, is mainly composed of eating and sleeping?"

"What else—our policy is one of drifting."

"You are extraordinarily good to me, Mr. Curtis."

"It is 'Jack' in the compact."

She sighed.

"Alas, this compact reads only one way. It means that you give and I receive. Will you—will you believe, in the future, that despair alone could have driven me to the course I have pursued?"

"No," he said sturdily.

"No? That is the only unkind thing you have said."

"I refuse to vilify happy chance in the name of black despair. But— here is Marcelle, and slaves bearing packages. I hear thuds in the next room."

And, indeed, the waiter entering just then with coffee, Marcelle's voice reached them sharply from the corridor:

"Now, you boy, be careful with that hat-box! Do you think you are an express man, or what?"

CHAPTER VI

NINE-THIRTY

Chance is often a skilled stage manager, and chance had arranged a really effective scene in the hall of the Central Hotel. The Earl of Valletort seemed to be somewhat unwilling to take up any of the gauntlets so readily thrown down by Devar and the Curtis family, and, for a few seconds, the ring of reporters was held spellbound by a situation which promised most excellently with regard to the all-important question of "copy."

Then the police captain, after waiting for Steingall to take the lead, nudged his silent colleague, and said gruffly:

"This thing cannot be gone into here. Those who can bring forward testimony of any value ought to come with Mr. Steingall and myself to the precinct station-house."

"Why lose time which cannot be overtaken later?" urged the Earl, appealing to Steingall, since it was the detective who had spoken to him in the first instance.

"We appear to be at cross purposes," said Steingall. "How did you two gentlemen get to know that a murder had been committed?"

"Murder!" gasped Count Vassilan.

"We are not talking of a murder, but of a most scandalous abduction, which will provide only one of a number of most serious charges against this person, Curtis," cried the Earl.

Vassilan seized him by the arm excitedly.

"Don't you understand, dear friend," he muttered in French. "The rascal must have killed de Courtois in order to gain possession of the marriage certificate."

"It will save trouble, sir, if you speak English here," said Steingall. Then he turned to the hotel clerk.

"Place a room at our disposal at once. Lord Valletort is quite right. We have not a second to waste."

A murmur of protest arose from the pressmen, though it was obvious that the police could not conduct the inquiry in the midst of an ever-growing crowd of residents and servants.

"Say, Steingall," whispered the reporter who had spoken for the others earlier, "can't you let us into this? We'll suppress anything you wish—I'll guarantee that, absolutely without reservation."

"*I* have no objection, but these high-toned strangers may not like it," said the detective quietly.

The Earl, when the point was referred to him, made no difficulty whatsoever about the presence of the journalists—in fact, he rather welcomed publicity.

"It is better that the truth should appear than a garbled and misleading version," he said affably. "I want your help, gentlemen. I know enough of newspaper ways to feel sure that a story of some sort will be star-headed in every news sheet in New York to-morrow, so my friend, Count Vassilan, and I are more than willing that you should be well informed."

Now, that phase of the problem was precisely what Count Ladislas Vassilan seemed to be exceedingly disconcerted about. He was singularly ill at ease. His florid face had paled to a dusky wanness when he heard the ugly word "Murder," and each passing moment served only to increase his agitation. Steingall, to all intents and purposes paying less heed to the man than to any other person present, had not missed one labored breath, one twitch of an eyelid, one nervous gesture. His phenomenal instinct in the detection of crime had fastened unerringly on a singular coincidence. Curtis had hazarded a guess that the real malefactors were Hungarians, and here was a Hungarian Count denouncing Curtis. Certainly that question of nationality promised remarkable developments.

When the whole party, consisting of some fifteen persons, had gathered behind the closed door of the hotel's private office, Steingall took the lead in directing the proceedings.

"It will help straighten out a tangle if I say exactly what has taken place here to-night—that is, to the best of our knowledge," he said. "There is every reason to believe that Mr. John D. Curtis arrived in New York this afternoon from Europe——"

"Right," broke in Devar. "I traveled with him on the *Lusitania*."

"Yes, his presence on board was announced in most of the papers," added a journalist.

"Please don't interrupt," said the detective. "You will be heard in your turn. Now, this Mr. Curtis was allotted room No. 605, and there is evidence to prove that he behaved like any ordinary individual who had just come from shipboard. He superintended the unpacking of his clothes, gave out a quantity of linen for the laundry, changed into evening dress, and dined alone. Thus far, there is ample corroboration of his own story, because his movements can be checked by the observation of half-a-dozen hotel employés. He says, by the way, that while buying some stamps at the cigar counter before going to the restaurant, he was jostled by a rough-looking foreigner, who apologized in broken French, and whom he took to be a Czech or Hungarian. No one seems to have witnessed this incident, but I have not questioned the man who sold him the stamps. Anyhow, after dinner, at twenty minutes of eight to be exact, he came into the lobby, intending to inform the clerk that he had closed the bedroom door and left his key in the room. We have ascertained that this statement is true; the door had to be forced, because a bag of golf clubs had fallen and become wedged between the door and the side of a steel trunk. Curtis never did speak to the clerk about the key; at that instant, he says, his attention was drawn to the queer behavior of the foreigner who had pushed against him, and who had been joined in the meantime by another man of similar type. They seemed to be very excited, and were apparently expecting someone to turn up, either in the street or from the hotel—Curtis fancied that they were on the look-out for interruption, or news, from both quarters. The porter on duty at the door, who is not quite intelligible to-night, remembers asking these men if they wanted a taxi, but they gave no heed to him. Then, according to Curtis's version of the affair, an automobile dashed up outside, and a young man in evening dress, carrying an overcoat, stepped out, and told the chauffeur to keep the engine going, as he would not be detained more than a minute. At that instant the two foreigners—Hungarians according to Curtis—sprang at the newcomer, and endeavored to force him back into the auto. Failing in this, one of them drew a knife, and stabbed him so severely that he died within a few minutes, and without uttering an intelligible word. Curtis ran to help, but was too far away to prevent the crime, and was further balked in an attempt to seize either of the wretches by having the dying man's body flung in his way. He endeavored to hinder the escape of the scoundrels in the automobile, but failed, because the chauffeur was evidently in league with them, and, when he came back to the crowd which had collected around the prostrate man, it would appear that someone gave him, by mistake, the victim's overcoat in place of his own. This error was not discovered until the police came to search the dead man's clothing, when various documents showed beyond question that the overcoat believed to be his was really Curtis's. Curtis told his story in a clear and straightforward way, and I, for one, have not seen any reason to doubt it. It is odd that he should have disappeared so completely since a few minutes after the crime, but that may be capable of a simple explanation, while it is possible that he has not as yet discovered the change of overcoats, or he must surely have returned and informed us of the mistake. I am assuming, of course, that he would act as one would expect of any reasonable minded citizen who had witnessed a serious crime.... Now, Lord Valletort, what have you to say about Mr. Curtis?"

A guttural exclamation from Count Vassilan drew all eyes to him. He seemed to be on the verge of collapse, and was positively livid with fright. In other conditions than those obtaining at the moment, such a display of terror on the part of a truculent looking, strongly built man would have been almost ludicrous; but Steingall found no humor in the spectacle. He was gazing at the Hungarian with a curious concentration, and the police captain, who had begun by thinking his colleague was saying far too much, and who was inclined to disagree with some of his conclusions, now thought he could discern method in his madness.

Again did Vassilan murmur something to the Earl in a strange tongue, and Valletort, with difficulty repressing his annoyance, explained that his friend was feeling the effects of a blow received earlier in the evening, and wished to retire at once to his room in the Waldorf-Astoria Hotel.

"By all means," said Steingall suavely. "I gather that Count Vassilan has no connection with the inquiry—in fact, he is not interested in it."

"He is, in a sense——" began the Earl, but Vassilan grasped his arm, and evidently besought him to come away without another word. Though Valletort was in a towering rage, he obviously thought fit to fall in with his companion's views.

"You see how it is," he said, with a nonchalant gesture that was belied by his grating tone. "I am afraid I must postpone my branch of this inquiry till a later hour—probably until the morning."

"Do you withdraw all charges against John D. Curtis?" demanded Devar, and his clear, incisive voice was distinctly hostile in its icy precision.

"No, sir. I do not," was the angry retort.

"Well, I guess you know best why you and the Hungarian potentate have developed this sudden attack of cold feet, but——"

"I'll thank you not to interfere, Mr. Devar," said Steingall determinedly. "If Lord Valletort thinks his business can wait till Count Vassilan has recovered from an indisposition, that is his affair only."

"I think nothing of the sort," snapped the Earl. "You all see that the Count is ill, and common humanity impels me to attend to him first. It may serve to curb this young gentleman's tongue if I say — —"

But Vassilan would not permit him to say anything. Though he was the ailing man, he literally dragged Valletort out of the room and into the street.

Steingall looked at the police captain, who quitted the apartment instantly. Then the detective gazed around at the others with a placid smile which seemed to show that he, for one, was well content with the unusual turn taken by events.

"I suppose you boys have verbatim notes of all that was said," he inquired, tossing the remark collectively to the group of pressmen.

"Every word," came the assurance.

"Well, now, I want you to keep all that out of the papers."

"If we do that, Steingall, what is there left?" said one of them good-humoredly.

"The biggest thing you have dropped on to this year; unless I am greatly mistaken, the scoop of scoops for those who happen to be present. I'm not going to pretend that any of you are blind or deaf, and it will assist the police materially if no comment is made on what you have heard and seen. I don't like to put it otherwise than as a friendly hint; but I may want the whole bunch as witnesses before this thing is through, so your mouths should be closed effectually with regard to incidents in this room."

A half-hearted laugh went around, and someone asked:

"We must put up a readable story of some kind—if we cut out certain details, surely we can use others?"

"I said 'incidents in this room,'" repeated the detective.

"Then we can mention the arrival of the Earl and the Count on the scene?"

"Why not?"

"One minute, sir," put in Mr. Horace P. Curtis. "If these gentlemen take you at your word, the charge made against my nephew will be published throughout the length and breadth of the United States to-morrow."

"I don't see how something of the sort is to be avoided," said Steingall.

"Then, in common fairness, the newspapers ought to state that my wife and I, as well as Mr. Devar, as good as told the Earl that he was lying."

"I imagine you can leave the matter safely in the very capable hands of the reporters present," said Steingall.

"Remember, please, that no charge was actually named against Curtis," said Devar. "The Earl of Valletort demanded that he should be found and arrested, and described him as a dangerous adventurer, but gave no shred of proof of his wild-cat statement that Curtis had been engaged in a scandalous abduction, and, when asked for it, discovered that he had urgent business elsewhere."

Steingall held up a hand in quiet reproof.

"My own view is that it would be best, at this stage, to say merely that the two noblemen came here inquiring for Curtis, and leave it at that. I am not trying to deprive the press of a sensation. Surely there is enough in Chapter One for to-night, and those reporters who have had the luck to be present will be able to fill in gaps in Chapters Two and Three when they come along to-morrow or next day."

"Right," said the journalist who, by tacit agreement, seemed to represent his confrères. "There are one or two items we want you to clear up, if you don't mind. First, did Curtis, or anybody else, note the number of the automobile?"

"Yes," said Steingall instantly. "The number is X24-305, and Curtis heard the man who was murdered address the chauffeur as 'Anatole.' He spoke French to the man, too."

"You omitted both of those interesting facts from your summary," commented the reporter with a smile.

"Did I? That was a piece of sheer forgetfulness on my part."

"You didn't forget to rope us all in here as witnesses when the Hungarian prince came on the boards. I knew you had something up your sleeve the moment you began to fill in details. But, as to the crime itself—have you found out the name of the man who was killed?"

"No. There were no papers in his clothes, but that may be accounted for by the singular accident of the exchange of overcoats. His linen was marked 'H. R. H.'"

"'H. R. H.,'" cried a bespectacled journalist who had been a silent listener hitherto. "That's rather odd. Those are the initials of Henry R. Hunter, a member of our staff. The news editor wanted him to take hold in the first instance when the fact that a murder had been committed was 'phoned to the office, but he could not be found anywhere, so I am here in his stead."

"I don't recall anyone of that name," said Steingall sharply.

"No, you wouldn't. He was in our Chicago office till the beginning of September. He did one or two bright things there that caught the chief's eye, so he was brought to New York.... By Jove, Hunter is a good French scholar. It was on that account he got on the track of a gang of Chicago anarchists."

A curious stillness fell on the gathering. It was as though a spirit of evil had suddenly made its presence felt; even the electric lamps seemed to have grown dimmer.

"Describe Hunter."

Steingall's voice rang out incisively; the reporter took off his spectacles, and began to burnish them, for his face was glistening with perspiration.

"He is about five feet ten inches in height, and weighs somewhere in the neighborhood of 150 pounds. He is straight and well-built, and his face is finely molded, with big, luminous eyes, deeply recessed, and — —"

"Has he a white scar across the left eyebrow?"

"Yes."

For some reason, the journalist carried his description of Hunter's personal appearance no farther. It was unnecessary. Before Steingall uttered another word everyone in the room had a foreboding that they were on the threshold of a discovery which lifted this tragedy into a prominence far beyond aught they had yet dreamed of.

Except for that momentary touch of amazement in the detective's tone they could gather nothing from his manner. But his invariable habit was to speak to the point, and without the least suggestion of ambiguity in his words.

"I am very much afraid, gentlemen, that the murdered man is Mr. Henry B. Hunter," he said. "I must trouble you to come with me, and place the question of identity beyond doubt. I hope that you, Mr. and Mrs. Curtis, and you, Mr. Devar, will make it convenient to await my return. There are matters on which you can give me valuable information."

In a few seconds the three found themselves alone. The clerk had business to attend to, but he courteously invited them to remain in the office until the detective came back.

"Did you ever hear such nonsense as this talk about Curtis being mixed up in an abduction?" began Devar, eager to dispossess his friend's relatives of any false impressions they might have formed. "Why, he didn't know a soul in the States—except yourselves," he added tactfully.

The uncle, who had been polishing his domed forehead with a large handkerchief at intervals during the past quarter of an hour, cleared his throat as a preliminary to some important announcement, but his better half had only kept silent because of a real fear that her nephew had been engaged in the commission of serious crime from the instant he set foot in New York, and she entered the fray vigorously now.

"We don't know much about him, and that's the truth, Mr. Devar," she cried. "There was some family disagreement years ago, and the brothers lost track of each other, but Horace here never forgets a name, and why should he, seeing that John was his father's name, and Delancy his mother's, and our nephew has both, so the minute we saw that paragraph in the Chicago papers about the eminent American engineer who had been building railways in China being on board the *Lusitania*, I says to Horace: 'Horace, it would be shame on us if we allowed your brother's son and your own nephew to arrive in New York without some of his kith and kin to bid him welcome,' and with that we hustled to catch the next train east, but the steamer did the trip quicker'n we counted on, and we just missed being at the docks, so if it hadn't been for our good luck in finding the man who helped John with his baggage, and who remembered the name of the hotel he gave the taxi-driver, we might have been searching New York all this blessed night without dreaming of coming to such a place as this, because the newspapers spoke so highly of John that we made sure he would be stopping in one of the Fifth Avenue hotels like the Waldorf-Astoria or Hoffman House, or perhaps higher uptown, in the Ritz-Carlton or the Plaza."

Mrs. Curtis was stout, so she yielded perforce to lack of breath, and Devar was able to explain smilingly that he, and none other, was responsible for the item in the newspapers.

"The fact is that I took a great liking to John D.," he said. "He is such a real good fellow, and so sublimely unconscious of his own merits, that I wanted to surprise him by starting a modest boom in the press, so I sent a wireless message about him to a journalistic friend in New York. I wondered why the reporters did not get hold of him when they came aboard at the quarantine station, but I remember now that, by some curious trick of fate, he and I stowed ourselves away in a part of the ship where no one was likely to find us, and I clean forgot to put them on his track when I went below."

"I guess my nephew has attended to the booming proposition on his own account," said Horace, getting under way at last.

Devar laughed, but Mrs. Curtis was shocked.

"Horace!" she cried indignantly, "that's the only unkind thing I've heard you say in years. Oh, yes,"—for her husband had spread his hands in mild protest—"I know you didn't mean it, but barbed shafts of humor often fall in places where they hurt, and it is terrible to think of your nephew being mixed up in a murder, and an abduction, and——"

She broke off in mid-career, and fixed a stern eye on Devar.

"Are you quite sure he didn't get flirting with some giddy young thing on board?" she demanded. "I've heard and read of some strange goings-on among people crossing the Atlantic. I could tell you of two marriages and no less than five divorces which——"

Devar was a polite young man, but he thought the situation called for firmness.

"To the best of my belief, your nephew never so much as spoke to any lady on the ship," he vowed. "He read a good deal, and played cards occasionally, and walked the decks with me when the weather permitted, but he did not even mention a woman's name except your own, madam."

"The marvel is that he mentioned us at all," said Horace.

Devar thought in his own mind, that the elder Curtis might be ponderous in body and speech but he certainly revealed horse sense when he opened his mouth.

"And whose fault was that, I should like to know?" cried Mrs. Curtis. "Didn't your own brother quarrel with you because you said he ought to have married a woman of some stability of character, and not a pretty, feather-headed girl who spent her days reading poetry and her nights in attending lectures, and who didn't begin to understand the A.B.C. of a wife's domestic duties?"

"Maybe I was wrong and he was right," said her husband.

"Horace!"

Mrs. Curtis was marshaling her forces for a mighty effort when the door opened, and Steingall entered, accompanied by a tall, well set-up man in evening dress, and wearing an open overcoat and green Homburg hat.

"Well," cried Devar, springing forward with outstretched hand, "I'm mighty glad to see you, John D.!"

The newcomer's face lit with pleasure, but before he could utter a responsive word Mrs. Curtis gurgled:

"John D.!... Are you John Delancy Curtis?... Horace, is this your nephew?"

"Judging from his looks, Louisa, he ought to be," said the stout man, gazing at the stranger with wide-eyed astonishment.

The Christian names of the couple acted like a galvanic battery on Curtis. At first, he could hardly believe his ears, but some resemblance in the portly Curtis to his own father warned him that this night of nights had not yet exhausted its store of stupefying surprises.

"Why!" he exclaimed, smiling cheerfully, "you must be my uncle and aunt from Bloomington, Indiana!"

"If you're John Delancy Curtis, that's our correct description," said Horace.

"Of course he is," chortled Mrs. Curtis. "He's as like you the day I married you as two peas in a pod, and if our little Horace had been spared he would have been his living image. Nephew, I'm proud to meet you," and Mrs. Curtis folded her relation in an ample embrace.

Curtis carried off a difficult situation with ease. He kissed his aunt, shook hands with his uncle, and was about to answer the lady's torrent of questions with regard to himself and his own people when Steingall interfered.

"Sorry to interrupt you," he said, "but the turn taken by to-night's crime demands your immediate attention, Mr. Curtis. Do you know you are wearing the dead man's overcoat?"

"Yes. I discovered that fact some time ago."

Curtis's prompt admission was more favorable to his cause than he could possibly realize then, though he had seen that the detective's extraordinarily brilliant eyes were fixed on the garment's blood-stained sleeve.

"And have you learnt the owner's name?" went on Steingall quietly.

"Yes, that is, I believe so, owing to a document I found in one of the pockets."

"Ah, what was that?"

"It concerned another person, but I am prepared to tell you its nature if it is absolutely essential."

"Believe me, there must be no concealment—now."

Something in the detective's tone conveyed a hint of peril, of suspicion, to the ears of one so accustomed to dealing with his fellow-men as was Curtis. But he shook off the premonition of ill, and decided, once and for all, to be candor itself where the authorities were concerned.

"It was a marriage license," he said.

"And the names on it?"

"They were those of a Frenchman, Jean de Courtois, and of an English lady, Hermione Beauregard Grandison."

"So you have imagined that the man who was killed was this Monsieur Jean de Courtois?"

For the life of him, Curtis could not prevent the tumultuous pumping of his heart from drawing some of the color from his face.

"Who else?" he inquired, never flinching from Steingall's searching gaze.

"No matter who owned the coat, or whom the license was intended for, the murdered man was no Frenchman, but a New York journalist named Henry R. Hunter," said Steingall.

Then Curtis yielded to the swift conviction that he had unwittingly trapped Lady Hermione into a marriage on grounds that were inadequate and false.

"Good God!" he muttered, and, for the moment, it was impossible for his hearers to resist the dreadful inference that, in some shape or form, he was implicated in the outrage which bulked so large in their minds. Mrs. Curtis wanted to scream aloud, but she dared not. Even Devar was staggered by his friend's unaccountable attitude. The only outwardly unmoved individual present was Horace P. Curtis. He turned and pressed an electric bell; Steingall glared at him, so he explained his action.

"I feel like a highball," he said blandly. "I guess Mrs. Curtis could do with one also. In fact, five highballs would be a bully good notion."

CHAPTER VII

TEN O'CLOCK

Curtis had seized the opportunity while Hermione was in her room before dinner to rub the blood-stained sleeve of the overcoat with a wet cloth. He had not, of course, been able to eradicate the ghastly dye wholly from the thick material, but the garment was now wearable, at any rate by night, and he had little fear of attracting attention as he crossed the brilliantly lighted foyer of the hotel.

Passing out by the Fifth Avenue exit, he began the second cigar of the evening, and stood in the porch for a moment to collect his faculties. The time was five minutes of ten, and he had been married about an hour and a half. He had just finished his second dinner, and for the guerdon of companionship with the charming and gracious girl whom fate had figuratively thrown into his arms he would cheerfully have tackled a third meal without any personal qualms as to subsequent indigestion.

But, joking apart, he was married. That was the overwhelming feature of life, a feature which dwarfed every other circumstance much as grimly gigantic Windsor Castle dominates the puny town beneath its walls. The mere tying of the matrimonial knot had not troubled him. He was heart whole and fancy free then—or, not to strain the metaphor, he could have boasted those attributes a little earlier in the evening—and he recked nothing of the really serious legal disabilities incurred by the adventure. But, like every other young man, his thoughts had turned sometimes to a young woman—not any special young woman, but that nebulous entity which is necessarily bound up with the notion that some day, somewhere, somehow, a man will encounter the maid in whose limpid eyes lurks his destiny. He had pictured the desirable one in day-dreams, and, merely because of his violent antipathy towards the Eurasian element in the Far East, the dulcissima had appeared invariably as a tall, slender creature, with the lightest of flaxen hair and the grayest of gray eyes. Now, some alchemy devised by the magician spirit of New York had fashioned his ideal, though slender, not so tall, and she owned a wealth of brown hair, hair that shone and glistened in every changing light, while her eyes were either blue or violet, just as one happened to catch the glint of them. And she had fascinating ways, too, which the lady of his fantasy could never have displayed, or he would not have abandoned the vision so readily. When she smiled, it was with lips and eyes in unison. When she spoke he heard harmonies not framed in mere words, whereas the other fair dame was unquestionably a deaf mute.

Indeed, while his glance was dwelling, to all outward semblance, on the passing traffic of one of New York's busiest thoroughfares, he was admitting to himself that he was deeply, irrevocably, in love, and the knowledge was almost stupefying. To one of Curtis's temperament it seemed to be a wildly fanciful thing that he should have yielded so swiftly. Two hours ago he had not seen Hermione, did not even know her name, whereas now he breathed it with devout reverence, though, with a perverseness seldom attached to such circumstances, the amazing fact that she was his wife formed a stubborn barrier against which the flood of new-born desire must rage in vain. For, above all else, he held dear his plighted word. He knew now that the marriage offered an almost insuperable obstacle to any effort on his part to win the girl's affections. In her despair she had trusted him, and he awoke with a guilty start to consciousness of that winsome face being wrung with a new terror if for one instant she had reason to suspect him of other than the altruistic motives he had professed in giving her the protection of his name.

Perhaps, in time—well, he was done now with moon-madness, and he stepped briskly down the avenue, firm set in purpose to risk everything for his wife's sake, and let the future rest in the lap of the gods.

This, be it noted, was his first stroll in New York. The night was fine and clear, for Rafferty's diagnosis of "a touch of frost in the air" was becoming justified, and no thoroughfare in the world could lend itself more completely to the romance of that walk than the wonderful promenade which leads from Central Park to Madison Square. With few exceptions, the nineteenth century plutocrat has been ousted from that section of Fifth Avenue; a giant democracy has reared its own palaces in the shape of hotels and office buildings which pierce the skies, stores which rival the proudest mansions of Venice in its heyday and Florence under Lorenzo Medici. Never in after life did Curtis forget that intimate glimpse of the grandeur and wealth of his native place. Coming up the harbor by daylight he had been overwhelmed by New York's proud defiance of the limits imposed by nature, but now, partly veiled by the mystery of night, the city displayed a feminine beauty at once entrancing and elusive.

At a cross street he paused for a moment to admire a gem of architecture wrenched bodily from its Cinque Cento setting by Brunelleschi, and transplanted to this new land to serve the opulent need of a vendor of precious stones and metals. In the strip of dark blue firmament visible above the admirably proportioned cornice he caught sight of two planets flaming high in the west, and in close juxtaposition. Necessity had made him somewhat of an astronomer, and he had studied Chinese astrology as a pastime. He recognized these lamps of the empyrean as Mars and Venus, and, up-to-date American though he was, drew comfort from that favoring augury. Then, in stepping from the roadway to the sidewalk, he stumbled over a heavy curb, and laughed at the reminder that star-gazing did not reveal pitfalls before unwary feet.

The incident knocked some of the poetry out of him, and it was a quite normal and level-headed young man who walked into the Central Hotel soon after ten o'clock, and found Detective Steingall's gaze resting on him contemplatively from the neighborhood of the cigar counter.

Before rejoining the waiting trio in the office, Steingall was interviewing the youth in charge of the tobacco and current literature department.

Such story as the boy had to tell was hardly in favor of Curtis.

"The gentleman came here to buy some stamps, and he and a man who was reading in the café said something to each other in a foreign lingo," ran the recital. "No, I don't think I would recognize French if I heard it—American is good enough for me—but there was no argument, nothing in the shape of a quarrel. The Englishman spoke twice, and the other fellar three times."

"Mr. Curtis is an American," Steingall explained.

"Well, he doesn't talk like one, anyhow," pronounced young New York—in this instance, of a pronounced Jewish type—which is perhaps the most dogmatic juvenility extant.

Then Curtis entered. He glanced around, and seemed to be gratified by the discovery that the hotel had lost its inquisitive crowd. He did not realize that every newspaper office in New York was alive with conjecture of which he was the chief figure, and that telegraph and telephone were carrying his name and fame across the length and breadth of the country.

"Hello!" he said, hailing Steingall affably, "you here still? Has anything turned up with regard to those scoundrels and their automobile?"

"Not a word—about them," said the detective.

The purveyor of cigars and news was positively awe-stricken. He was aware of Steingall's repute as the "man with the microscopic eye," and he fully expected that the "sleuth's" penetrating organ had already discerned the word "murderer" branded on Curtis's shirt front.

"What time will you want me in the morning?" went on Curtis, looking in the direction of the office. He was really thinking about the mislaid key; not for an instant did he imagine that by that simple gesture he had almost eradicated from Steingall's mind the germ of doubt which events had certainly conspired to plant there.

"I want you now," came the somewhat startling answer.

"Eh, why?"

"Some friends of yours are anxious to see you. They are in the private office over there," and Steingall thrust out his chin in the indicative manner which the Romans used to call *annuens*.

"Oh, Howard Devar, I suppose. But who else?"

"Come along, Mr. Curtis. You can stand a pleasant surprise, I am sure," and, with that, the detective led the way across the hall, leaving the youthful Jew in a maze of conflicting emotions, for, according to all the rules of the game as played in the dime novel, the tec' should have sprung on his prey like a tiger. Another person whose nervous system received a shock was the super-clerk. He, like the boy, knew of the network of suspicion which had closed on Curtis during the past two hours, and he had watched the cordial meeting between the two men with something akin to stupefaction.

But neither of these onlookers had grasped the really essential fact that Steingall did not say one word as to the hue and cry which resulted from Curtis's strange disappearance. The detective was a master of the art of restraint. In his own way, he applied to his profession the maxim of Horace — *Ars est celare artem*.

And he had his reward in that cry of dismay, almost of horror, which burst from Curtis's lips when he heard the true name of the murdered man.

Uncle Horace's seemingly maladroit interruption (it raised him to a pinnacle of esteem in Devar's mind from which he was never dislodged subsequently) prevented any striking development until a glad-eyed waiter had entered and taken an order for four highballs. Even Mrs. Curtis admitted the need of a stimulant, but Curtis steadily refused any intoxicant, even the mildest. Steingall endured the delay stoically. He actually held back a sufficient time to allow Horace P. Curtis to empty his glass with one well-sustained effort. Then he came to close quarters with Napoleonic directness.

"I take it you assumed that the dead man was the Jean de Courtois mentioned in the marriage license?" he said.

He gave that question pride of place in pursuance of a queer thought which had leaped into his brain during the enforced interval. But, if he had been thinking hard, so had Curtis, and the latter had outlined a plan of action which was fated to disrupt Steingall's, much as a harmless looking percussion cap may interfere with the smug torpor of a powder magazine.

"Yes," said Curtis, with the judicial nod of a man who states a comparatively obvious fact.

"Have you that license?"

"No."

"Where is it?"

"Reposing in the writing-desk of the Rev. Thomas J. Hughes, a minister of the Protestant Episcopal Church, who lives in 56th Street, near Seventh Avenue."

"And what is it doing there, pray?"

"I used it. I have married Lady Hermione Grandison."

Steingall permitted himself the rare luxury of a semi-hysterical break in his voice.

"What!" he cried. "Is she the daughter of the Earl of Valletort?"

"Precisely, though you astonish me by the ease with which you connect two such widely different names. Such knowledge usually implies a close acquaintance with the amiable foibles of the British aristocracy."

Certainly it was well that Mrs. Horace P. Curtis had partaken of a tonic in the shape of a highball.

"Well!" she gasped.

For once she was practically speechless, but she gave the astounded Devar a pitiless glance which said plainly:

"Wait till I get my breath, young man, and I'll take some of the cocksureness out of you!"

Steingall soon gathered his scattered wits.

"Are you really speaking seriously, Mr. Curtis?" he asked.

"Quite seriously."

"Was this marriage an arranged affair?"

"Oh, yes. The marriage itself was prearranged."

"Candidly, I don't understand you."

"No? I am not surprised. But I do not wish you to remain under any misapprehension as to the true state of affairs. Lady Hermione Grandison meant to marry a French music-master named Jean de Courtois. I thought, thought honestly but mistakenly, that the man was dead, and, as it was of vital importance that her ladyship should get married to-night, I offered my services as Jean de Courtois' substitute, and they were accepted."

"Am I to take that statement as literally true?"

"Absolutely."

"You were not acquainted with the lady earlier?"

"No."

"Never seen or heard of her?"

"No."

"How did you come to engage in this—this freak marriage, then?"

Curtis measured Steingall with a contemplative eye.

"You are called on to assimilate a novel idea, and, in consequence, are choosing your words badly," he said. "It was not a freak marriage. Although I may have broken the laws of the State of New York by using a license issued to some other person, Lady Hermione and I are legally husband and wife, and no power on earth can dissolve the union without the expressed consent of one or both of us."

"Do you mean me to accept the bald theory that you first learnt the lady's name and address from a document discovered in another man's overcoat, that you went to her house, told her the man was dead, and suggested that you should become the bridegroom in his stead?"

"As an adjective, 'bald' is—well, bald. But you've got the affair sized up accurately otherwise."

"Oh, the shameless hussy!" broke in Mrs. Horace vehemently.

Steingall turned on her with a certain heat of manner.

"Do not interrupt, madam, I beg," he exclaimed.

"Better reserve judgment, aunt, until you have met my wife," said Curtis. He spoke gently enough. He had appraised his relatives almost at a glance, and was sufficiently broad-minded to allow for the natural distress of a respectable middle-aged lady who had been whirled, as it were, out of her wonted environment, and rapt into the realms of necromancy and Arabian Nights.

Steingall swept aside this intermission with the emphatic hand of a cross-examining lawyer.

"You say it was 'of vital importance that the lady should be married to-night.' What does that imply?"

"Do you wish me to put it in different language?"

"I want to know what the vitally important reason was. I presume she furnished one?"

"Ah, but how does that concern the New York police, Mr. Steingall?"

"Every element in this business concerns us. The license was in Hunter's possession—was he bringing it to someone named de Courtois? Or was he masquerading under an alias?"

"Answering your second question, I imagine not. I have the best of reasons for believing that Jean de Courtois exists. I wish now I hadn't. Don't you see, Steingall, I am in a deuce of a fix? I married the lady under a misapprehension. She might have really preferred this fellow, de Courtois."

Steingall liked a joke as well as any man in New York, and was not at all averse from chaffing some of his less gifted colleagues when their obtuseness or faithful adherence to the letter of instructions permitted a criminal to befool them; but he resented the levity of Curtis's tone now, though, deep in his heart, he felt that he liked the man.

"You don't seem to realize the peculiarly awkward position in which you stand," he said, with due official gravity.

"On the contrary, I feel it acutely. What am I to say to my wife——?"

"I am not wrung with agony over the lady's sensitiveness," broke in the detective dryly. "A good many people believe that you were concerned in this murder. There are not lacking circumstantial details which warrant that view. I am not saying too much when I tell you that some men, in my shoes, would arrest you forthwith."

Curtis looked at Steingall quizzically, and even laughed with a whole-hearted appreciation of the jest.

"Lucky for me I have fallen into the hands of a sensible person," he said.

"Allow me to remark," put in Uncle Horace solemnly, "that Mr. Steingall has won my unstinted admiration by the way in which he has conducted this inquiry."

Devar was beginning to enjoy himself. He alone was able to estimate Curtis at his true worth; even that astounding marriage was losing some of its bizarre attributes since Curtis had begun to talk about it.

"Good for you, Mr. Curtis, senior," he crowed delightedly. "If Indiana knew what it really wanted it would run you for Governor."

Steingall nearly became angry. Indeed, it is probable that he would have expressed his sentiments in strong language were it not for the presence of Mrs. Curtis.

"Now, sir," he said, with a perceptible stiffening of manner, "let us have done with pretense. You strike me as being sane, yet you ask me to believe that you have acted like a lunatic. Well, let it go at that. Who is this Jean de Courtois, whom Lady Hermione Grandison was to have married to-night?"

"My wife tells me that he is a French music-master whom she hired to marry her in order that she might escape from a pestiferous person named Count Ladislas Vassilan," replied Curtis with cool directness. "She brought the obliging individual with her from Paris for the purpose, and paid him a thousand dollars as a sort of retaining fee. From what little I have seen of her, she impresses me as a charming girl wholly without experience of a world which, though not altogether wicked, is nevertheless callous and self-seeking.

Among other drawbacks, she embarked on a fantastic project with a most disingenuous belief in the good faith of a Frenchman. Now, I admire France as a nation, but where women are concerned, I distrust Frenchmen as a race, and I suspect—mind you, I am merely guessing—but I repeat that I suspect the honesty of Monsieur Jean de Courtois in this matter. There was no earthly reason why he should not have married Lady Hermione some weeks ago, but it is clear that he has used every artifice to delay the ceremony until to-night—and, it may be found when we learn the facts, was prepared to put it off once more till to-morrow or next day. Why? In my opinion, the reason is not far to seek. The Earl of Valletort and Count Ladislas Vassilan were crossing the Atlantic hot in pursuit of the unwilling bride. They arrived in New York to-night, and were so well posted in events, both past and prospective, that they headed straight for the flat in which Lady Hermione was living with her maid. Naturally, I am keenly interested in the causes which led up to a peculiarly brutal and uncalled-for murder, and, as my wife's husband, I have the further incentive of hoping to bring to justice certain of her persecutors whom I cannot help connecting indirectly with the crime of which I was, I suppose, one of the most credible and intelligent witnesses. Now, before I was aware that such a winsome creature existed as the present Lady Hermione Curtis, I had estimated the murderers as Hungarians, two of them at any rate, since I am hardly prepared to vouch for the chauffeur. Count Ladislas Vassilan is a Hungarian. The poor fellow who was killed, though his name is American enough, spoke French with a pure accent. One of the Hungarians spoke French, fluently but vilely. Jean de Courtois is admittedly a Frenchman. I am not a detective, Mr. Steingall, but as a plain man of affairs I am forced to the conclusion that there has seldom been a similarly mysterious crime in which certain lines of inquiry thrust themselves more pertinently on the imagination. To sum up, I advise you to find Jean de Courtois— unless, indeed, he, too, has been killed—and you will be in close touch with the origin of the whole ugly business."

"Good egg!" cried the irresistible Devar. "It's a pity you were not with us on the *Lusitania*, Mr. Steingall, or you would realize that when John D. rears up on his hind legs, and talks like that, there is nothing more to be said."

"Is Lady Hermione a pretty girl?" demanded Mrs. Curtis eagerly. Her democratic soul was rejoicing in the discovery that her nephew's wife did not lose her title because of the marriage. Of course, no one ever before heard of such folly as this matrimonial leap in the dark, but, once taken, there was satisfaction in the thought that the bride was an earl's daughter. Moreover, she had read of such queer goings on among the British Aristocracy that a wedding at sight was a comparatively venial offense.

Curtis assured his aunt that Hermione was the most beautiful and fascinating person he had ever met, and Steingall listened to the eulogy with a grinning rictus of jaw. In the whole course of his professional experience he had never encountered anything on a par with this capricious blend of comedy and tragedy.

Of course, it did not escape his acute brain that Curtis was right in assuming that the *clou* of the situation lay with Jean de Courtois. Dead or alive, the Frenchman must be found, and found quickly. The extraordinary story told by Curtis, if true—and the detective was persuaded that this curiously constituted young man was not trying to hoodwink him in any particular—pointed a ready way toward investigation. The unfortunate journalist, Hunter, was about to enter the Central Hotel when he was attacked so mercilessly. As a consequence, some knowledge of de Courtois was probably awaiting the first questioner at the inquiry counter. What a whimsical incongruity it would be if he were told that the French music-master around whom the inquiry pivoted was within arm's length all the time! He had actually turned to the door in order to summon the hotel clerk when that worthy himself knocked and entered.

"The Earl of Valletort is here, and wishes to have a word with you, Mr. Steingall," he said.

The detective's present grim conceit ran somewhat to the effect that if he remained long enough in the Central Hotel he would accumulate sufficient evidence to electrocute three criminals, at least, and send others to the penitentiary, but he merely nodded and said:

"Show his lordship right in."

He was conscious of a dramatic pause in the conversation which had broken out between the others. Once again had Mrs. Curtis been rendered dumb by the shock of an unforeseen development. Devar, who was having the night of his life, leaned back against the wainscot, Uncle Horace peered hopelessly into an empty tumbler, but dared not suggest a second highball, while Curtis, after one sharp glance at the detective, whom he credited with having arranged this surprise in some inexplicable way, thrust his hands into his trousers' pockets and awaited the advent of Hermione's father with a calmness that he himself could hardly account for. Hitherto, his adventurous life had been made up of strenuous effort tempered by the Anglo-Saxon phlegm which disregards dangers and difficulties. Prolonged strain of an emotional nature was new to him. He understood, but did not apply the knowledge, that when the human vessel is full to the brim with excitement, the earth may rock and the heavens roll together in fury without the power to add one more drop of gall or distress to the completed measure. At that instant, if the Earl of Valletort had been accompanied by the embodied ghosts of his ancestors, Curtis would have viewed the procession with unconcern.

The Earl, a handsome slightly built, erect man of fifty, hawk-nosed, keen-eyed, with drooping mustache and carefully arranged thin gray hair, glanced at Curtis as he might have regarded any other stranger.

"I have disposed of my friend," he said to Steingall, "and I hurried back here on off-chance that you might still be engaged in——"

"Before your lordship enters into details, allow me to introduce Mr. John D. Curtis," said Steingall, silently thanking the fates which had brought about a meeting so opportune to his own task if embarrassing to its chief actors.

"Mr. John D. Curtis, the—the person who conspired with my daughter to contract an illegal marriage!" barked the Earl, instantly dropping the repose of Vere de Vere.

"John Delancy Curtis, at any rate," said Curtis gravely. "As your son-in-law, may I remark that a few minutes' conversation with a lawyer will enable you to correct two misstatements in the rest of your description? There was no conspiracy, and the ceremony was unquestionably legal."

The Earl gave him one searching and envenomed look, and appealed forthwith to the detective.

"I charge that man with abduction and personation," he cried, and his voice grew husky with wrath. "There can be no gainsaying the facts. My daughter, it is true, had arranged a marriage with a Monsieur Jean de Courtois. It was provisionally fixed to take place this evening at eight o'clock, but, by some means not known to me, the marriage license came into the hands of this admitted law-breaker, and he evidently persuaded a foolish and impetuous girl to accept him instead of de Courtois. I am not an authority on the laws of the State of New York, but I stake my reputation on the belief that a flagrant offense has been committed against the social ordinances of any well regulated community. I now call on you to arrest him, or, if official process is needed, to direct me to the proper authority."

"Have you any proof of the charge?" said Steingall, who had not failed to observe Curtis's air of unconcern under the Earl's fiery denunciation.

"Proof in plenty," came the snarling answer. "I have seen the license and the signed register, and Monsieur de Courtois is known to me personally. Besides, have you not this rascal's own admission?"

"Why omit the equally damning evidence of conspiracy?" demanded Curtis.

"What do you mean, you, you— —"

"Interloper. How will that serve? It was you who spoke of conspiring, though I grant you seem to have dropped that item of the indictment. But Mr. Steingall, as representing the law, should hear the full tale of villainy. If your lordship will produce de Courtois's letters, cablegrams, and wireless messages to yourself and your confederate, Count Ladislas Vassilan, he will begin to appreciate the true bearing of a rather intricate inquiry."

It was a chance shot, but it went home. Curtis had not spent ten years in counteracting Manchu scheming and duplicity without arriving at certain basic principles in laying bare the methods of double-dealing, and the Earl of Valletort was manifestly disturbed by this cold analysis of facts which he imagined were known to an exceedingly limited circle in New York.

But he had the presence of mind to waive aside Curtis's allegations as unworthy of discussion.

"I address myself to you," he said to Steingall. "Have I made my request clear, or shall I repeat it?"

"Have you any objection to answering a few questions, my lord?" said the detective.

"None whatsoever."

"When did you and Count Vassilan arrive in New York?"

"At twenty minutes after eight to-night."

"How did you ascertain what was happening with regard to your daughter?"

"By inquiry."

"Of course, but from whom?"

"From the minister who performed an unauthorized ceremony."

"How did you know where to go so promptly to secure information?"

"I was kept informed of my daughter's movements by agents."

"Who were they?"

"Their names will be given at the right time."

"The right time is now."

"You are not a magistrate. I take it you are a police officer."

"Your lordship may feel well assured on that point. It is exactly because I am a police officer that I press for a reply. Your grievance against Mr. John D. Curtis is much more of a matter for a civil than a criminal court. I guess he has broken the law, but the machinery for putting it in motion is not under my control. I am investigating a murder, and every word you have said confirms my belief that your daughter's contemplated marriage was the indirect but none the less certain cause of the crime. Now, Lord Valletort, who were your inquiry agents?"

"Ha!" muttered Uncle Horace.

It was a simple enough ejaculation, but it served to drive home the nail which the detective's outspoken declaration had hammered into the Earl's startled consciousness. Here, in truth, was a new and disturbing phase of the matrimonial problem contrived by Hermione, aided and abetted by that mischievous scoundrel, Curtis. Still, he was not one to be driven easily into a corner.

"You practically refer me to a lawyer for advice; I take you at your word," he said, with a quick return to the self-controlled attitude of an experienced man of the world.

"You decline, then, to answer the only vitally important question I have put to you?" said Steingall.

"I decline to answer that question until I have consulted someone better able—or shall I say, more willing?—to instruct me as to the speediest means of punishing a malefactor."

"The noble lord is disqualified," broke in Devar. "This is the second time since the flag fell that he has refused his fences."

"If you interrupt again I shall turn you out of the room, Mr. Devar," cried Steingall vexedly.

"But, dash it all, Steingall, somebody must see that John D. has fair play. He only swerved once, and then for a single stride, while he——"

"I shall not warn you a second time," and Devar knew that the detective meant what he said, and kept quiet.

"May I ask where the police headquarters are situated?" said the Earl in the frostiest tone he could command at the moment.

"At the corner of Center Street and Grand," said Steingall indifferently. He was about to add the unpleasing fact—unpleasing to Lord Valletort, that is—that the man on duty at the Detective Bureau would certainly refer an inquirer to him, Steingall, when the clerk reappeared.

"A patrolman has brought a note for you," he said, handing Steingall a sealed letter, which the detective opened instantly after glancing at the superscription. It was from the police captain, and ran:

"Count Vassilan has just left the Waldorf-Astoria in a taxi. Clancy is driving."

Steingall's face betrayed no more expression than that of the Sphinx, though inwardly he was consumed with laughter; he himself was chief of the Bureau, and Clancy was his most trusted assistant! Certainly, the gods were contriving a spicy dish for the news-loving inhabitants of New York.

CHAPTER VIII

TEN-THIRTY

The Earl of Valletort turned on his heel, and went out abruptly. Therefore, he missed Steingall's first words to the hotel clerk, which would have given him furiously to think, while it is reasonable to suppose that he would have paid quite a large sum of money to have heard the clerk's answer.

For the detective said:

"Do you happen to know anything about a Frenchman, name of Jean de Courtois?"

And the clerk replied:

"Why, yes. He's in his room now, I believe."

"In his room—where?"

"Here, of course. He came in about 6.30, took his key and a Marconigram, and has not showed up since."

Uncle Horace could withstand the strain no longer.

"Would you mind sending the waiter again?" he gasped. "If I don't get a pick-me-up of some sort quickly, I'll collapse."

Aunt Louisa would dearly have loved to put in a word, but she knew not what to say. Life at Bloomington supplied no parallel to the rapidity of existence in New York that evening. She was aware of statements being made in language which rang familiarly in her ears, but they had no more coherence in her clogged understanding than the gabble of dementia.

Steingall was the least surprised of the five people who listened to the clerk's words. The notion that de Courtois might be close at hand had dawned on him already; still, he was not prepared to hear that the man was actually a resident in the hotel.

"Has Monsieur de Courtois lived here some time?" he asked, not without a sharp glance at Curtis to see how the suspect was taking this new phase in his adventure.

"About a month," said the clerk.

"Has he received many visitors?"

"A few, mostly foreigners. A Mr. Hunter called here occasionally, and they dined together last evening. I believe Mr. Hunter is connected with the press."

The clerk wondered why he was being catechized about the Frenchman. He had no more notion that de Courtois and Hunter were connected with the tragedy than the man in the moon.

"Take me to Monsieur de Courtois's room," Said Steingall, after a momentary pause.

"May I come with you?" inquired Curtis.

"Why?"

"I am deeply interested in de Courtois, and I may be able to help you in questioning him. I speak French well."

"So do I," said Steingall. "But, come if you like."

"For the love of Heaven, don't leave me out of this, Steingall," pleaded Devar.

The detective was blessed with a sense of humor; he realized that the inquiry had long since passed the bounds of official decorum, and its irregularities had proved so illuminative that he was not anxious to check them yet a while.

"Yes," he said, "you'll do no harm if you keep a still tongue in your head."

"You'll come back to us, John, won't you?" broke in Mrs. Curtis, desperately contributing the first commonplace remark that occurred to her bemused brain.

"Yes, aunt. I'll rejoin you here. Shall I have some supper sent in for both of you?"

"No, my boy," said Uncle Horace, who had revived under the prospect of a long drink. "If any feasting is to be done later it is up to me to arrange it. The night is young. I hope to have the honor of toasting your wife before I go to bed."

Curtis smiled at that, but made no reply, the moment being inopportune for explanations, but Devar murmured, as they crossed the lobby with Steingall and the clerk:

"That uncle of yours is a peach, John D. He points the moral like a Greek chorus."

"I fear he will regard me as a hare-brained nephew," said Curtis. "As for my aunt, poor lady, she must think me the most extraordinary human being she has ever set eyes on. What puzzles me most is—"

"Wow! I know what aunts are capable of," broke in Devar rapidly, for he was doubtful now how his friend would regard the publicity he had not desired. "Mrs. Curtis, senior, is thanking her stars at this minute that she will have a chance of paralyzing Bloomington with full details of her nephew's marriage into the ranks of the British aristocracy. The odd thing is that I'm tickled to death by the notion that I, little Howard, put you in for this night's gorgeous doings. Didn't you wonder why I passed up an introduction to *my* aunt and my cousins in the Customs shed? Man alive, if Mrs. Morgan Apjohn had made your acquaintance to-day she would have insisted on your dining with the family to-night, and at 7.30 P.M. your feet would have been safely tucked under the mahogany in her home on Riverside Drive instead of leading you into the maze you seem to have found so readily. All I wanted was an excuse to get away soon. Gee whizz! What a fireworks display you've put up in the meantime!"

"Fifth," said the clerk to the elevator attendant, and the four men shot skyward.

As each floor above the street level was a replica of the next higher one, Curtis happened to note that the route followed to the Frenchman's room was similar to that leading to 605.

"What number does Monsieur de Courtois occupy?" he inquired.

"505," said the clerk.

"Then it is directly beneath mine?"

"Yes, sir. He must have heard us breaking open your door."

"I beg your pardon. Heard what?"

"We committed some minor offenses with regard to your property during your absence," said Steingall, "but they were of slight account as compared with your own extravagances. Let me warn you not to say too much before de Courtois. Even taking your version of events, Mr. Curtis, Lord Valletort will probably raise a wasps' nest about your ears in the morning."

"But why *break open* the door? Surely, there was a pass key——"

"Sh-s-sh! Here we are!"

Steingall tapped lightly on a panel of 505, and the four listened silently for any response. None came—that is, there was nothing which could be recognized as the sound of a voice or of human movement inside the room. Nevertheless, they fancied they heard something, and the detective knocked again, somewhat more insistently. Now they were intent for the slightest noise behind that closed door, and they caught a subdued groan or whine, followed by the metallic creak of a bed-frame.

At that instant a chamber-maid hurried up.

"I was just going to 'phone the office," she said to the clerk. "A little while ago I tried to enter that room, but my key would not turn in the lock."

"Did you hear anyone stirring within?" asked the clerk.

"No, sir. I knocked, and there was no answer."

"Listen now, then."

A third time did Steingall rap on the door, and the strange whine was repeated, while there could be no question that a bed was being dragged or shoved to and fro on a carpeted floor.

"My land!" whispered the girl in an awed tone. "There's something wrong in there!"

"Let me try your key," said the clerk. He rattled the master-key in the keyhole, but with no avail.

"I suppose it acts all right in every other lock?" he growled.

"Oh, yes, sir. I've been using it all the evening."

"Someone has tampered with the lock from the outside," he said savagely. "There is nothing for it but to send for the engineer. Before we're through with this business we'll pull the d—d hotel to pieces. A nice reputation the place will get if all this door-forcing appears in the papers to-morrow."

Certainly the clerk was to be pitied. Never before had the decorum of the Central Hotel been so outraged. Its air of smug respectability seemed to have vanished. Even to the clerk's own disturbed imagination the establishment had suddenly grown raffish, and its dingy paint and drab upholstery resembled the make-up and cloak of a scowling tragedian.

A strong-armed workman came joyously. He had already figured as a personage below stairs, because of his earlier experiences, and it was a cheering thing to be called on twice in one night to participate in a mystery which was undoubtedly connected with the murder in the street.

Before adopting more strenuous methods he inserted a piece of strong wire into the keyhole, thinking to pick the lock by that means; but he soon desisted.

"Some joker has been at that game before me," he announced. "A chunk of wire has been forced in there after the door was locked."

"From the outside?" inquired Steingall.

"Yes, sir. These locks work by a key only from without. There is a handle inside.... Well, here goes!"

A few blows with a sharp chisel soon cut away sufficient of the frame to allow the door to be forced open. On this occasion, there being no wedge in the center, it was not necessary to attack the hinges, and, once the lock was freed, the door swung back readily into the interior darkness.

The engineer, remembering his needless alarm at falling head foremost into Curtis's room, went forward boldly enough now, and paid for his temerity. He was so anxious to be the first to discover whatever horror existed there that he made for the center of the apartment without waiting to turn on the light, and, as a consequence, when he stumbled over something which he knew was a human body, and was greeted with a subdued though savage whine, he was even more frightened than before.

But no one was concerned about him or his feelings when Steingall touched an electric switch and revealed a bound and gagged man fastened to a leg of the bed. At first, owing to the extraordinary posture of the body, it was feared that another tragedy had been enacted. The victim of an uncanny outrage was lying on his side, and his arms and legs were roughly but skillfully tied with a stout rope in such wise that he resembled a fowl trussed for the oven. After securing him in this fashion, his assailants had fastened the ends of the rope to the iron frame of the bed, and his only possible movement was an ignominious half roll, back and forth, in a space of less than eight inches. This maneuver he had evidently been engaged in as soon as he heard voices and knocking outside, but he had been gagged with such brutal efficacy that his sole effort at speech was a species of whinny through his nose.

The detective's knife speedily liberated him; when he was lifted from the floor and laid gently on the bed, he remained there, quite speechless and overcome.

Steingall turned to the agitated chambermaid, whose eyes were round with terror, and who would certainly have alarmed the hotel with her screams had she come upon the occupant of the room in the course of her rounds.

"Bring a glass of hot milk, as quickly as you can," he said, and the girl sped away to the service telephone.

"Wouldn't brandy be better?" inquired Devar.

"No. Milk is the most soothing liquid in a case like this. The man's jaws are sore and aching. Probably, too, he is faint from fright and want of food. If we can get him to sip some milk he will be able to tell us, perhaps, just what has happened."

While they awaited the return of the chamber-maid, the party of rescuers gazed curiously at the prostrate figure on the bed. They saw a small, slight, neatly built man, attired in evening dress, whose sallow face was in harmony with a shock of black hair. A large and somewhat vicious mouth was partly concealed by a heavy black mustache, and the long-fingered, nervous hands were sure tokens of the artistic temperament. There could be no manner of doubt that this hapless individual was Jean de Courtois. He looked exactly what he was, a French musician, while initials on his boxes, and a number of letters on the dressing-table, all testified to his identity.

Curtis, Devar, and the hotel clerk seemed to be more interested in the appearance of the half-insensible de Courtois than Steingall. He gave him one penetrating glance, and would have known the man again after ten years had they been parted that instant; but, if he favored the Frenchman with scant attention, he made no scruples about examining the documents on the table, though his first care was to thank the workman, and send him from the room.

"Now," he muttered to the others in a low tone, "leave the questioning to me, and mention no names."

He picked up a Marconigram lying among the letters, and read it. Without a word, but smiling slightly, he handed it unobtrusively to Curtis. It bore that day's date, and the decoded time of delivery was 4 P.M.

"Arriving to-night," it ran. "Coming direct Fifty-Ninth Street. Expect us there about eight-thirty."

Curtis smiled, too. He grasped the detective's unspoken thought. Steingall had as good as said that the message bore out Curtis's counter charge against Count Vassilan and the Earl of Valletort of conspiring with de Courtois himself to defeat Lady Hermione's marriage project. Indeed, before replacing the slip of paper on the table, the detective produced a note-book, and entered therein particulars which would secure proof of the Marconigram's origin if necessary.

The maid hurried in with the milk, and Steingall, why had covered more ground among the Frenchman's correspondence than the others gave him credit for, now acted as nurse. With some difficulty he succeeded in persuading the stricken man on the bed to relax his firmly closed jaws and endeavor to swallow the fluid. It was a tedious business, but progress became more rapid when de Courtois realized that he was in the hands of those who meant well by him. It was noticeable, too, as his senses returned and the panic glare left his eyes, that his expression changed from one of abject fear to a lowering look of suspicious uncertainty. He peered at Steingall and the hotel clerk many times, but gave Curtis and Devar only a perfunctory glance. Oddly enough, the fact that the two latter were in evening dress seemed to reassure him, and it became evident later that the presence of the clerk led him to regard these strangers as guests in the hotel who had been attracted to his room by the mere accident of propinquity.

His first intelligible words, uttered in broken English, were:

"Vat time ees eet?"

"Ten-thirty," said Steingall.

"*Ah, cré nom d'un nom*! I haf to go, queek!"

"Where to?"

"No mattaire. I tank you all to-morrow. I explain eferyting den. Now, I go."

"You had better stay where you are, Monsieur de Courtois," said Steingall in French. "Milord Valletort and Count Vassilan have arrived. I have seen them, and nothing more can be done with respect to their affair tonight. I am the chief of the New York Detective Bureau, and I want you to tell me how you came to be in the state in which you were found."

But de Courtois was regaining his wits rapidly, and the clarifying of his senses rendered him obviously unwilling to give any information as to the cause of his own plight. Nor would he speak French. For some reason, probably because of a permissible vagueness in statements couched in a foreign tongue, he insisted on using English.

"Eef you haf seen my frien's you tell me vare I fin' dem. I come your office to-morrow, an' make ze complete explanation," he said.

"I must trouble you to-night, please," insisted Steingall quietly. "You don't understand what has occurred while you were fastened up here. You know Mr. Henry R. Hunter?"

"Yes, yes. I know heem."

"Well, he was stabbed while alighting from an automobile outside this hotel shortly before eight o'clock, and I imagine he was coming to see you."

"Stabbed! Did zey keel heem?"

"Yes. Now, tell me who 'they' were."

Monsieur Jean de Courtois was taken instantly and violently ill. He dropped back on the bed, from which he had risen valiantly in his eagerness to be stirring, and faintly proclaimed his inability to grasp what the detective was saying.

"Ah, *Grand Dieu!*" he murmured. "I am eel; fetch a doctaire. My brain, eet ees, vat you say, *étourdi.*"

"You will soon recover from your illness. Come, now, pull yourself together, and tell me who the men were who tied you up, and why, if you can give a reason."

The Frenchman shut his eyes, and groaned.

"I am stranjare here, Monsieur le Commissaire," he said brokenly. "I know no ones, nodings. Milor' Valletort, he ees acquaint. Send for heem, and bring ze doctaire."

"Don't you understand that your friend, Mr. Hunter, the journalist who was helping you in the matter of Lady Hermione Grandison's marriage, has been murdered?"

The other men in the room caught a new quality in Steingall's voice. Contempt, disgust, utter disdain of a type of rascal whom he would prefer to deal with most fittingly by kicking him, were revealed in each syllable; but Jean de Courtois was apparently deaf to the mean opinion his conduct was inducing among those who had extricated him from a disagreeable if not actually dangerous predicament. He squirmed convulsively, and half sobbed his inability to realize the true nature of anything that had happened either to himself or to any other person.

"Very well," said the detective, "if you are so thoroughly knocked out I'll see that you are kept quiet for the rest of the evening."

He turned to the clerk.

"Kindly arrange that two trustworthy men shall undress this ill-used gentleman. He may be given anything to eat or drink that he requires, but if he shows signs of delirium, such as a desire to go out, or write letters, or use the telephone, he must be stopped, forcibly if necessary. Should he become violent, ring up the nearest police station-house. I'll send a doctor to him in a few minutes."

De Courtois revived slightly under the stimulus of these emphatic directions.

"I haf not done ze wrong," he protested. "Eet ees me who suffare, and I do not permeet dis interference wid my leebairty."

"You see," said Steingall coolly. "His mind is wandering already. Just 'phone for a couple of attendants, will you, and I'll give them instructions. I take full responsibility, of course."

"But, monsieur——" cried the Frenchman.

"Would you mind getting a move on? I am losing time here," said Steingall quietly to the clerk.

"I claim ze protection of my consul," sputtered de Courtois.

"Poor fellow! He is quite light-headed," said the detective sympathetically, addressing the company at large but speaking in French. "I do hope most sincerely that I may arrest those infernal Hungarians to-night. Not only did they kill Hunter but they have brought this little man to death's door."

The effect of these few harmless sounding words was electrical. Monsieur de Courtois' angry demeanor suddenly changed to that of a sufferer almost as seriously injured as Steingall made out. He collapsed utterly, and never lifted his head even when most drastic measures were enjoined on a couple of sturdy negroes as to the care that must be devoted to the invalid.

Steingall was astonishingly outspoken to Curtis and Devar while they were walking to the elevator.

"I am surprised that that miserable whelp escaped with his life," he said. "Usually, in cases of this sort, the rascal who betrays his friends receives short shrift from those who make use of him. He knows too much for their safety, and gets a knife between his ribs as soon as his services cease to be valuable."

"I must confess that I don't begin to grasp the bearings of this affair," admitted Curtis. "It is almost grotesque to imagine that a number of men could be found in New York who would stop short of no crime, however daring, simply to prevent a young lady from marrying in despite of her father's wishes."

126

"Of course, the young lady figures large in your eyes," said Steingall with a dry laugh. "You haven't thought this matter out, Mr. Curtis. When you have slept on it, and the fact dawns on you that there are other people in the world than the charming Lady Hermione, you will realize that she is a mere pawn around whom a number of very important persons are contending. I don't wish to say a word to depreciate her as a star of the first magnitude, but I am greatly mistaken if there is not another woman, either here or in Europe, whose personality, if known, would attract far more attention from the police.... By the way, has it occurred to you that Providence has certainly befriended you to-night? The dare-devils who murdered Hunter were inclined to kill you in error.... Now, I want you to concentrate your mind on the face and expression of that chauffeur, Anatole. Keep him constantly in your thoughts. If you can swear to him when we parade him before you with half-a-dozen other men, I shall soon strip the inquiry of its mystery."

In the hall they were surrounded by a squad of reporters, and three photographers took flashlight pictures.

"Hello!" muttered the detective to Curtis, "they've found you! Now we must use our brains to get you out of this."

They escaped the journalists by closing the door of the office on them. Then the clerk was summoned, and solved the first difficulty by revealing a back-stairs exit by way of the basement. An attendant was sent to Curtis's room, to pack a grip with some clothes and linen, and, by adroit maneuvering, the whole party got away from the hotel.

Steingall insisted on interviewing Lady Hermione that night. He pointed out, reasonably enough, that she might possess a good deal of valuable information concerning Count Ladislas Vassilan; if, as Curtis believed was the case, she had already retired to rest, she must be aroused. The hour was not so late, and Vassilan's movements in New York might be elucidated by knowledge of his previous career.

So Curtis announced that his bride was installed in the Plaza Hotel, and, while he and Devar escaped through the cellars, Steingall took Uncle Horace and Aunt Louisa boldly through the lobby. A taxi was waiting there, and he gave the driver the address of the police headquarters downtown, but re-directed him when they were safe from pursuit, and the three, so oddly assorted as companions, arrived at the Plaza within a minute of the two young men.

Steingall went straight to the telephone room, and Curtis ascended to his suite of apartments. He knocked at Hermione's door, and her "Yes, who is there?" came with disconcerting speed. Evidently, she was far from being asleep yet.

"It is I—dear," said Curtis, in whom the mere sense of being near his "wife" induced a species of vertigo. Indeed, he was horribly nervous, since he could not form the slightest notion as to the manner in which she would receive the latest news of de Courtois.

The door was opened without delay, and Hermione appeared, dressed exactly as she was when he bade her farewell.

"I am sorry to disturb you," he said, "but it cannot be helped. Things have been happening since I left you."

Her face blanched, but she tried to smile, though the corners of her mouth drooped piteously.

"They are not here already?" she cried, and he had no occasion to ask who "they" were.

"No," he said, with a cheerfulness he was far from feeling. "The fact is I—I—have brought some friends to see you. That is, some of them will, I hope, be your very good friends—my uncle and aunt, and young Howard Devar, whom I spoke about earlier. There is a detective, too—a very decent fellow named Steingall. Shall I bring them here? It will be pleasanter than being stared at in a crowded supper room."

She was surprised, but the relief in her tone was unmistakable.

"I don't want any supper," she said. "I shall be glad to meet your relatives, of course, though——"

"Though you think I might have mentioned them sooner? Well, the strangest part of the business is that they should be in New York at all. I haven't the remotest idea as to why they are here, or how they dropped across me. But isn't it a rather fortunate thing? They may prove useful in a hundred ways."

"Please don't keep them waiting. What does the detective want?"

"Every syllable you can tell him about Count Vassilan."

"I hardly know the man at all. I always avoided him in Paris."

"You may be astonished by the number of facts you will produce when Steingall questions you. And, I had better warn you that my uncle is even now consulting the head-waiter about a wedding feast. He has adopted you without reservation on my poor description."

His frankly admiring look brought a blush to her cheeks; but she only laughed a little constrainedly, and murmured that she would try to be as complacent as the occasion demanded. Events were certainly in league to lend her wedding night a remarkably close semblance to the real thing. And as Curtis descended to the foyer to summon their waiting guests he decided then and there not to mar the festivities by any explanations concerning Jean de Courtois's second time on earth. Steingall had practically settled the question by confining the Frenchman to his room for the remainder of the night. Why interfere with an admirable arrangement? Let the wretched intriguer be forgotten till the morrow, at any rate!

CHAPTER IX

ELEVEN O'CLOCK

"In multitude of counselors there is safety," says the Book of Proverbs. Usually, the philosophy attributed to Solomon exhibits a soundness of judgment which is unrivaled, so it is reasonable to assume that in Hebrew gnomic thought four do not constitute a multitude, because four people agreed with Curtis that there was not the slightest need to mention Jean de Courtois to Hermione that evening, and five people were wrong, though in ninety-nine cases out of a hundred they might have been right. Hermione herself admitted afterwards that she would have believed Curtis implicitly had he explained the circumstances which accounted for his undoubted conviction that de Courtois was dead; indeed, she went so far as to say that, as a matter of choice, she infinitely preferred the American to the Frenchman in the role of a husband *pro tem*. She had never regarded de Courtois from any other point of view than as her paid ally, and she was beginning to share Curtis's belief that the man was a double-dealer, a fact which helped to modify her natural regret at the report of his death in her behalf.

In a calmer mood, too, Curtis would have been quick to realize that a girl who had reposed such supreme confidence in his probity was entitled to share his fullest knowledge of the extraordinary bond which united them, but for one half-hour he was swayed by expediency, and expediency often exercises a disrupting influence on a friendship founded on faith. He only meant to spare her the dismay which could hardly fail to manifest itself when she heard that de Courtois was alive, and that additional complications must now arise with reference to the wrongful use of the marriage license; in reality, he was doing himself a bitter injustice.

But, having elected for a definite course, he was not a man who would deviate from it by a hair's breadth. When the junta in the vestibule of the Plaza Hotel had promised to remain mute on the topic of de Courtois, he dismissed the matter from his mind as having no further influence on the night's doings.

"Is there any means of recovering my overcoat?" he asked Steingall, remembering the change of garments when a waiter asked if the gentlemen cared to deposit their hats and coats in the cloak-room.

"Yes," said the detective. "Just empty the pockets of the coat you are wearing, and I'll send a messenger to the police station-house with a note. You won't mind if I retain your documents till after the inquest? One never knows what questions will be asked, and you must remember that an attempt may be made to fasten the crime upon you."

Curtis laughed at the absurdity of any such notion, but, for the first time, he examined the contents of the dead man's coat pockets methodically. The pocket in which the license had reposed was empty. Its fellow contained a notebook and pencil. There were also some newspaper cuttings—items of current interest in New York, but devoid of bearing on the crime or its cognate developments.

An elastic band caused the book to open at a definite page, and Steingall, who knew a little of everything, and a great deal of all matters appertaining to his profession, deciphered some shorthand characters which promised enlightenment. He passed no comment, however, but pocketed the book, scribbled a few lines on a sheet of paper bearing the name of the hotel, and intrusted coat and letter to an attendant.

Uncle Horace, after a momentary qualm, gave instructions to the head-waiter in the approved manner of a trust magnate.

"We're up against it now, Louisa," he whispered confidentially to his wife, "so let's have one wonderful night if we never have another."

Mrs. Curtis nodded her complete agreement. She would have sanctioned a mortgage on her home rather than forego any material part of an experience which would command the breathless attention of many a future gathering of matrons and maids in faraway Bloomington.

Lady Hermione received her visitors with a shy cordiality which won their prompt approval. Aunt Louisa had been perplexed by indecision as to what she was to say or how she was to act when she met the bride, but one glance of her keen, motherly eyes at the blushing and timid girl resolved any doubts on both scores.

"God bless you, my dear!" she said, throwing her arms around Hermione's neck and kissing her heartily. "Perhaps everything is for the best, and, anyway, you've married into a family of honest men and true women."

"Ma'am," said Uncle Horace, when his turn came to be introduced, "strange as it may sound, I know less about my nephew than you yourself, but if he resembles his father in character as he does in appearance, you've chosen well, and let me add, ma'am, that *he* seems to have made a first-rate selection at sight."

Of course, such congratulations were woefully misplaced, but Hermione was too well-bred to reveal any cause for disquietude other than the normal embarrassment any young woman would display in like conditions.

Curtis, too, put in a quiet word which threw light on the situation.

"As I told you a few minutes since, I was not aware that my uncle and aunt were in New York," he said. "I cannot even guess how they came to find me so opportunely, and we have hardly been able to say a word to each other yet, because they were in the thick of the police inquiry when I met them in my hotel."

"Why, that's the easiest thing," declared Aunt Louisa, rejoicing in a long-looked-for opportunity to hear her own voice in full volume. "This young gentleman here," and she nodded at the dismayed Devar, "told us that he cottoned to your husband, my dear, something remarkable on board the steamer, so he sent a message by wireless to the editor of a New York paper, asking him to let America know that one of her citizens who had won distinction in China was homeward bound, and the editor circulated a real nice paragraph about it. It quite took my breath away when Mrs. Harvey, our mayor's wife—such a charming woman, my dear, and I do hope I may have the pleasure of bringing you to one of her delightful tea-and-bridge afternoons—said to me on Monday: 'Surely, Mrs. Curtis, this John Delancy Curtis who is on board the *Lusitania* must be a son of that brother of your husband who died in China some years ago?' and I said: 'What in the world are you talking about, Mrs. Harvey?' so she showed me the newspaper, and I was that taken aback that I revoked in the next hand, and the only mean player we have in the club claimed three tricks 'without,' and went game, being a woman herself who hasn't chick nor child, but devotes far too much time and money to toy dogs; anyhow, I couldn't give my mind to cards any more that day, so off I rushed home and 'phoned Horace, and here we are, after such a flurry as you never would imagine, what between packing in a hurry for the trip east, and missing the steamer's arrival by nearly an hour, and turning up in the Central Hotel just in time to hear——" Then Aunt Louisa, assuredly at no loss for words, but remembering in a hazy way the compact made in the vestibule, found it incumbent on her to break away from the main trend of the narrative, so she concluded: "Just in time to hear things being said about our nephew which we felt bound to deny, both for his sake and our own."

Curtis had favored Devar with a questioning scowl when he learnt how his advent had been heralded in the press, but Devar merely vouchsafed a brazen wink, and in the next breath Hermione herself became his unconscious and most persuasive advocate.

"I have been bothering my brains to discover when or where I had seen Mr. Curtis's name before—before we met to-night," she said, smiling at the ridiculous vagueness of her own phrase. "Now I remember. I used to read the newspaper reports about every ship that arrived, and I noticed that identical paragraph."

"Thank you, Lady Hermione," cried Devar, crowing inwardly over his friend's discomfiture. "John D. will begin to believe soon what I have been telling him during the last half-hour—that I am the real *Deus ex machinâ* of the whole business. Why, if it hadn't been for me you two would never have got married, and this merry party couldn't have happened!"

A knock at the door caused Hermione to turn with a startled look. Try as she might, she dreaded every such incident as the preliminary to a stormy interview with her father.

"Unless I am greatly mistaken, ma'am," interposed Uncle Horace blandly, "this will be a waiter coming to tell us that supper is ready."

As usual, he said the correct thing, and Steingall drew Hermione aside while the table was being spread for the feast. He lost no time in coming to the point. His first demand showed that he took nothing for granted.

"I am bound to speak plainly, your ladyship," he said. "Is the remarkable story told by Mr. John D. Curtis true?"

"Regarding the marriage?" said Hermione promptly.

"Yes."

"Well, as I do not know what he may have said, you can decide that matter for yourself after you have heard my version. I am a fugitive from Paris, where my father was endeavoring to force me into a detestable union: I am practically a complete stranger in New York: I had arranged with Monsieur de Courtois to become my husband, under a clear agreement for money paid that the marriage should serve only as a shield against my pursuers; he was prevented by some dreadful men from keeping to-night's appointment, and Mr. Curtis came to me, intending to break the news somewhat more gently than one might look for otherwise. He heard my sad little explanation, and was sorry for me. As it happened, he appreciated the real nature of my predicament, and, having no ties to prevent such a daring step, offered me the protection of his name until such time as I become my own mistress and am free to secure a dissolution of the marriage."

"Will you tell me exactly what you mean?" said the detective. His voice was kindly, and his expression gravely sympathetic, and Hermione could not read the amused tolerance lurking behind the mask of those keen eyes.

"I mean that I am yet what lawyers call an infant. In six months I shall be twenty-one, and the coercion which has been used to force me into marrying Count Ladislas Vassilan will be no longer possible."

"Do you forfeit an inheritance by refusing to obey Lord Valletort's wishes?"

"No, unless with respect to my father's estate. My mother was wealthy, and her money is settled on me most securely."

"In trust?"

"Yes, I have trustees, an English banker and a clergyman."

"But, if they are men of good standing, they ought to have protected you from undue interference."

"An earl is of good standing, too, in my country, and Count Vassilan claims royal rank in Hungary. I loathe the man, yet every one of my friends and relatives urged me to accept him."

"Why?"

"Because he has a chance of obtaining a throne when the Austro-Hungarian Empire breaks up, and my wealth will help his cause materially."

Steingall allowed himself to appear surprised.

"Is your income so large, then?" he said.

"Yes, I suppose so. My trustees tell me that I am worth nearly a hundred thousand a year."

"Dollars?"

"No—pounds sterling."

They were conversing in subdued tones, yet the detective behaved like a commonplace mortal in giving a rabbit-peep sideways to ascertain if the girl's astounding statement had been overheard by the others. But the members of the Curtis family of honest men and true women had withdrawn purposely to the far side of the room, and Devar was laboring to convince his friend that he had acted wisely in placarding his name and fame throughout the United States.

"To your knowledge, Lady Hermione, is any other person in New York aware that you are several times a millionaire?"

"I think not. Poor Jean de Courtois may have had some notion of the fact, but I lived so unostentatiously in Paris that he would necessarily be inclined to minimize the amount of my fortune. Tell me, Mr. Steingall, do you really think he — —"

The detective shook his head, and laughed with official dryness.

"Forgive me, Lady Hermione," he said, "but I must not advance any theories, at present. Now, as to Count Vassilan—how long have you known him?"

"About a year."

"Has he been your suitor practically all that time?"

"Yes. The first day we met I was told by my father that I ought to be proud if he chose me as his wife. So I hated him from the very beginning."

"You took a dislike to him, I suppose?"

"Yes, an instant and violent dislike. But that is not all. There are things I cannot mention, though they are the common property of anyone who has mixed in Parisian society during the past twelve months. Surely you will be able to find men and women in this great city who can supply enough of Paris gossip to show you clearly what manner of man this Hungarian prince really is!"

Hermione's face showed the distress she felt, and Steingall's disposition was far too generous to permit of any further probing in this direction when the inquiry gave pain to a young and innocent-minded girl.

"To-morrow," he said grimly, "I may read several chapters of Count Vassilan's life. But so much depends on this night's work. At any minute—certainly within an hour—I shall have news which may be affected most markedly by some chance hint supplied by you. I want you to understand, Lady Hermione, that Mr. Curtis's share in the queer tangle of the past few hours is not so simple or unimportant as you seem to imagine. I believe he has been actuated by the best of motives——"

"Oh, yes, I am sure of it," she broke in eagerly. "If I am fated never to see him again after to-night I shall always remember him as a true friend and gallant gentleman."

Steingall bit back the words which rose unbidden to his lips. He had certainly been wallowing in romance since the telephone called him to the Central Hotel, but even in the pages of fiction he had never found a more wildly improbable theory than the likelihood of John Delancy Curtis allowing any consideration short of death to separate him from such a bride as Lady Hermione within the short space of time she apparently regarded as the possible span of her married life.

"Ah," he murmured, "if he is wise he will call you to give evidence in his behalf. Judges exercise a good deal of latitude in these matters."

"But will he be arrested for marrying me? If any wrong has been done with respect to the marriage license, I am equally to blame," she said loyally.

Steingall frowned judicially. Their conversation was approaching perilously near the forbidden topic of de Courtois.

"In law, as in most affairs of life, it does no good to meet trouble half way, your ladyship," he said. "Now, reverting to the Hungarian prince—do you remember the names of any persons, of either sex, whom he associated with in Paris? Of course, such a man would be widely known in what is called society, but I want you to try and recall some of his intimate friends."

"I believe you would find his boon companions in certain cafés on the Grand Boulevard and in the vaudeville theaters on Montmartre; but would it not help you a little if I told you of his enemies?"

"Most certainly."

"Well, I do happen to know that he is hated most cordially by the Countess Marie Zapolya, who lives in the Hotel Ritz."

"In Paris?"

"Yes. She advised me to shun him as I would the plague."

"Did she give any reason?"

"It may sound strange, but I really believe she wants him to marry her daughter."

"Ah, that is interesting. Pray go on."

"I never understood the thing rightly, but I heard once, through a servant, that Count Vassilan was expected to wed Elizabetta Zapolya—the succession to the Hungarian monarchy, if ever it were revived, was involved—but Count Vassilan spurned the lady. The Countess is furious because her daughter was slighted, yet wishes to compel him to fulfill his obligations."

"In that event, she would be anxious to see you safely married to some other person?"

"Oh, she was. She visited me, several times, and advised me not to risk a life-long unhappiness by becoming mixed up in the maze of Mid-Europe politics. And—there is something else. Poor Elizabetta Zapolya, who is somewhat older than me, is in love with an attaché at the Austro-Hungarian Embassy in Paris."

"Have you his name?"

"Yes. Captain Eugene de Karely."

"How does he stand with regard to Count Vassilan?"

"I am told that he has challenged him repeatedly to a duel, but Count Vassilan cannot meet him because they are not equals in the grades of Hungarian aristocracy. I am glad that Mr. Curtis did not wait to consult the Almanach de Gotha when *he* encountered the wretch. Has he told you that he hit him?"

"I have seen the Count," said Steingall.

"Where?"

The detective was not deaf to the note of alarm in her voice, but the matter must be broached some time, and why not now?

"At the Central Hotel, about an hour ago," he said.

"Was my father with him?"

"Yes. The Earl has also had the pleasure of a few minutes' talk with Mr. Curtis."

Hermione was open-eyed with surprise.

"Mr. Curtis has not said a word of this to me," she cried, and her louder tone traveled across the room.

"Said a word about what?" inquired Curtis, being not unwilling to break in on the conversation, which he thought had lasted quite long enough.

"That my father and Count Vassilan had met you at your hotel."

"No, not Count Vassilan," explained the detective. "He had gone before Mr. Curtis came, but Lord Valletort returned."

"Did he ask you where I was?" demanded the girl breathlessly, addressing Curtis.

"No. He tried to have me arrested, and failed. I think he looked on me as an unlikely subject to yield unnecessary information."

"Supper is served, sir," said a maître d'hôtel to Uncle Horace, and further discussion of Count Vassilan's tangled matrimonial schemes became difficult for the moment.

Steingall was pressed to join the party—without prejudice to any official duties he might be called on to perform next day, as Curtis put it pleasantly—and consented. Once again had his instinct been justified, for he was sure that Lady Hermione's Parisian reminiscences would prove important in some way not yet determinable. Moreover, his colleagues knew he was at the Plaza Hotel, and he was content to remain there while his trusted aide, Clancy, was acting as chauffeur during Count Vassilan's belated excursion.

The police captain was keeping an eye on the Waldorf-Astoria, a detective was searching the apartment rented by the murdered journalist, and other men of the Bureau were hunting the record of the automobile, though Steingall was convinced that this branch of the inquiry would end in a blind alley, because the car had undoubtedly been stolen, and its lawful owner would only be able to identify it, and declare that, to the best of his belief, it was locked in a garage at the time it was being used for the commission of a crime. Steingall assumed that the unfortunate Hunter—or it might have been de Courtois—was led to hire this particular vehicle by adroit misrepresentation on the part of some unknown scoundrels who were aware of the contemplated marriage. The shorthand notes in Hunter's book bore out this theory, because they were obviously data supplied by de Courtois which would have enabled the journalist to write a thoroughly sensational story next day. He was convinced, when the truth was known, it would be discovered that Hunter made the Frenchman's acquaintance owing to his habit of mixing with the strange underworld from the Continent of Europe which has its lost legion in New York. De Courtois was just the sort of vainglorious little man who would welcome the notoriety of such an adventure as the prevented marriage ceremony, wherein his name would figure with those of distinguished people, and the last thing he counted on was the murder of the scribe who had promised him columns of descriptive matter in the press. The pert musician was not the first, nor would he be the last, to find that the role of cat's-paw is apt to prove more exacting than was anticipated. To his chagrin, he saw himself changed suddenly from a trusted agent into a dupe, and his utter collapse on hearing of the murder fitted in exactly with the theory taking shape in the detective's mind—that there were two implacable forces at war in New York that night, that Lady Hermione's marriage to Count Vassilan or the Frenchman provided the immediate bone of contention, and that the struggle had been complicated by a too literal interpretation of instructions carried out by bitter partisans.

In the midst of a lively conversation, the telephone jangled its imperative message from a wall bracket in the room. Devar was nearest the instrument, and he answered the call.

"It's for you, Mr. Steingall," he said.

SCENES FROM THE PHOTO-DRAMA.

The detective would have preferred greater privacy, but he rose at once and answered.

"And who is Mr. Krantz?" he demanded. Then, after a pause: "Oh, yes.... Is he?... You needn't trouble at all about that. The police surgeon, at my request, has dosed him with sufficient bromide to keep him quiet till to-morrow morning.... Yes, I understand. Tell them it can't be done, and refer them to the Centre-street Bureau.... What?... No, so far as I can guess, the engineer won't be wanted again to-night."

He hung up the receiver, and returned to his seat, though he had just been informed that the Earl of Valletort and another person, having ascertained by some means that de Courtois still lived, were raising a commotion at the Central Hotel and demanding access to the Frenchman's room.

"Please, am I mixed up with Mr. Krantz?" inquired Hermione, smiling, for it was a bizarre experience to find herself interested in all sorts and conditions of people whom she had never heard of.

"Mr. Krantz is the reception clerk at the Central Hotel," was the answer, which conveyed fuller information to other ears than the girl's. Then Steingall glanced at his watch.

"I think some of you people must be tired after a strenuous day," he said. "I expect to be called away soon, and it is possible that I may want to disturb you, Mr. Curtis, before you retire for the night. Do you intend to remain here?"

"Yes."

For an instant, an appreciable constraint manifested its presence, and Uncle Horace did not display his wonted tact when he accentuated it by a dry chuckle, *à propos* of nothing in particular. Curtis relieved the situation after a slight hesitation.

"Lady Hermione, I take it, will now go to bed," he said coolly, "and, if she is wise, will refuse to unlock her door again till her maid comes in the morning. I purpose changing my clothes, in case I may have to accompany you on some midnight expedition. My uncle and aunt will tell us where they are staying, and arrange to meet us here at lunch to-morrow. You, Devar, being an approved night hawk, will join me in a cigar. How is that for a reasonable disposal of the company, Mr. Steingall?"

As though in reply, the telephone rang again, and the detective lifted the receiver from its hook.

"Hello! That you, Clancy?" he said. "Right. I'll come along by the subway from 59th Street—that will be quicker than a taxi … yes … yes."

He turned, and the five people in the room saw that his face was glowing with the fire of action.

"You can defer that change of suits, Mr. Curtis. We must be off at once.… Mr. Devar, have you an automobile? Can you get hold of it now? Well, 'phone your chauffeur to be at Centre-street headquarters in as much under half-an-hour as he can manage. Taxi-drivers gossip among themselves, so a private car is better.… Excuse the rush, Lady Hermione, and you, too, Mrs. Curtis. I haven't another minute to spare."

Luckily, Curtis found his overcoat awaiting him in the cloak room, or he might have been in a difficulty, for New York in November is not a city which encourages midnight journeys in evening dress.

Uncle Horace and Aunt Louisa were hurried into a taxi, and as they were being whisked off to the quiet hotel to which their baggage had been consigned, the stout man began polishing his domed forehead once more.

"Lou," he said, "I can't make head nor tail of this business. Can you?"

"Not yet, Horace," was the hopeful response.

"But—what sort of marriage is this, anyway?"

"Oh, that's all right. Those two haven't begun courting yet. But it won't be long before they start. Did you notice— —"

And details observed by Aunt Louisa endured till the taxi stopped.

CHAPTER X

MIDNIGHT

After a quick journey by New York's unrivaled system of rapid transit, the three men alighted at Spring Street, and a couple of minutes' brisk walk brought them to a large, white-fronted building of severe architecture. Above the main entrance two green lamps stared solemnly into the night, and their monitory gleam seemed to bid evildoers "Beware!"; nor was there aught far-fetched in the notion, because from this imposing center New York's guardians kept watch and ward over the city.

"Clancy still waiting?" demanded Steingall of a policeman in uniform who was on duty in an inquiry office.

"Yes, sir. He asked me to be on the lookout in case you turned up unexpectedly, as he didn't want to miss you."

The Chief Inspector led his companions straight to the Detective Bureau, taking good care to avoid the room in which the "covering" reporters were gathered, because the Police Headquarters of New York, unlike any similar department outside the bounds of the United States, makes the press welcome, and gives details of all arrests, fires, accidents and other occurrences of a noteworthy nature as soon as the facts are telegraphed or telephoned from outlying districts.

Passing through the general office, Steingall entered his own sanctum. A small, slightly built man was bent over a table and scrutinizing a Rogues' Gallery of photographs in a large album. He turned as the door opened, straightened himself, and revealed a wizened face, somewhat of the actor type, its prominent features being an expressive mouth, a thin, hooked nose, and a pair of singularly piercing and deeply sunken eyes.

"Hello, Bob," he said to Steingall. Then, without a moment's hesitation, he added: "Good-evening, Mr. Curtis—glad to see you, Mr. Devar."

"Good-evening, Mr. Clancy," said Curtis, not to be outdone in this exchange of compliments, though he could not imagine how a person who had never seen him should not only know his name but apply it so confidently.

"May we smoke here?" asked Devar, who had lighted a cigar on emerging from the subway station.

"Oh, yes," said Steingall. "Make yourselves at home in that respect. I am a hard smoker. Let me offer you a good American cigar, Mr. Curtis."

"Thank you. Perhaps you will try one of mine. I bought them in London, but they are of a fair brand. You, too, Mr. Clancy?"

"I'll take one, with pleasure, though I don't smoke," said the little man. Seeing the question on the faces of both visitors, he cackled, in a queer, high-pitched voice:

"I refuse to poison my gastric juices with nicotine, but I like the smell of tobacco. Poor old Steingall there has pretty fair eyesight, but his nose wouldn't sniff brimstone in a volcano, all because he insists on smoking."

"Gastric juice!" laughed Steingall. "You don't possess the article. Skin, bones, and tongue are your chief constituents. I'm not surprised you make an occasional hit as a detective, because the average crook would never suspect a funny little gazook like you of being that celebrated sleuth, Eugene Clancy."

Clancy's long, nervous fingers had cracked the wrapper of the cigar given him by Curtis, and he was now passing it to and fro beneath his nostrils.

"You will observe the difference, gentlemen, between beef and brains," he said, nodding derisively at the bulky Chief Inspector. "He rubbers along because he looks like a prize-fighter, and can drive his fist through a three-quarter inch pine plank. But we hunt well together, being a unique combination of science and brute force.... By the way, that reminds me. If I have got the story right, Count Ladislas Vassilan only landed in New York to-night. Did he drive straight to a boxing contest, or what?"

"Wait a second, Clancy," interrupted Steingall. "Is there anything doing? How much time have we?"

"Exactly twenty minutes. At twelve-thirty I must be in East Broadway."

"Good. Now, Mr. Curtis, tell Clancy exactly what happened since you put on poor Hunter's overcoat at the corner of Broadway and 27th Street."

Curtis obeyed, though he fancied he had never encountered a more unofficial official than Clancy. Shrewd judge of character as he was, he could hardly be expected to guess, after such a momentary glimpse of a man of extraordinary genius in unraveling crime, that Clancy was never more discursive, never more prone to chaff and sneer at his special friend, Steingall, than when hot on the trail of some particularly acute and daring malefactor. The Chief of the Bureau, of course, knew by these signs that his trusted *aide* had obtained information of a really startling nature, but neither Curtis nor Devar was aware of Clancy's idiosyncrasies, and some few minutes elapsed before they began to suspect that he had a good deal more up his sleeve than they gave him credit for at first.

From the outset he took an original view of Curtis's marriage.

"The girl is young and good-looking, you say?" was his opening question.

"Not yet twenty-one, and remarkably attractive," said Curtis, though hardly prepared for the detective's interest in this direction.

"Well educated and lady-like, I suppose?"

"Yes, as befits her position."

"Cut out her position, which doesn't amount to a row of beans where intellect is concerned.... Well, a man never knows much about a woman anyway, and what little he learns is acquired by a process of rejection after marriage."

"May I ask what you mean?"

"Judging from your history and apparent age, Mr. Curtis, I take it you have not had time to go fooling about after girls?"

"You are certainly right in that respect."

"Naturally, or you wouldn't be so ignorant concerning the dear creatures. You are to be congratulated, 'pon my soul. You will have the rare experience of constructing a divinity out of a wife, whereas the average man begins by choosing a divinity and finds he has only secured a wife."

Curtis laughed, but met the detective's penetrating gaze frankly.

"Your bitter philosophy may be sound, Mr. Clancy," he said, "but it is built on a false premiss. My marriage is only a matter of form. It may be legal—indeed, I believe it is—but there can be no dispute as to the nature of the bond between Lady Hermione and myself. She regards me as a husband in name only, and will dissolve the tie at her own convenience."

"You'll place no obstacles in her way?"

"None."

"Quite sure?"

"Absolutely."

Clancy giggled, as though he were a comedian who had scored a point with his audience.

"Then you're married for keeps," he announced, with the grin of a man who has solved a humorous riddle. "By refusing to thwart the lady you throw away your last slender chance of freedom, and you will find her waiting at the gate of the State Penitentiary when you come out. By Jove, you've been pretty rapid, though. No wonder people say the East is waking up. Are there many more like you in China?"

Curtis was not altogether pleased by this banter, nor did he trouble to conceal his opinion that the New York Detective Bureau was treating a grave crime with scandalous levity.

"Whether Lady Hermione married me or Jean de Courtois is a rather immaterial side issue," he said, somewhat emphatically. "From what little I can grasp of a curiously involved affair, it seems to me that there are weightier interests than ours at stake. And, if I may venture to differ from you, a lot of things may happen before I see the inside of a prison."

"After your meteoric career during the past few hours I am inclined to agree with that last remark," and Clancy's tone became so serious that Devar laughed outright. "Don't misunderstand me, Mr. Curtis. I am lost in admiration of your nerve, but you have told me just what I wanted to make sure of."

"I have expressed no opinions. I confined myself to actual facts."

"And isn't it a highly significant fact that you are over head and ears in love with your wife? *Nom d'un pipe!* Doesn't that complicate the thing worse than a Chinese puzzle?"

"I really don't see——" began Curtis, yielding to a feeling of annoyance which was not altogether unwarrantable, but Clancy jerked out his hands as though they were attached to arms moved by the strings of a marionette.

"Of course, you don't!" he cried. "You're in love! You're gorged with the amococcus microbe! It's the worst case I've ever heard of. I once knew a man who met a girl for the first time at the Park Row end of Brooklyn Bridge and proposed to her before they had crossed the East River, but you've set up a record that will never be beaten. You find a marriage license in the pockets of a murdered man, rush off in a taxi to the address of the lady named therein, marry her, punch a frantic rival on the nose, take the fair one to a hotel, flout her father, a British peer, and hold a banquet at which the Chief of the New York Detective Bureau is an honored guest; and then you have the hardihood to tell me that your actions constitute an immaterial side issue in the biggest sensation New York has produced this year. Young man, wait till the interviewers get hold of you to-morrow! Wait till the sob sisters begin gushing over your bride—a pretty one—with a title! Name of good little gray man! They'll whoop your side issues into a scare-head front page! Before you know where you are they'll have you bleating about the color of her eyes, the exquisite curve of her Cupid's Bow lips, and the way her hair shone when the electric light fell on it, while she, on her part, will be confiding, with a suspicious break in her voice, what a perfectly darling specimen of the American man at his best you are. Mr. Curtis, you're married good and hard, and if you want to cinch the job you ought to go to jail for a while."

Unquestionably, the two civilians present thought that Clancy was slightly mad, so Steingall intervened.

"Hop off your perch, Eugene," he said, "and tell us how you came to drive Count Vassilan's taxi, and where you took him."

"It was a case of intelligent anticipation of forthcoming events," said Clancy, whose excitability disappeared instantly, leaving him calm and extremely lucid of speech. "When Evans (the police captain) gave me the bearings of the affair—though, of course, being a creature of handcuffs and bludgeons, he thought our friend Curtis was the real scoundrel—I realized at once that Vassilan's indisposition was a bad attack of blue funk. Such a man could no more remain quietly in his room at the hotel than a fox terrier could pass a dog fight without taking hold. As soon as I saw the Earl go out alone, and heard him direct the taxi to the Central Hotel in 27th Street, I decided that my best place was at the driving wheel of another taxi. I picked out a man on the rank who was about my size, and might be mistaken for me in a half-light, and got him to lend me his coat and cap. He took mine, and a word to the door-porter fixed things so that I was whistled up quite naturally when his countship appeared. He had changed his clothes and linen, but one glance at his nose showed that I had marked my bird, even if the porter hadn't given me the mystic sign at the right moment. I received my orders, and off we went, a second cab following, with the driver of my taxi as a fare. Evidently, the Count was not well posted in New York distances, because he grew restive, and wondered where I was taking him. He tried to be artful, too, and when we reached East Broadway he pulled me up at the corner of Market Street, told me to wait, and lodged a five-dollar bill as security, saying I would have annozzaire when we got back to the hotel. Didn't that make things easy? He plunged into the crowd—you know what a bunch of Russians, Hungarians, and Polish Jews get together in East Broadway about ten-thirty—so I rushed to the second cab, swapped coats and hats again, gave the taxi-man the five-spot, and put him in charge of his own cab. In less than a minute I overtook the Count, just as he was crossing the street, and saw him enter a house, after saying something to a second-hand clothes man who was bawling out his goods from the open store on the ground floor. By the time I had bought two silk handkerchiefs and a pair of boots, and was haggling like mad over a collection of linen collars, size 16—a present for you, Steingall—his nobility came downstairs, but not alone; there was a girl with him. Luckily, she was no Hungarian, but Italian, and they talked in broken English. 'They no come-a here-a now-a-time, Excellenza,' she said, 'but you-a fin' dem at Morris Siegelman's restaurant at 'alf-a-pass twelve.' He said something choice—in pure Magyar, I guess—and headed for the taxi. That is all, or practically all. I tried to go back on my bargains with the Israelite in the store, but he made such a row that I paid him, and when I reached the second cab the driver told me that my man nodded as he passed, showing that Vassilan was returning to the hotel. So I came here, and 'phoned you."

Steingall glanced at a clock on the mantel-piece. He rose, threw open a door, and switched on a light.

"Mr. Curtis," he said, "we must risk something, but I think I can make you up sufficiently to escape recognition, not so much by the Count as by others who may attend that supper party. You come, too, Mr. Devar. There is safety in numbers."

With a deftness that was worthy of a theatrical costumier, the detectives converted themselves and the two young men into ship's firemen. No more effective or simpler disguise could have been devised on the spur of the moment, nor one that might be assumed more readily. Boots offered the main difficulty, but Clancy's purchase fitted Devar, and Curtis made the best of a pair of canvas shoes, while a mixture of grease and coffee extract applied to face and hands changed four respectable looking persons into a gang which would certainly attract the attention of the police anywhere outside the bounds of just such a locality as they were bound for.

In case the exigencies of the chase separated them, Steingall gave some instructions to the man in the inquiry office, and Devar tested the realism of his appearance by disregarding the chauffeur of the splendidly appointed automobile waiting at the exit. Walking up to the car, he opened the door and said gruffly:

"Jump in, boys!"

The chauffeur wriggled out of his seat instantly, and leaped to the pavement.

"Here, what the — —" he began, whereupon Devar laughed.

"It's all right, Arthur," he said.

"What's all right? This car is here for Mr. Howard Devar," cried the man angrily.

"Well, you cuckoo, and who am I?"

Something familiar in the voice caused the chauffeur to look closely at the speaker, whom he had not seen for a considerable time except for a fleeting glimpse on the arrival of the *Lusitania* at New York that afternoon. He was perplexed, but was evidently not devoid of humor.

"It's either you or your ghost, sir," he said, "and if it's your ghost you must have been badly treated in the next world."

A roundsman was entering headquarters at the moment, and gave the quartette a sharp glance.

"Here, Parker," said Steingall, "tell this man my name."

The policeman came up, looked at the detective, and laughed.

"This is Mr. Steingall, chief of the Detective Bureau," he said to the bewildered driver, who resumed charge of the car without further ado, but nevertheless remained uneasy in his mind. And not without cause. He, poor fellow, all unconsciously, was now gathered into the net which had spread its meshes so wide in New York that night. He could not understand why his employer's son should be gallivanting around the city in company with such questionable looking characters, even though one of them might be the famous "man with the microscopic eye," but he was far from realizing that he and his car would help to make history before morning.

In obedience to orders, he ran along Grand Street, and halted the car on the south side of W. H. Seward Park.

"Remain here, if we do not return earlier, till one o'clock," Steingall told him, "and then run slowly along East Broadway to the corner of Montgomery Street. We are going to Morris Siegelman's restaurant, which is a few doors higher up, on the north side. If we stroll past you, pay no heed, but follow at a little distance. Have you got that right?"

"Yes, sir."

Devar was hugely delighted by the man's discomfited tone.

"Cheer up, Arthur," he said. "You'll be tickled to death to-morrow when you read the newspapers, and discover the part you played in a big news item."

"Now, don't forget to lurch about the sidewalk," was Steingall's next injunction to the amateurs. "Think of all the bad language you ever heard, and use it. We're toughs, and must behave as such. Can either of you sing?"

"I can," admitted Curtis.

"That will help some. Strike up any sort of sailor's chanty when we're in the restaurant."

Late as the hour, East Broadway was full to repletion with a cosmopolitan crowd. It was a Thursday evening, and the Hebrew Sabbath began at sunset on the following day, so the poor Jews of the quarter were out in their thousands, either buying provisions for the coming holiday or attracted by the light and bustle. Heavy looking Russians, olive-skinned Italians, placid Germans, wild-eyed and pallid Czechs, lounged along the thoroughfare, chatting with compatriots, or gathering in amused groups to hear the strange patter of some voluble merchant retailing goods from a barrow. From the interiors of tiny shops and cellars came eldritch voices crying the nature and remarkable qualities of the wares within. Every hand-cart carried a flaring naphtha-lamp, and the glare of these innumerable torches created strong lights and flickering shadows which would have gladdened the heart of Rembrandt were his artistic wraith permitted to roam the by-ways of a city which, perhaps, he never heard of, even in its early Dutch guise as New Amsterdam.

The lofty tenement houses seemed to be crowded as the streets. Within a square mile of that section of New York a quarter of a million people find habitation, food, and employment. They supply each other's needs, speak their own weird tongues, and by slow degrees become absorbed by the great continent which harbors them, and then only when a second or third generation becomes Americanized.

In such a motley throng four prowling stokers, ashore for a night's spree, attracted scant attention, and Morris Siegelman's hospitable door was reached without incident. A taxi-cab was standing by the curb, and the driver, gazing at the living panorama of the street, little guessed that he had changed garments with one of the half-drunken firemen two hours earlier.

"Here y'are, mattes!" cried Steingall, joyously surveying a printed legend displayed among the bottles of a dingy bar running along the side of an apartment which had once been the parlor of a pretentious house, "this is the right sort o' dope—vodka—same as is supplied to the Czar of all the Roossias. Get a pint of vodka into yer gizzards an' you'll think you've swallowed a lump of red-hot clinker."

Clancy hopped on to a high stool, and curled himself up on the rounded seat in the accepted posture of Buddha, while Devar, who was by way of being a gymnast, stood on his hands and beat a tattoo with his feet against the edge of the counter. Not to be outdone, Curtis began to sing. He had a good baritone voice, and entered with zest into the mad spirit of the frolic. The song he chose was redolent of the sea. It related a tar's escapades among witches, cruisers, and girls. Three of the latter claimed him at one and the same time—so "What was a sailor-boy to do? Yeo-ho, Yeo-ho, Yeo-ho!" The chorus decided the point:

"Why, we went strolling down by the rolling,
Down by the rolling sea.
If you can't be true to One or Two,
You're much better off with Three."

Evidently, the roysterers' antics commanded the general approval of
Morris Siegelman's patrons, and loud cries of "Brava!" "Encore!"
"Bis!" "Herrlich!" rewarded Curtis's lyrical effort. Some thirty
people or more were scattered about the room, mostly in small
parties seated around marble-topped tables. Beer was the favorite
beverage; a minority was eating, the menu being strange and
wondrous, and everyone was smoking cigarettes. When Curtis
received his share of the poisonous decoction so vaunted by
Steingall, he faced the company, glass in hand, and saw Count
Vassilan seated in a corner close to a window. With him were a
good-looking Italian girl and a youth, and the three were deep in
eager converse, giving no heed to the other revelers, but rather
taking advantage of the prevalent clatter of talk and drinking
utensils to discuss whatever topic it was which proved so
interesting.

Steingall's eyes carried a question, and Curtis shook his head.
Vassilan's male companion bore only the slight resemblance of a
kindred nationality to the men who committed the murder, while he
differed essentially from the treacherous "Anatole."

"I wish your best girl could see you now, John D.," whispered
Devar, who had just recovered from a violent fit of coughing
induced by the raw whisky which Siegelman dispensed under the
seal of vodka. Curtis laughed at the conceit, which was grotesque in
its very essence. Wild and bizarre as his experiences had been that
night, none was more whimsical than this bawling of a ballad in an
East Broadway saloon while posing as a sailor with three sheets in
the wind.

"Mostly Hungarians here," muttered Steingall. "We seem to be in
the right place, anyhow."

"Let's eat," said Clancy suddenly.

Reflected in a cracked mirror he had seen a man and two women rise and leave a table in the corner occupied by the Count. He skipped off the stool, and made for the vacant place; the others followed, and Curtis had several glasses raised to his honor as he passed through the merry-makers.

Clancy noisily summoned a waitress, and ordered four plates of spaghetti with tomatoes. He sat with his back to the absorbed party beneath the window, and apologized with exaggerated politeness when his chair touched that of the Italian girl, though his accent, needless to say, was redolent of the East side.

"They do not come, then?" he heard Vassilan say impatiently.

"P'raps notta to-night," said the girl, "but you sure meet-a dem here, mebbe to-morrow, mebbe de nex' day."

The Count tore a leaf from a notebook and scribbled something rapidly. When he spoke, it was to the Hungarian, and in Magyar, but it was easy to guess that he was giving earnest directions as to the delivery of the note.

"Now would be a good time to raise a row if we could manage it," growled Steingall.

Curtis was toying with his fourth meal since sunset, and admitted that he was ready for anything rather than spaghetti à la tomato.

"If there's enough varieties of Hungarians and Slavs in the street I can start a riot in less than no time," confided Devar.

"How?" asked the detective.

"This way," and Devar began to sing. He owned a light tenor, clear and melodious, and the air had a curiously barbaric lilt which, musically considered, was reminiscent of the gypsies' chorus in "The

Bohemian Girl." But the words were couched in a strange tongue, sonorous and full voweled, and the Hungarians in the room became greatly stirred when it dawned on them that a semi-intoxicated American stoker was chanting a forbidden national melody. Far better than he knew, he sounded uncharted deeps in human nature. Andrew Fletcher of Saltoun stated an eternal truth when he wrote to the Marquis of Montrose: "I know a very wise man that believed that if a man were permitted to make all the ballads he need not care who should make the laws of a nation." Before Devar had finished the first verse people from the street were crowding in through the open door, and flashing eyes and strange ejaculations showed that the Czechs thought they were witnessing a miracle. As the second verse rang out, vibrant and challenging, the mob, eager to share in the interior excitement, rushed the entrance. Many could hear, but few could see, and all were roused to exaltation by a melody the public singing of which would have brought imprisonment or death in their own land.

"Now for it!" roared Steingall, and over went table and crockery with a crash. Of course, this added to the turmoil, and some women in the café began to shriek. Not knowing in the least what was causing the commotion, the crowd surged into that particular corner, and Steingall, apparently frenzied, sprang to the window, opened it, and said to Count Vassilan:

"Get out, quick! They'll be knifing you in a minute!"

The Italian girl screamed at that, so she was lifted into the safety of the street. Vassilan followed, or rather was practically thrown out, and the young Hungarian could have climbed after him nimbly enough had not Curtis insisted on helping him, and, pinioning his arms, forced him head foremost over the sill, but not so rapidly that Steingall should be unable to "go through him" scientifically for the note.

"Be off, you two! Take the car and go home!"

It was no time for argument. Both Curtis and Devar read into Steingall's muttered injunction the belief that the hunt had ended for the night. They knew that the detectives could take care of themselves, and they had scrambled through the window and made off swiftly in the direction of the waiting automobile before the despoiled Hungarian regained his feet. The hour yet wanted nearly ten minutes of being one o'clock, so the chauffeur had not budged from his post in the park. Devar told him to start the engine, and be ready to jump off without delay. Then they waited, and watched the corner of the square intersected by East Broadway, but neither Steingall nor Clancy appeared, so they judged it best to obey orders, and make for the Police Headquarters. There they washed and resumed their own clothes, an operation which consumed another quarter of an hour. Still there was no sign of the detectives, and they decided, somewhat reluctantly, to do as they had been bidden, and go home.

"What sort of witches' shibboleth was that which you brought off in Siegelman's?" asked Curtis, while the car was humming placidly up Broadway.

"Oh, that was an inspiration," chuckled Devar.

"An inspiration founded on a solid basis of fact. Now, out with it!"

"Well, I was a year at Heidelberg, you know, and a fellow there told me that one evening, in a café at Temesvar, a student kicked up a shindy by singing that song. In less than a minute an officer had been stabbed with his own sword, and a policeman shot, and it took a squadron of cavalry to clear the street. He learnt the blessed ditty, out of sheer curiosity, and I picked it up from him."

"What is it all about?"

"I don't know. I believe it tells the Austrians their real name, but I couldn't translate a line of it to save my life."

Curtis leaned back in the car and laughed.

"You are by way of being a genius," he said. "I have seen a crowd go stark, staring mad because some idiot waved a black flag, but that was a symbol of the Boxer rebellion, and it meant something. In this instance, among people so far away from their own country, one would hardly expect — —"

He broke off suddenly, and leaned forward.

The car had just entered Madison Square, at the junction of Broadway and Fifth Avenue, south of 23rd Street. A Columbus Avenue street-car had halted to allow traffic to pass, and a gray automobile which was coming out of Fifth Avenue had been held up by a policeman stationed there. Curtis's attention was caught by the color and shape of the vehicle, and in the flood of light cast by the powerful lamps and brilliant electric devices concentrated on that important crossing, he obtained a vivid glimpse of the chauffeur's face.

"Devar," he said, and some electrical quality in his voice startled his mercurial companion, "tell your man to overtake that car and run it into the sidewalk. The driver is 'Anatole,' and it is our duty to stop him!"

At that instant the policeman signaled the uptown traffic to move on.

CHAPTER XI

ONE O'CLOCK

Devar had the nimble wits of a fox, and the blood which raced in his veins was volatile as quicksilver. The same glance which showed him the gray automobile stealing softly across the network of car-lines of one of the city's main thoroughfares revealed a roundsman crossing the square.

"Friend Anatole may be heeled," he said. "Let's get help."

Leaning out, he shouted to Arthur, whose other name was Brodie:

"Pull in alongside the cop. I want to speak to him."

The chauffeur obeyed, and the policeman turned a questioning eye on the car, thinking some idiot meant to run him down. Devar had the door open in a second.

"Have you heard of the murder in 27th Street, outside the Central Hotel?" he said, almost bewildering the man by his eager directness.

"Of course I have," came the answer, quickly enough.

"Well, the car mixed up in it is right ahead. There it is, making for Fifth Avenue. Jump in! We'll explain as we go."

The roundsman needed no second invitation. Obviously, unless some brainless young fool was trying to be humorous, there was no time to spare for words. He sprang inside, and Devar cried to the surprised chauffeur:

"Follow that gray auto. Don't kill anybody, but hit up the speed until we are close behind it, and then I'll tell you what next to do."

Little recking what this order really meant, for its true inwardness was hidden at the moment from the ken of those far better versed than he in the tangle of events, Brodie changed gear and touched the accelerator, and the machine whirred past Admiral Farragut's statue at a pace which would have caused even doughty "Old Salamander" to blink with astonishment.

While four pairs of eyes were watching the fast moving vehicle in front, Curtis gave the policeman a brief resume of the night's doings since he and Devar had gone with Steingall to the Police Headquarters. There was no need to say much about the actual crime, because the man had full details, with descriptions of the man-slayers, in his notebook.

He was a shrewd person, too. His name was McCulloch; his father had emigrated from Belfast, and a man of such ancestry seldom takes anything for granted.

"I suppose you are not quite certain, Mr. Curtis, that the chauffeur driving that car ahead is the 'Anatole' concerned in the death of Mr. Hunter?" he asked.

But Curtis was of a cautious temperament, too.

"No," he said, "that is more than I dare state, even if I had an opportunity to look at him closely. As it is, I merely received what I may term 'an impression' of him. That, together with the marked similarity of the car to the one I saw outside the hotel, seems to offer reasonable ground for inquiry at any rate."

"Did you notice the number of this car?"

"No, not exactly. I believe it differs from that which I undoubtedly did see and put on record."

"Of course, the plate must have been changed or he would never venture in this locality again. If you are right, sir, the fellow must possess a mighty cool nerve, because he is just passing 27th Street, within a few yards of the hotel."

Somehow, the fact had escaped Curtis's remembrance; excellent though his topographical sense might be, he was still sufficient of a stranger in New York not to appreciate the bearings of particular localities with the prompt discrimination necessarily displayed by the policeman.

During the succeeding few seconds none of the occupants of the limousine spoke. Devar was kneeling on one of the front seats, and the roundsman, who had removed his uniform hat to avoid attracting notice when a lamp shone directly into the interior, quietly took stock of the men who had so unceremoniously called him off his tour of inspection. Evidently he satisfied himself that he was not being dragged into a wild-goose chase. Their tense manner could hardly have been assumed: they were in desperate and deadly earnest; so he thanked the stars which had brought him into active connection with an important crime, and gave his mind strictly to the business in hand. Several knotty points demanded careful if speedy decision. The chased automobile might prove to be an innocent vehicle, driven by a chauffeur above suspicion, and if its owner appeared in the guise of some highly influential person he, the roundsman, might be called to sharp account for exceeding his duty in making an arrest, or, if he stopped short of that extreme course, in conducting an offensive inquiry.

Brodie took his instructions literally, and the distance between the two cars was diminishing sensibly. It seemed, too, as though the driver of the gray car slackened pace after passing 27th Street, although Fifth Avenue was fairly clear of traffic, which, such as it was, consisted mainly of motors going uptown — that is to say, in the same direction as pursued and pursuer.

At 34th Street came a check. A cross-town street-car caused the gray automobile to swerve rapidly in order to avoid a collision, and Brodie, a methodical person of law-abiding instincts, lost nearly fifty yards in allowing the streetcar to pass.

"Whoever he may be, he is not going to make any unnecessary stops," commented the roundsman, fully alive to the significance of the incident, since ninety-nine drivers out of a hundred would have applied the brake and allowed the heavy public conveyance to get out of the way.

"Unless the Hungarian assassins of New York are bang up-to-date in the benzine part of their stock-in-trade, our car will make good in the next two blocks," said Devar, over his shoulder.

And, indeed, it almost appeared that Brodie had heard what was said. He bent forward slightly, touched a few taps with skilled fingers, squared his shoulders, and set about the race with the air of a man who thought it had lasted long enough.

Nearing 42nd Street, he had reduced the gap to little more than twice the length of the car, and the three men saw the number plate clearly. Not only did the number differ, but it was of another series.

"That's a New Jersey car," announced the policeman.

"It may be a New Jersey number," Curtis corrected him, "but I still retain my belief that we are following the right man and the right car."

Just then no less than four cross-town electric cars loomed into sight, and completely blocked the avenue at its intersection with 42nd Street. The gray automobile had to pull up very quickly, and Brodie was compelled to execute a neat half-turn to clear the rear wheels. In the result, both cars halted side by side, but Curtis found himself just short of a position whence he could obtain a second look at the suspected man.

The policeman had bent low in his seat, lest his uniform should be seen, but he, like his companions, gave a sharp glance into the interior of the other car. It was empty.

He was seated on the near side, however, and he noticed that the lower panel behind the door had been cleaned since the remainder of the paint-work was touched, and the step bore signs of a recent washing.

Devar lowered one of the front sashes a couple of inches.

"Don't look round, Arthur," he said in a low tone, "and don't take any notice of the chauffeur, but creep forward a foot or two, and then let him go ahead again."

Brodie sat like a sphinx, and apparently did nothing, yet the car moved. Sacrificing himself, Roundsman McCulloch fell back into his corner, and left the window clear for Curtis.

"Well?" he inquired, and, surfeited though he might be with New York sensations, the others were conscious of just a hint of excitement in his voice.

"That is Anatole, I am nearly sure," said Curtis.

"Why not jump out and grab him now?" suggested Devar.

"Do you gentlemen mind following him for a time?" asked the policeman.

"No, I'm game for anything. And you, Curtis?"

"Oh, I feel ready to start the night all over again."

The street-cars went on, and the gray automobile darted through the first possible opening.

"You see, it is this way," explained the official. "I am prepared to arrest the man on Mr. Curtis's evidence, because I couldn't have better testimony than that of the chief witness. But I've been chewing on this thing for the past few minutes, and it strikes me that we gain nothing by acting in a hurry. You may be sure that this fellow, even if he is the person we want, will deny it, and a day or two may be lost in proving his identity, or collecting facts which would support the theory that he was the chauffeur connected with the crime. Now, if we let him go on, we shall certainly have a better hold over him. We'll find out his destination—perhaps secure a very useful address, or, with real luck, discover that he is keeping a fixture with some other individual."

"In a word, we must watch and pray," said Devar.

"Well, we can wait and see, anyhow," said the practical minded McCulloch.

His counsel sounded good, and the others agreed with him, thereby letting themselves and the patient Brodie in for some remarkable developments in a pursuit which began by a simple coincidence and was destined to end in a manner which none of them dreamed of.

Devar opened the window again.

"Arthur," he said, "did you happen to notice whether or not that fellow is carrying a reflector?"

"Yes, sir. He has one. I saw him looking into it when I drew alongside."

"Ah, that puts a different complexion on the affair, as the young man said when he kissed his best girl and tasted Somebody's Beauty Powder. Don't press, Arthur. Just keep him in sight till I consult the law."

As the outcome of a hurried discussion, Brodie received a fresh mandate. During the straightaway run he was not to approach the gray car nearer than sixty yards or thereabouts—in effect, remaining within the same block if possible, but, if the gray car stopped in front of any dwelling, he was to slacken speed and pass it, taking the middle of the road, and holding himself in instant readiness to halt or turn as directed.

"By the way, how are you fixed for petrol?" added Devar.

"I filled the tanks, sir, before leaving the garage. We're good for the trip to Albany and back."

Brodie's tone was quite cheerful. He, too, had been reviewing the situation, and the presence of a uniformed policeman had dispelled the last shred of suspicion that some stupid joke had been worked off outside the Police Headquarters when a fearsome looking tough was introduced to him as the Chief of the New York Detective Bureau.

Devar was about to congratulate the roundsman on the prospect of an all-night journey if Brodie's chance phrase were fated to come true, when he glanced at Curtis, and elected to remain silent. They were passing the Plaza Hotel, and his friend was peering up at its square white bulk. Obviously, he was striving to locate Hermione's room. Most probably he failed, for it is no easy matter to pick out the windows of any particular set of rooms in a huge building while rushing along at twenty-five or more miles an hour. Further, it was now past one o'clock in the morning, and most respectable people were in bed, so the solemn mass of the hotel was enlivened by very few rectangles of light.

But Curtis fancied, as did Devar also, that the illuminated blinds of three windows on the second floor might possibly be those of Suite F., and each wondered, if the surmise were correct, why her ladyship was remaining up so late.

Devar resolved to say nothing, but Curtis felt that he must talk, if only for the sake of hearing his own voice. Usually a man of taciturn habit, the outcome of long vigils among an alien and often hostile race in a semi-civilized land, he had gone through so much during the five and a half hours which had unfolded their marvels since he quitted the dining-room of the Central Hotel, that he ached for human sympathy, even in a trivial matter of this sort.

"I thought I saw a light in my wife's rooms," he said.

"As you mention it, so did I," agreed Devar.

"I hope she is not awaiting my return?"

"Perhaps she is anxious about you?"

"But why?"

"Women are given that way. She knows you went out with Steingall, and he is a dangerous character."

"Is Mrs. Curtis staying in the Plaza?" asked the puzzled McCulloch.

"Yes."

"But I thought you occupied a room at the Central Hotel in 27th Street?"

"I did, but I got married at half-past eight, and we went to the Plaza."

"Married at half-past eight—just after the murder!" The policeman's words formed a crescendo of sheer surprise. For some indefinable reason this curious conjunction of a crime and a wedding went beyond his comprehension.

"Yes, it happened so. It might have been avoided, yet, looking back now over the whole of the circumstances, it would appear that I have followed a beaten track inevitable as death."

Of course, the roundsman could not grasp the somber thought underlying Curtis's words, but a species of indeterminate suspicion prompted his next question.

"You came from the Plaza with Mr. Steingall, I believe, sir?"

"Yes. We were having supper there, with Mr. Devar and my uncle and aunt, when Mr. Clancy rang him up on the telephone, and he invited us to accompany him to the Police Headquarters. The rest you know."

Certainly, the explanation sounded quite satisfactory. The attitude of these two young men and their chauffeur was perfectly correct, and the policeman's views had been strengthened materially by the tell-tale tokens he had noted on the gray car, which, however, he had not thought fit to mention. If Steingall had attended the supper in the Plaza he must have convinced himself that there was nothing unusual, or, at any rate, doubtful, about the queer fact that a man who was mixed up in a remarkable murder should have gone straight from the scene of the tragedy and got married.

Just to dispel a little of the mist that befogged his brain, he waited a while and then said:

"Which side of the car was opposite the doorway when those two men attacked Mr. Hunter?"

"The left. The car had entered the street from Broadway."

"Why do you ask?" inquired Devar, instantly alive to the queerness of this alteration of topics.

"My mind went back to the job we have in hand," said the roundsman readily. "I was wondering just what sort of glimpse Mr. Curtis obtained of the chauffeur. Of course, I see now that he was looking at the man exactly under similar conditions when we made that stop at 42nd Street."

Thus, unknown to either of the parties to the alliance, a minor crisis was averted, because it may safely be conceded that the hard-headed policeman would have refused then and there to accept any sort of statement from such a lunatic as John Delancy Curtis, if he were given a full, true, and particular account of the night's proceedings while being whirled up Fifth Avenue in a fast moving automobile.

Romance, if it is to be accepted without question, requires the setting of a comfortable armchair or tree-shaded nook in a summer garden. There, forgetting and forgotten by the world, man or maid may indeed be carried far on the Magic Carpet of Tangu, but, when served out by two strangers to a prosaic policeman seated in a humming car, and bound Heaven knew whither long after midnight, it is apt to savor of the moon and witchcraft.

Away up the straight vista of Fifth Avenue sped the two cars. On the left lay the black solitude of Central Park, on the right the varied architecture of New York's millionaire dwellings.

Devar and the policeman talked cheerfully enough, but Curtis was wrapped in his own musings till the rear lamp of the gray car suddenly curved to the left and vanished.

"He has turned into the Parkway at 110th Street," said McCulloch, and Curtis awoke with a start to a sense of his surroundings.

"I suppose he's making for St. Nicholas Avenue," went on the roundsman.

"Why?" demanded Curtis, whose recollections of map-study would have reminded him, in other conditions, that the avenue named by McCulloch is one of the few which slant across the city's rectangles.

"Well, sir, it's only a guess, but St. Nicholas Avenue is a short cut to Washington Heights, and cars often follow that route. Yes, there he goes!"

For an instant they caught a fleeting glimpse of Lenox Avenue, which runs parallel with Fifth, and then they were bowling along St. Nicholas Avenue. After a half-mile or less, they crossed Eighth Avenue at an acute angle, but the gray car kept steadily on, and soon was skirting St. Nicholas Park.

Thenceforth another mile and a half counted as little until the flying automobile gained the Harlem River Speedway. Here the pace improved. There was practically no traffic to interfere with progress now, and Brodie had to maintain an equable rate of forty miles an hour in order to keep within sight of his quarry.

At last, by way of Nagle and Amsterdam Avenues, they regained Broadway itself, at the point where its many sinuosities end at the bridges over the Harlem River and Spuyten Creek.

By this time, McCulloch was undeniably anxious. Many a mile separated him from the busy activities of Madison Square and its surroundings, and the main roads of the State of New York were opening up their possibilities. Still, he was of Scotch-Irish stock, and even the most ardent Nationalist would be slow to maintain that the men from beyond the Boyne are what is popularly and tersely described as "quitters."

"I'd be better pleased if I had any sort of notion where that joker was heading for," he said, with a grim smile. "I didn't count on taking a joy-ride at this hour of the morning."

That was his sole concession to outraged official decorum. He accepted a cigar, and forthwith resigned himself to the exigencies of the chase, which lay not with him but with the dark and devious purposes of the sinister Anatole.

The end, however, was nearer than any of them was now inclined to imagine. A rapid run along the main road through Yonkers brought them to Hastings and the bank of the Hudson River. The comparatively level grades of New York were replaced by hilly ground, and if they would avoid courting observation beyond any doubt of error it was essential that the gray car should be allowed greater latitude. In fact, it was almost demonstrable that an alert criminal like the man they were pursuing—if he really were the ally of Hunter's slayers—could hardly have failed to realize much earlier that he was being followed. Moreover, being an expert motorist, he would know that the car in the rear could not only hold him in the race but close up with him whenever its occupants were so minded. He would not be lulled into false security by the present widening of the gap, because that was an obvious maneuver due to altered circumstances. In a word, there was now no hope or prospect of running him to earth at a rendezvous, but, giving him credit for the possession and use of a criminal's brains, it became an urgent matter to overtake him and compel a halt by deliberately blocking the way.

They debated the point fully, and Devar was about to tell Brodie to act when the gray car disappeared.

Not wishing to interfere at a critical moment, Devar drew back from the window. Brodie spurted down a hill and along a short level lined with suburban villas; he slowed to take a sharp corner, and the car ran along a winding lane which could lead nowhere but to the water's edge. It was pitch dark, and a mist from the Hudson filled the valley. Common sense urged a careful pace, because it had never been possible to stop and adjust the powerful headlights, while the luminous haze of an occasional street lamp served only to reveal the narrowness of the road and the presence of shacks and warehouses.

The descent was fairly steep, so Brodie shut off the engine, and the big car crept on with a stealthy and noiseless rapidity which seemed to betoken an actual sense of danger.

Suddenly they heard a loud splash, accompanied by a muffled explosion, and McCulloch relieved his feelings by a few words, the use of which is expressly forbidden by the police manual. But their purport was ridiculously clear; the gray car had plunged into the Hudson, and who could tell whether or not Anatole had gone with it? Curtis was the first to adopt a definite line of reasoning: he assumed command now with the confidence of one accustomed to be in tight places and to depend on his own wits for extrication.

"Go forward slowly until the buildings stop, Brodie," he said, for the two front windows were lowered, and the three men were crowded at them. "That fellow knew exactly where he was going. When you pull up, light the acetylene lamps, and we will take the other pair and search the wharf from which that car was shot into the stream."

Within a few yards the brakes went on with a jerk, and a tall crane loomed up vaguely in front. All four men sprang to the ground, and while the chauffeur busied himself with the big lamps Curtis and Devar disconnected the smaller ones.

They found themselves standing on a wooden quay, evidently used for the trans-shipment of building materials, and a quick scrutiny showed that the lane supplied the only practicable means of egress. Some gaunt sheds blocked one end of the wharf and piles of dressed stone cumbered the other. The tiny wavelets of the river murmured and gurgled amid the heavy piles which shored up the landing-place, and Devar's sharp eyes soon detected a corner of the gray-colored limousine round which a ripple had formed. In all probability the heated cylinders had burst when the water rushed in, and the explosion had tilted the chassis, else the river, necessarily deep by the side of the quay, would have concealed the wreckage completely.

From out of the mist came a white glare. Brodie had set the lamps going, and now the square section of the submerged car became distinctly visible. A little to one side a barge was moored, and the policeman, who had produced a serviceable looking revolver, determined to search it.

A plank spanned the foot or so of interstice between the quay and the rough deck, and, in the flurry of the moment, the three men crossed without warning the chauffeur as to their movements. The squat craft had an open well amidships, but there were two covered-in ends, and McCulloch, taking one of the lamps, peered down into the nearest hatchway.

"If anyone is below there, speak," he said, "or I give you warning that I shall shoot at sight."

There was no answer; he knelt down, lowered the lamp, and peered inside.

"Empty!" he announced. "Now for the other one."

He repeated the same tactics, but the cavity revealed no lurking form within. Naturally, his companions were absorbed in McCulloch's actions, because they knew that any instant a blinding sheet of flame might leap out of the darkness and a bullet send him prostrate and writhing. Of the three, Curtis was most inured to an environment that was unusual and weird, and he it was who first noticed that the barge was altering its position with regard to the white discs of light which the lamps of the automobile formed in the mist, and a splash caused by the falling plank confirmed his frenzied doubt.

One glance showed what had happened. Already they were ten or twelve feet from the quay, which stood fully two feet above the deck of the barge. Even while the fantastic notion flashed through his mind, a shoreward jump barely achievable by a first-rate athlete became a sheer impossibility.

"Good Lord!" he cried, almost laughing with vexation. "The barge has been cast off from her moorings!"

Devar and McCulloch greeted the discovery with appropriate remarks, but the situation called for deeds rather than words. The cumbrous craft was swinging gayly out into the stream, displaying a light-hearted energy and ease of motion which would certainly not have been forthcoming had it been the object of her unwilling crew to get her under way.

The whereabouts of Brodie and the automobile were still vaguely discernible by two fast converging luminous circles now some twenty yards distant, and the fact was painfully borne in on them that in another few seconds this landmark would be swallowed in a sea of mist and swirling waters.

Curtis, accustomed to the vagaries of Chinese junks in the swift currents of the Yang-tse-Kiang, adopted the only measures which promised any degree of success. He ran to the helm, which had been lashed on the starboard side to keep it from fouling any submerged piles near the bank. Casting it loose, he put it hard a-port, and shouted to the policeman and Devar to bring a couple of boards from the floor of the well, and use them to sheer in the hulk to the bank.

The night was pitch dark, the mist fell on them like an impenetrable veil, and the wooded heights which dominated both banks of the river prevented any ray of light from coming to their assistance. Still, they had two lamps, which at least enabled them to see each other, and Curtis could judge with reasonable accuracy of the direction they were taking by the set of the stream. They seemed to have been toiling a weary time before the helmsman fancied he could see something looming out of the void. He believed that, however slowly, they were surely forging inshore again, and was about to ask Devar to abandon his valiant efforts to convert a long plank into a paddle and go forward in order to keep a lookout, when the barge crashed heavily into the stern of a ship of some sort, and simultaneously bumped into a wharf. The noise was terrific, coming so unexpectedly out of the silence, and their argosy careened dangerously under some obstruction forward.

No orders were needed now. They scrambled ashore, abandoning one of the lamps in their desperate hurry, and the policeman instantly extinguished the light of the other by pressing the glass closely to his breast when a rumble of curses heralded the coming on deck of two men who had been aroused from sleep on board the vessel by the thunderous onset of the colliding barge.

CHAPTER XII

TWO-THIRTY A. M.

Few men or women of sympathetic nature, and gifted with ordinary powers of observation, can go through life without learning, at some time or other in the course of their careers, that circumstances wholly beyond human control can display on occasion a fiendish faculty of converting patent honesty into apparent dishonesty — and that which is true of motive holds equally good in the case of conduct.

The three men standing breathless and unmoved on some unknown wharf on the left bank of the Hudson might fairly be described as superlatively honest persons, nor had they done any act which could be construed as wrongful by the most captious critic; yet McCulloch's concealment of the lamp suggested something thievish and illicit, and, though he alone could give a valid reason for exercising extreme discretion, because he realized, better than the others, what a choice morsel this adventure would supply to the press if ever it became known, both Curtis and Devar listened like himself with bated breath to the oaths and ejaculations which came from the after part of the moored vessel.

"Howly war!" cried one of the startled crew. "See what's butted into us — the divvle's own battherin'-ram av a scow, an' wid an ilegant lanthern shtuck on her mangy hide, if ye plaze."

A ship's lamp bobbed up and down in the gloom, and another voice said gruffly:

"Mighty good job we had those fenders out, or she would have knocked a hole in us. She seems to be wedged in good and hard under our mooring rope; but shin over, Pat, an' make her fast. Somebody owns the brute, an' there'll be damages to pay for this, an' p'raps salvage as well."

The Irishman dropped down into the barge. The silent trio on the quay heard him walking to the lamp, and saw its dull orb of radiance lifted from the deck.

"Begob, but this is a bit of a fairy tale," came the comment. "Here is none o' yer tin-cint Standard Ile prapositions, but a rale dandy uv a lamp, fit for a lady's cabin on Vandherbilt's yacht. An', for the luv o' Hiven, look at the make uv it, wid a handle where the bottom ought to be, an' all polished up like the pewther in Casey's saloon."

"Oh, get a move on, Pat, an' tie her up," said the other voice. "It's the Lord knows what o'clock, an' we've a long day before us to-morrow."

The lamp moved astern, and the Irishman investigated matters further.

"There's bin black wur-rk here, George," he shouted. "The moorin' rope nivver bruk. It was cut."

A sharp hiss of breath between McCulloch's teeth betrayed the stress of his emotions. To think that he, a smart roundsman of the Broadway squad, should have been bested so thoroughly by a miserable alien chauffeur! The man had merely slipped over the edge of the quay, and clung like a limpet to the rough baulks of timber which faced it; when his pursuers were safely disposed of on board the barge, one cut of a sharp knife had sent them adrift by the stern, while the forward rope, released of any strain, had probably uncoiled itself from a stanchion with the diabolical ingenuity which inanimate objects can display at unlooked-for moments.

"Fling a coil uv line here," continued the speaker. "This fag ind is no good, at all at all."

The thud of a falling rope, and various grunts and comments from the Irishman, showed that the barge was being secured. Still the three waited. The primary display of secrecy, the instinct to remain unseen, had passed, but there was nothing to be gained by entering into a long and difficult explanation with the ship's hands, while it would be a simple matter to recoup the owner of the barge for any charge which might be levied on him for injury to the vessel, provided the liability rested with him and not with others.

Swearing and grumbling, Pat stumbled along the quay, carrying the lamp. He passed within a few feet of the motionless group, and soon they heard him and his mate descending the companionway to their bunks.

"Now for a light," said the policeman, "and let's get out of this!"

Taking heed not to turn the lamp toward the ship, lest their movements should be overheard and a head pop up out of the hatch, he led the way quietly to the rear of the wharf. A rough road climbed the hill to the left, and, as this direction offered the only probable means of regaining the car, they took it.

After a long climb they reached a better road, which ultimately brought them into a main thoroughfare. Then Curtis bethought him of looking at his watch, and was astonished to find that the hour was half-past two o'clock.

"By Jove!" he cried. "We must have consumed fully half an hour over that trip. I wonder whether your man has waited, Devar; or would he give us up as lost, and go home?"

"What! Arthur return alone, and tell my aunt that the last he saw of me I was adrift on the Hudson River in a barge with a policeman and a swashbuckler from Pekin? Not much!"

"I hope you are right, sir," said McCulloch. "Even when we reach New York I must trouble you two gentlemen to come to the station-house and report the whole affair, as I was due there an hour ago, and the entire precinct will have been scoured for news of me by this time."

Devar laughed loudly.

"I don't want to alarm you, McCulloch—not that you are of the neurotic habit, judging by the way you took a chance of having a hole bored through you while searching that blessed barge—but if you believe you can frame a cut-and-dried programme during the time you have retained John D. Curtis's services as guide, philosopher, and friend, you are hugging a delusion. I started out from a happy home last evening intending to pick up a friendless stranger and show him the orthodox sights of New York. Gee whizz! Look at me now! I missed John D. by a few minutes, but found myself gaping with the crowd at the scene of a murder in which he had figured heavily. Since then I have helped to break open hotel doors, discovered a villain tied and gagged by other villains, stood on my head in Morris Siegelman's joint, started a riot in East Broadway, helped a detective to commit a larceny, cheeked a British lord, and scoffed at a Hungarian prince, to say nothing of the present racket. So don't you go making plans for the night yet a while, McCulloch, because John D. will keep you busy without any call for you exercising your brain cells in that respect."

The roundsman did not try to grasp the inner significance of this rigmarole. He was unfeignedly glad to have escaped from an awkward predicament.

"Anyhow," he said briefly, "if it comes to the worst I can ring up my captain from the nearest station-house, and at least he will know where I am."

"Don't be too sure of that, either. Suppose you had 'phoned your captain before you went on board the barge, would he be any the wiser now? Just to prove the exceeding wisdom of my remarks, do you know where you are at the present moment? Because I don't."

The policeman stopped short, and gazed ahead with a new anxiety. The mist was thinner here, and pin-points of light from a row of lamps showed in a straight line for a considerable distance. For an instant there was an embarrassed pause, because all three failed to remember covering any similar stretch of level road after descending the hill and turning into the lane leading to the Hudson.

"Did you notice a few minutes since that a low wall bounded the road on both sides?" said Curtis, breaking a somewhat strained silence.

Yes, each had seen it.

"Well, I am inclined to believe," he went on, "that that wall formed part of an accommodation bridge, under which the car passed in the dark without our being aware of it. Indeed, I feel confident that if we turn back along this main road, we shall meet our lane on the right, and about three hundred yards from this very point."

They agreed to make the experiment, and Devar grinned broadly when the lane presented itself exactly as Curtis had predicted.

"What did I tell you?" he cackled to the roundsman. "John D. is a Chinese necromancer. I'm getting used to his tricks, and you will catch the habit in another hour or two. By four o'clock you won't be the least bit surprised if you find yourself flying across the New Jersey flats in an aeroplane, or having a cup of hot coffee on board the pilot steamer off Sandy Hook."

"I'll risk either of those unlikely things, sir, if we find your car where we left it," They stepped out briskly. When all was said and done, none of the three wished to be stranded in some unknown byway of Westchester County at that ungodly hour, and their relief was great when the stark outline of the crane became visible in an otherwise impenetrable wall of darkness.

"By Jove! The car is here all right," crowed Devar joyously.

In the next few strides the automobile came in sight, the blaze of its headlights casting a cheerful glow over the wharf. Brodie was standing where the barge had been moored, and gazing blankly at the river; he turned when he heard their footsteps, and ran quickly to the car.

"It's O. K., Arthur," cried Devar, realizing that the chauffeur might be dreading an attack from the rear, "little Willie has returned, and won't go boating again in a derelict barge at two o'clock in the morning if he can help it."

"Oh, it's you, sir!" came the answer in a tone of vast relief. "My, but I'm glad to see you! I didn't know what to do. I thought you were safe enough, because I heard your voices as you drifted away, and I fancied you might make the shore again lower down, but it seemed to be a hopeless job to go in search of you, so, after things had calmed down a bit, I decided to stop right here."

After the first gasp of excitement, there had crept into the placid Brodie's voice a note of quiet jubilation which hinted at developments.

"Did anything happen after we sailed away?" asked Devar.

"Did you see anyone?" demanded the policeman.

"Things were quiet as the grave for quite a time after you gentlemen disappeared," said Brodie, speaking with the unctuous slowness of a man who has been vouchsafed the opportunity of his life and has grabbed it with both hands.

"Something *did* occur, then?" put in Devar impatiently.

"Nothing to speak of, sir—at first," came the irritating answer. "I watched you go on board the barge, and I noticed her edging out into the river, and it was easy enough to know that none of you had cast her off, because what you said showed that you were even more surprised than I was. So, sez I to meself, 'Arthur, me boy, barges don't untie themselves from wharves in that casual sort of way, and at just the right minute, too, for anyone who wanted to dispose of a cop,' begging your pardon, Mr. Policeman, but that was the line of argument I had with meself."

"Try the accelerator, Arthur," groaned Devar.

"If ever I meet with a bit of an accident, sir, I always pull up and plan the wheel-marks; I carry a tape for the purpose, and it saves a lot of hard swearing in court afterwards." Brodie spoke seriously, and Devar vowed that he would interrupt no more, since he merely succeeded in stimulating the man's torpid wits.

Even now, the chauffeur waited to allow his philosophy to sink into minds which might prove unreceptive. Finding that there was no likelihood of debate, he went on:

"It struck me, too, that a feller who didn't hesitate about shoving a good car into a river must be a rank tough, the kind of character who would jump at the chance of plugging me with a bullet, or two, for that matter, and hiking off with the car, without anybody being the wiser, so I nipped out from behind the wheel, and, taking care to keep away from the light, crept in behind that pile of rock there," and he nodded to the mass of dressed stone which filled one end of the wharf.

He waited, as though to make sure that they appreciated his generalship. Devar's teeth grated, and McCulloch stirred uneasily, but no one spoke.

"You'll notice that it is only a few feet away," he said, measuring the distance with a thoughtful eye, "but, to make sure of reaching anybody who might try to monkey with the car, I groped around until I had found two half bricks. Then I waited. By that time, which was really less than it takes me to tell you about it, there wasn't a sound to be heard but the lapping of the river. The last thing I heard you say, Mr. Howard, was— —"

"I used language which no self-respecting chauffeur could possibly repeat," broke in Devar despairingly.

"That's as may be, sir. Circumstances alter cases, as you will see before I've done. Well, I listened to the river, which resembled nothing in all the world so much as the sobbing of a child, but no one stirred for such a time that I began to feel stiff, and I was thinking that I might be acting like a fool for my pains when a head popped up over the edge of the wharf."

Obviously, this sentence demanded a dramatic pause, and Brodie knew his business. Perhaps he expected cries of horror from his audience, but none was forthcoming, so, with a sigh, he continued:

"That cured the stiffness, gentlemen, I can assure you. I balanced one of the half bricks in my left hand—I'm a left-handed man in many things—and watched the head, while it was easy to see that the head watched the car. 'Now,' sez I to meself, 'that's the whelp who mistreated a car which had served him well, and he's reckoning in his own mind that my car would suit his needs just as well as the one he has lost.' I do believe I read that man's mind correctly. He might have said out loud: 'That party of sports were muts. They're all aboard the Hudson River liner, chauffeur and all.' I beg your pardon, gentlemen, if I have put it awkwardly, but I am sort of feeling my way towards the feller's sentiments, groping in the dark, as you might say."

Notwithstanding his effort at self-restraint, Devar felt that he must speak or explode.

"Go right ahead, Arthur," he said. "Explain the position thoroughly. The fog is lifting, and we have heaps of time before sunrise."

"The whole affair is a mighty queer business, sir," said Brodie seriously. "The roundsman here will tell you how careful one has to be in such matters. I have had a law-case or two in my time, and them lawyers turn you inside out if you begin romancing. For instance, what I've just told you isn't evidence. The man said nothing; neither did I. We played a fine game of cat and mouse, only it happened that I was the cat.... Well, it is getting late, so I'll get on with the story. The head didn't budge for quite a while, but at last it made a move, and soon the identical chauffeur who hit up the pace from 23rd Street climbed on to the wharf and dodged in behind the crane. He had something in his right hand, too, that I didn't like the look of, so I gripped my chunk of brick mighty hard. This time he didn't wait so long, but crept forward like a stage murderer, peeping this way and that, but making for the car. Once he looked straight at where I was crouching, and I was scared stiff, because a brick ain't any fair match for one of them new-fangled pistols at six yards or so; but I guess he was a bit nervy himself, and he didn't make out anything unusual in my direction. Then he dodged right round the car to the back, and returned on the side nearest to me. I suppose he reckoned all was safe by that time, so he took hold of the crank and began to start the engine. 'Now or never!' says I to meself, so up I gets, and my knee joints cracked like—well, they cracked so loud that only the turning of the crank stopped him from hearing them. With that, I let drive with the half brick, and caught him square in the small of the back. Down he went with a yell, and me on top of him. I had the second half brick ready to batter his skull in if he showed fight, but the first one had laid him out sufficient for my purpose, which was to get hold of this."

Brodie's hand dived into a pocket, and he produced a particularly vicious looking automatic pistol.

Then McCulloch said imperatively:

"You've got him. Where is he?"

Brodie was really an artist. Some men would have smirked with triumph, but he merely jerked a thumb casually toward the automobile:

"In there!" he said.

The policeman ran to a door and wrenched it open. He turned the rays of the lamp which he still held in his hand on to a figure, lying kneeling on the floor in an extraordinary attitude. From a white face a pair of gleaming eyes met his in a glance of hate and fear, but no words came from the thin lips set in a line, and a moment's scrutiny showed that the captive was bound hand and foot. Indeed, hands and feet were fastened together with a stout cord, which had been passed around the man's neck subsequently, so that he was in some danger of suffocation if he endeavored to wriggle loose, or even straighten his back, which was bent over his heels.

"He's all right," said Brodie, who had strolled leisurely after the others. "I told him I was taking no chances, and was compelled to make him uncomfortable, but that he wouldn't choke if he kept quiet. Of course, he has had a rather trying wait, but I couldn't help that, could I?"

"We give you best," growled McCulloch. "Did you stiffen him with the half brick, then, that you were able to hunt around for a rope?"

"That helped some, but I also remarked that, if he moved, this toy of his would surely go off by accident, and he seemed to think it might hurt."

McCulloch held the lamp close to the livid, twisted face.

"Is this Anatole?" he said suddenly.

"Yes," said Curtis, with instant appreciation of his adroitness.

They were rewarded by the scowl which convulsed the mask-like face, and terror set its unmistakable seal there. A harsh metallic voice came from the huddled-up form.

"Cut this d—d rope, and let me stand on my feet!"

"There's no special hurry," said the policeman coolly. "We won't object to making things more pleasant for you if you promise to take us straight to your Hungarian friends."

Again that wave of dread which betokens the quailing heart of the detected felon swept over the man's features, but he only swore again, and protested that they had no right to torture him.

McCulloch saw that he had to deal with a hardened criminal, from whom no conscience stricken confession would be forthcoming. He gave the lamp to Curtis, stooped, and lifted the prisoner out on to the ground. Untying the rope, except at the man's ankles, he brought the listless hands in front, and placed a pair of handcuffs on the wrists.

"Now," he said, "if you have any sense left, you'll keep quiet and enjoy the ride back to New York."

"Why am I arrested? I have a right to know?" The words were yelped at him rather than spoken.

"All in good time, Anatole. You'll have everything explained to you fair and square."

"That is not my name. That's a Frenchman's name."

"It fitted you all right in 27th Street a few hours ago."

"I was not there. I can prove it."

"Of course you can. You'd be a poor sort of crook if you couldn't. But what's this?" the roundsman had found some letters and a pocketbook in an inner pocket of the chauffeur's closely buttoned jacket—"M. Anatole Labergerie, care of Morris Siegelman, saloon-keeper, East Broadway, N. Y.," he said. "You know someone named Anatole, anyhow, so we are warm, as the kids say," he went on sarcastically.

"I say nothing. I admit nothing. I demand the presence of a lawyer," was the defiant reply.

"You'll see a heap of lawyers before the State of New York has no further use for you. Now, I'll take you to a nice, quiet hotel for the night. In with you.... Mind the step. Let me give you a friendly hand.... No, that seat, if you please, close up in the corner. I'll go next. Mr. Curtis, you don't object to being squeezed a little, I'm sure, though the three of us will crowd the back seat, and if the gentleman who says nothing and admits nothing will only change his mind, and tell us exactly how he has spent a rather exciting evening, the story will help pass the journey quite pleasantly."

But Anatole Labergerie, whose accent was that of a Frenchman with a very complete knowledge of English, had evidently determined on a policy of silence, and no word crossed his lips during the greater part of the long run to the police station-house in 30th Street, in which precinct, the 23rd, the murder had occurred, and to which McCulloch was attached.

His presence in the car acted as an effectual damper on conversation in so far as Curtis and Devar were concerned. If their suspicions were justified, he was a principal in an atrocious crime, and mere propinquity with such a wretch induced a feeling of loathing comparable only with that shrinking from physical contact to which mankind yields when confronted with leprosy in its final forbidding form.

But McCulloch was jubilant. He regarded his prisoner with the almost friendly interest taken in his quarry by the slayer of wild beasts to whose rifle has fallen some peculiarly rare and dangerous "specimen." He enlivened the road with anecdotes of famous criminals, and each story invariably concluded with a facetious reference to the "chair" or a "lifer." Once or twice he gave details of the breaking up of some notorious gang owing to information extracted from one of its minor members, who, in consequence, either escaped punishment or received a light sentence; but the captive remained mute and apparently indifferent, whereupon Curtis, who had been revolving in his mind certain elements in a singularly complex mystery, broke fresh ground by saying:

"The strangest feature of this affair is probably unknown to you, Mr. McCulloch. To all intents and purposes, the men who killed the journalist were acting in concert with a Frenchman named Jean de Courtois, and their common object was to prevent a marriage arranged for last night. Yet this same de Courtois was found gagged and bound in his room at the Central Hotel shortly before midnight.

Someone had maltreated him badly, and the wonder is he was not killed outright."

Now, the roundsman, wedged close against the prisoner, felt the man give an almost unconscious and quite involuntary start when de Courtois was mentioned, and there could be no question that he was straining his ears to catch each syllable Curtis uttered.

Nudging the latter, McCulloch said:

"So it was a near thing that two weddings were not interfered with last night, sir?"

"No, not two, only one. I married the lady."

"You did!"

The policeman's undoubted bewilderment was convincingly genuine, but, despite his surprise, he was alert to catch the slightest move or sign of emotion on the part of the captive.

"Yes," said Curtis. "I married her before half-past eight."

"Then you must have possessed some knowledge of the parties mixed up in this business?"

"No, not in the sense you have in mind. I cannot supply full particulars now, but you will learn them in due course. The point I wish to emphasize is this—poor Mr. Hunter's death was absolutely needless. I imagine he only came into connection with the intrigue by exercising the journalistic instinct to obtain exclusive details of a sensational news item which involved several distinguished people. The miserable tools employed by men who wished to gain their own ends were not even true to each other, and they undoubtedly attacked Hunter by error."

"Did they mean to kill you, then?"

"Oh, no. They had never heard of me. I dropped from the skies, or the nearest thing to it, since I was on the Atlantic at this hour yesterday."

McCulloch was aware that the Frenchman had been profoundly disturbed by Curtis's statements, and kept the ball rolling. That name, de Courtois, seemed to supply the clew to the man's agitation, so he harped on it.

"Has Mr. Steingall seen de Courtois?" he asked.

"Yes. Mr. Devar and I accompanied him to de Courtois's room, and set the rascal free."

"That settles it," said the roundsman emphatically. "If the man with the camera eye has looked de Courtois over it is all up with the whole bunch. Are you listening, Anatole? This should be real lively hearing for you."

"Monsieur de Courtois is a friend of mine," came the sullen response.

"Oh, is he? Then you do know something about events in 27th Street, eh?"

"I tell you nothing, but why should I deny that I know Monsieur de Courtois?"

"Or that you are a Frenchman," put in Curtis quietly. "One of the few words in the French language which no foreigner can ever pronounce is that word 'Monsieur,' especially when it is followed by a 'de.' I speak French well enough to realize my limitations."

"Now, Anatole, cough it up," said McCulloch jocularly. "You've no more chance of winning through than a chunk of ice in hell's flames."

"Let me alone, I'm tired," said the other, relapsing into a stony inattention which did not end even when Brodie brought the car to a stand outside the police station-house in West 30th Street.

The advent of the roundsman with a prisoner and escort created some commotion among his colleagues. The police captain was the same official who had harbored suspicion against Curtis not so many hours ago, and his opinion was not entirely changed, only modified.

He glanced darkly at Curtis and Devar, but was manifestly cheered by sight of McCulloch with a chauffeur in custody.

"Hello!" he cried, "and where in Hades have *you* been?"

"A long way from home, Mr. Evans," said the roundsman. "But it was worth while. This is Anatole, whose other name is Labergerie, the man wanted for the murder in 27th Street."

"The deuce it is! Where did you get him?"

"Away up beyond Yonkers."

"Hold on a minute."

He swung round quickly to a telephone, and called up Headquarters.

"Hello, there," he said, when an answer came. "Mr. Steingall or Mr. Clancy in? Both? Well, put me through…. That you, Mr. Steingall? I'm Evans, 23rd precinct…. Sergeant McCulloch has just arrived with a prisoner, the chauffeur, Anatole; and Mr. Curtis is here, too…. Anatole Labergerie is the full name."

Some conversation followed. The others could hear the peculiar rasping sound of a voice otherwise undistinguishable, but it was evident that the police captain was greatly puzzled. At last he beckoned to Curtis.

"You're wanted," he said laconically.

Curtis went to the instrument, and Steingall's rather amused tone was soon explicable.

"There's a screw loose, somewhere," he said. "Anatole Labergerie is a respectable garage-keeper. I know him well. Half an hour ago I called him out of bed, chiefly on account of his front name, and he told me that Mr. Hunter hired a car from him last evening, but never showed up at the appointed place and time, and the chauffeur brought the car back to the garage to wait further orders."

"I have no wish to traduce Anatole Labergerie," said Curtis, "but I am quite sure that the man under arrest is the driver of the car in which the Hungarians made off. He has admitted, too, that Jean de Courtois is his friend."

A low whistle revealed Steingall's revised view of the situation.

"Don't go away," he said. "Clancy and I will be with you in less than quarter of an hour."

Curtis hung up the receiver, and announced the new development. The Frenchman did not betray any cognizance of it. He had collapsed into a chair, and looked the degenerate that he was.

But Devar slapped McCulloch's broad shoulders.

"Didn't I tell you?" he cried. "There's a whole lot of night ahead of us yet. Gee whizz! I'll write a book before I'm through with this!"

CHAPTER XIII

WHEREIN LADY HERMIONE "ACTS FOR THE BEST"

A dejected and disheveled super-clerk was called on to face a new crisis soon after he had apparently got rid of most of the persons concerned in the pandemonium which had raged for hours around that refuge of middle-class decorum and respectability, the Central Hotel in 27th Street.

As he was wont to explain in later days of blessed peacefulness:

"The queerest part of the whole business was that I never had the slightest notion as to what was going to happen next. Everything occurred like a flash of lightning, and imitated lightning by never striking twice in the same place."

It was not to be expected that a man of the Earl of Valletort's social standing and experience would allow himself to be brow-beaten by a police official and an uncertain miscellany of people like Devar and the members of the Curtis family. When the cool night air had tempered his indignation, and he was removed from the electrical atmosphere created by his son-in-law's positive disdain and Steingall's negative indifference, he began to survey the situation. Though not wholly a stranger in New York, he was far from being versed in the technicalities of legal and police methods, so he bethought him of securing skilled advice. The hour was late, but the fact merely presented a difficulty which was not insuperable to a person of even average intelligence. He turned into an imposing looking hotel on Broadway, produced his card, and asked for the manager.

An affable clerk hurried forward, thinking that his house was about to earn new laurels; if somewhat surprised by the Earl's explanation that he was in need of a lawyer of repute, and had applied to the proprietor of an important hotel as one most likely to further the quest, he responded with prompt civility.

"There are several lawyers guests in the hotel at this moment, my lord," he said. "Each is a notable man in one branch of practice or another. May I ask if you want advice in a matter of real estate, or some commercial claim, or a criminal charge?"

"The latter, in a sense," said the Earl. "A relative of mine has contracted a marriage under conditions which are illegal, or, at any rate, most irregular."

The clerk stroked his chin.

"Mr. Otto Schmidt has just concluded a remarkable nullity of marriage suit," he pondered.

"Just the man for my purpose. Is he in?"

Within five minutes the Earl was closeted with Mr. Otto Schmidt in the latter's private sitting-room. The lawyer was a short man, who bore a remarkable physical resemblance to an egg. Head, rotund body, and immensely fat legs tapering to very small feet, formed a complete oval, while his ivory-tinted skin, and a curious crease running round forehead and ears beneath a scalp wholly devoid of hair, suggested that the egg had been boiled, and the top cut off and replaced.

But he showed presently that the ovum was sound in quality. He listened in absolute silence until his lordship had told his story. All things considered, the recital was essentially true.

There were suppressions of fact, such as the lack of any mention of collusion between the distraught father and Count Ladislas Vassilan on the one hand and Jean de Courtois on the other, and there were wholly unwarrantable imputations against Curtis's character and attributes, but, on the whole, Mr. Schmidt was able, in his own phrase, "to size up the position" with fair accuracy.

Like every other man of common sense who became acquainted with the night's doings in a connected narrative, he began by expressing his astonishment.

"I have had some singular cases to handle during a long and varied professional career," he said, and eyelids almost devoid of lashes dropped for an instant over a pair of dark and curiously piercing eyes, "but I have never heard of anything quite like this. You say the name of the detective who gave you the account of the murder, and of the connection of this John Delancy Curtis with it, is Steingall?"

"Yes."

Again the eyelids fell, and, as Mr. Schmidt's face was also devoid of eyebrows, and was colorless in its pallor, and as his lips met in a thin seam above a chin which merged in folds of soft flesh where his neck ought to be, his features at such a moment assumed the disagreeable aspect of a death mask, though this impression vanished when those brilliant eyes peered forth from their bulbous sockets.

"But I know Steingall," he said. "He is at the head of the New York Detective Bureau, a man of the highest reputation, and one who commands confidence in the courts, not to speak of his department."

"He struck me as an able man, but I am quite sure he has failed to appreciate the share this fellow, Curtis, has borne in the affair," said the Earl testily.

"It seems to me that your daughter, Lady Hermione, could not possibly have been what is commonly described as 'in love' with de Courtois? Stupid as the comment may appear, I must search for a motive."

"My good sir, the notion is preposterous. I—I have reason to believe that she intended this marriage to serve as a shield, or cloak, for her own purposes, which were, I regret to say, largely inspired by a stubborn resolve not to marry a man who is suitable as a husband in every way—by birth, social position, and distinguished prospects."

195

"Her own purposes. What does that mean exactly?"

"It means that she was contracting a marriage as a matter of form. Don't you see that this consideration, and this alone, made it possible for an impertinent outsider like Curtis to offer his services as de Courtois's substitute, while my misguided daughter was equally prepared to accept them?"

"Ah!"

The eyelids shut tightly once more, and the Earl, feeling rather irritated and disturbed by this unpleasing habit, shifted his chair noisily. He found, however, that Mr. Schmidt merely kept the shutters down for a rather longer period than before, and, as the lawyer impressed him with a sense of power and ability, he resolved to put up with a peculiarity which was certainly disconcerting.

"May I ask if your daughter is what is popularly known as a pretty girl, my lord?" demanded Schmidt suddenly.

"Yes. She is remarkably good-looking, but — —"

"Motive, my lord, motive. I was wondering why Curtis should behave like a thundering idiot. Now, apart from your natural dislike to the man, how would you describe him?"

"He looks a gentleman, and, under ordinary conditions, I would regard him as a social equal," admitted the Earl.

"So, unfortunate as the circumstances may be, he is a more desirable *parti* than the French music-master?"

Then the noble lord flared into heat.

"Dash it all!" he cried. "You are almost as bad as that detective person. I am not bothering my brains as to Curtis's desirableness or otherwise, or comparing him with a worm like de Courtois. I want this marriage annulled. I want him arrested. I want the aid of the law to extricate my daughter from the consequences of her own folly. Surely, such a marriage cannot be legal!"

Schmidt weighed the point from behind the veil, and an unemotional reply soothed his fiery client.

"The idea is, perhaps, untenable—almost repulsive," he said, "but the law on the matter is governed by so many differing decisions that I cannot express a reasoned opinion offhand. You see, the question of consideration intervenes. And—and—where is the lady now?"

"I don't know."

"You left Curtis at the Central Hotel!"

"Yes."

"In company with Steingall, and two elderly Curtises, and young Devar?"

"Yes."

"Why didn't you demand your daughter's present address?"

"I—I was so stunned by what I regarded as official sanction of an outrage that I came away in a fury."

Mr. Otto Schmidt rose, or rather, raised his oblong shape from a slight incline on a chair to a horizontal position.

"Let us go to the hotel," he said. "And there must be no more fury. Leave the inquiry in my hands, my lord, and it will be strange if I do not succeed in elucidating points which are now baffling us—in fact, I may say, inducing mental disturbance."

Thus, it came to pass that Krantz, the reception clerk at the Central Hotel, had just seen the doctor sent to dose de Courtois with bromide leaving the building when the Earl and Mr. Schmidt entered.

As it happened, the lawyer was known to him, Schmidt having had legal charge of the corporation which reconstructed the hotel, so it was impossible for an employé to be reticent with him about the matters which were discussed forthwith.

"Mr. Steingall gone?" inquired Schmidt affably.

"Yes, sir. He left here nearly half an hour ago," said the clerk, outwardly self-possessed, but wondering inwardly what new bomb would be exploded in his weary brain.

"This murder, and its attendant circumstances, constitute a very extraordinary affair," said the lawyer.

"Yes, sir."

Krantz was not deceived. He had answered some such remark a hundred times that evening, but he would surely be put on the rack in a moment by some fantastic disclosure which none save a lunatic would dream of.

"Now, about this Mr. John Delancy Curtis," purred Schmidt, "has it been ascertained beyond all doubt that he arrived in New York from Europe this evening?"

"I think so, sir," was the jaded answer. "The police are satisfied on that point, I believe, and he himself gave his last address as Pekin."

"Pekin!"

"Yes, sir."

Everybody was invariably astonished when they heard of Pekin. Had Curtis described his recent residence as "the Moon" it would have been regarded as only a degree more recondite.

"Then," said Schmidt, closing his eyes, "assuming he is the stranger he represents himself as being, he could have no personal connection with the murder of Monsieur Jean de Courtois?"

There! Another comet had fallen in 27th Street. Krantz winced, as if the lawyer had struck him.

"Mr. de Courtois!" he gasped. "Who says he was murdered? He is— not very well, it is true, but for all that I can tell, he is sound asleep in bed at this minute."

"Sound asleep!" roared the Earl, who had been most positive in his opinion that Curtis must have brought about the Frenchman's death for his own fell purpose.

Otto Schmidt laid a restraining hand on his lordship's shoulder.

"Steady now," he murmured. "Remember my instructions. The inquiry is committed to me for the time."

"But, confound it, man— —"

"Yes, this is startling, this changes the whole aspect of the case. But you see the value of calm and judicious method."

The egg-shaped man was certainly entitled to take credit for the disclosure, and seldom failed to do so in many subsequent expositions to admiring friends of a singular case, but he never realized how thoroughly self-deluded the Earl had been by the original blunder.

"But, sir," protested the clerk, "it was never supposed that Mr. de Courtois had been killed. No one knew who the poor gentleman was at first, because Mr. Curtis's overcoat and his had been accidently exchanged in the flurry and excitement after the crime was committed. The police found the initials H. R. H. on his clothing, and that fact led to his being recognized as Mr. Henry R. Hunter, a well-known New York journalist. Had I seen him myself, I would have settled that point in a moment, because he often came here to visit Mr. de Courtois."

"Indeed! That is very interesting, most decidedly interesting."

"Are you quite certain that what you are saying is correct? Mr. Hunter, the murdered man, was acquainted with Monsieur de Courtois?"

The question came from the Earl of Valletort, whose angry bewilderment had suddenly given place to a gravity of demeanor that was significant of the serious complications involved in the clerk's statement.

Poor Krantz could have bitten his tongue for its too free wagging. He was thoroughly tired, and had intended to go to his room at the earliest moment and repair damages by a long night's rest. Now, to all appearance, he had unwittingly reopened the whole wretched imbroglio. But there was no help for it. Having put his hand to the plow he was obliged to turn the furrow.

"Yes, my lord, positive," he said between his teeth.

"Ah!" Schmidt was beginning to think that the amazing marriage promised to develop into a *cause célèbre*. "In that event, it becomes essential, indeed, I may say imperative, that his lordship and I should interview Monsieur de Courtois without delay."

"Sorry, sir," said the clerk, desperately availing himself of the detective's instructions, "but Mr. Steingall left orders that no one should be permitted to visit Mr. de Courtois to-night."

"Left orders? Is the man in this hotel?"

"Oh, yes, I was aware of that all the time," put in the Earl. "He lived here—don't you see, that accounts for the mistake I made in assuming that——"

"Forgive me." The lawyer's monitory hand rose again, and he turned to the clerk. "You can hardly expect me, Mr. Krantz, to regard Mr. Steingall's 'orders' as in any way controlling my actions. Kindly show his lordship and me to Monsieur de Courtois's room at once."

There was nothing for it but to obey. Krantz understood exactly how he would be jumped on and pulverized in the morning by irate stockholders in the hotel if any action of his should be adversely reported on by the great Otto Schmidt.

But the visit to de Courtois fizzled out unexpectedly. The Frenchman, still attired in evening dress, for that is the conventional wedding attire of his race, was lying on the bed sleeping the sleep of utter exhaustion supplemented by bromide. The two negro attendants, who were hoping for some more exciting experience, were squatted on the floor playing pinochle, and the strenuous efforts of Lord Valletort to arouse the slumberer were quite useless. But—and that was a vital thing—he had seen de Courtois, and knew beyond doubt that he was alive, and seemingly in good health, or, at any rate, physically uninjured.

"The man has been drugged," said the lawyer, watching the Earl's unavailing attempt to awaken the Frenchman. "Is, by any chance, Mr. Curtis's room situated near this one?"

"It is just overhead," said the clerk.

"Dear me!"

Schmidt looked up at the ceiling as though his eyes might discern a trap-door. "Is Mr. Curtis there now?"

"No, sir."

"Where is he?"

"He went out with a Mr. Devar."

"Oh! Do you know where he went to?"

Krantz was tempted to prevaricate, but Schmidt was a power in the Central Hotel.

"I believe, sir, he is at the Plaza."

"A large hotel, near Central Park, is it not?" demanded the Earl eagerly.

"My lord, pardon me." The lawyer was no believer in letting all the world into your secrets, and the clerk's manner showed that he was far from well posted in certain elements of the affair.

Valletort was for rushing forthwith off in a taxi to the Plaza; but Schmidt vetoed the notion. He shared the Earl's conviction that Hermione would be discovered there, but, before meeting her, he wanted to obtain a great many particulars the lack of which in his client's earlier story his legal acumen had already scented.

So he drew the impatient nobleman into a quiet corner of the restaurant, and extracted from his unwilling lips certain details as to Count Vassilan and the marriage project which had not been forthcoming before.

Krantz seized the opportunity to call up Steingall on the telephone and told him something, not all, of what had occurred. He did not say that the Earl and Schmidt had actually seen de Courtois, and suppressed any mention of his disclosure with reference to Curtis's whereabouts, not that he wished to mislead the detective willfully, but he felt that he had been indiscreet, and there was no need to proclaim the fact. Moreover, he had never heard Hermione's name mentioned, or he was gallant enough to have risked any trouble next day if a lady would be saved distress thereby.

Schmidt's lawyer-like caution was destined to have far-reaching effects on the night's history. It provided one of the minor rills of a torrent which was gaining irresistible momentum, and would submerge many people before its uncontrolled madness was exhausted. Had he yielded to the Earl, and hurried to the Plaza at once, he would have met Curtis and Steingall there, and those two men might have diverted the bursting current of events into a new channel. But, naturally enough, he wanted to understand precisely where he stood. In a word, the egg was excellent in its constituents, but lacked the exuberant freshness of the newly-laid article.

Hence, while the Earl nearly choked with indignation at sight of that entry in the visitors' book at the Plaza—"Mr. and Lady Hermione Curtis, Pekin,"—mistress and maid were once more discussing the astounding things which had taken place since the moment when John Delancy Curtis rang the bell at Flat 10 in Number 1000 59th Street.

"If only I knew how to act for the best!" wailed Hermione half tearfully. "I am afraid, Marcelle, I have been too egotistical, too much concerned about myself, I mean, and far too regardless of others. I have allowed Mr. Curtis to place himself in a dreadful position——"

"I'm sure, miladi, he doesn't think so," interrupted Marcelle breathlessly.

"That is the worst feature of it, to my thinking. He is making all the sacrifice."

"What! To get a wife like you, miladi!"

"I am *not* his wife."

"Well, you are not married like folk who go away for a honeymoon and find rice in their clothes every day for a week, but Mr. Curtis says, miladi, that you are his wife right enough in the eyes of the law, and I'm sure he admires you immensely already, so there's no telling——"

"Marcelle, do you imagine for one single instant that I would really marry any man who took me as a favor, who conferred an obligation on me, who came to my assistance in a moment of despair?"

"No, miladi, not if he thought those things. But I have a sort of notion that Mr. Curtis would hurt any other man who suggested any of them, and it is easy to see by the very way he looks at you——"

"Oh, have pity, and don't harp on that string! I can be nothing to him. You mistake his kindness for something which is so utterly impossible that it almost drives me to hysteria to hear it even spoken of."

Marcelle knew better. In some recess of her own acute mind she felt that Lady Hermione's heightened color and shining eyes were due to just that wild and irresponsible conceit which they were debating. Indeed, Hermione could not leave the topic alone. She forbade it, rejected it, stormed at its folly, yet came back to it like a child held spellbound by some terrifying yet fascinating object.

The maid was racking her brain for some feminine argument which should convince an impulsive mistress that Curtis might reasonably regard his matrimonial entanglement as by no means so incapable of a satisfactory outcome as his "wife" deemed it, when a knock at the door of the sitting-room alarmed both.

And, indeed, the ever-present dread which haunted them was justified, because a page announced "The Earl of Valletort and Mr. Otto Schmidt," and before the petrified Marcelle could utter a word of protest, the two men were in the room.

Marcelle said afterwards that no incident of those tumultuous hours surprised her more than the way in which Lady Hermione received her unbidden and unwelcome visitors. The instant before their arrival she was an irresponsible and doubting and vacillating girl, torn by emotion, and swayed hither and thither by gusts of perplexity which ranged from half-formed hope to blank despair, but now she came from her bedroom without a second's hesitancy, and faced her father and the lawyer with a proud serenity which obviously disconcerted them, and quite dumfounded Marcelle.

"Ah! At last!" said the Earl, trying to speak complacently, but failing rather badly, because his attitude and words were decidedly melodramatic.

"And too late!" said his daughter, letting her fine eyes dwell on Schmidt with the contemplative scrutiny she might bestow on an exhibit in a natural history museum.

"Pardon me, your ladyship, not too late, but just in time, I fancy."

Otto Schmidt met her gaze without flinching, and he was a man who undoubtedly commanded attention when he spoke. His tone was deferential but decisive. His black eyes were taking in this charming and intelligent woman in full measure. Her rare beauty, her unstudied pose, her slender elegance, the quiet harmonies of her costume—each and all made their appeal. He even waited for her reply, compelling it by some subtle transference of the knowledge that he would not endeavor to browbeat or misunderstand her.

"I have heard your name, but may I ask why you are here?" she said composedly.

It pleased him to find that he had not erred by underrating her intelligence.

"A very proper question, Lady Hermione," he said. "I am a lawyer, fairly well known in New York, and your father has consulted me with reference to the marriage you have contracted to-night."

"Since, as you say, the marriage has most certainly been contracted, the statement hardly explains your presence."

He smiled, and Lord Valletort, who had not seen Otto Schmidt smile once during the past hour, discovered that he had not begun to appraise his new ally's qualities at their due worth.

"It is a legal habit to state events in their order," he replied suavely. "But these are matters which we ought to discuss privately."

"No, Marcelle, do not go," said Hermione, hiding her fear under an assumption of icy indifference, and checking the maid's movement in response to the lawyer's hint. "Marcelle Leroux is fully in my confidence," she explained, "and you can say nothing which she may not listen to."

"I am obliged to your ladyship, but I had to mention her presence," said Schmidt. "Well, I am sorry to be the bearer of unpleasant news, but you were inveigled into a marriage ceremony with John Delancy Curtis by gross and fraudulent misrepresentation. He told you, I assume, that Monsieur Jean de Courtois was dead. That is not true. Monsieur de Courtois is alive, and in his room at the Central Hotel in 27th Street at this moment. He was detained there at the hour you awaited him—kept there forcibly, by means which must be investigated, but the really important fact now is that he lives. Need I tell you what that statement implies? Need I emphasize the lie with which this man Curtis attained his object? Your father, the Earl, and I myself, saw Jean de Courtois a few minutes since. Probably, and not without reason, you doubt my word. If that is so, will you kindly use the telephone yourself, ring up the Central Hotel, and ask if Monsieur de Courtois is there? You will hardly imagine that the hotel staff would enter into a conspiracy with us to deceive you. Again, you might send for the manager here. He knows me, and will assure you that I am not a person who would lend himself to subterfuge or falsehood."

"But some man was killed, was he not?"

Hermione's lips had whitened, but her courage was superb, though her poor heart was like to burst with its frenzied throbbing, for she was certain this self-possessed man was speaking truly, and, if he were, her hero with the head of gold had revealed feet of clay.

"Yes, unhappily, a journalist named Hunter."

Schmidt was an artist. He knew when to use few words.

"But Mr. Curtis himself may have been deceived."

"Mr. Curtis was among those who pretended to liberate de Courtois from his bonds. Your unfortunate friend was brutally tied and gagged in his room in the hotel, and is now recovering from the effects of the maltreatment he received."

"Mr. Curtis couldn't have known of this when he was here, little more than half an hour ago."

"He knew it two hours ago. Not only he, but Mr. Steingall knew it. Did neither of them tell you?"

In utter despair, broken-hearted now not by reason of her own plight, but rather because of a shattered faith, Hermione appealed to the Earl.

"Father, is this true?"

"Absolutely true, every syllable. I really think you ought to confirm Mr. Schmidt's statement by inquiry at the Central Hotel."

"And publish my unhappy story more widely!... Will you kindly leave me now? I must think, and act."

"One word, your ladyship, and I have done," said the lawyer, speaking with a slow seriousness that could not fail to be convincing. "The mischief is not irreparable—at present. But you must not remain here. You are registered in the books of the hotel as the wife of John Delancy Curtis, and, if I may say it with respect, your own sense of what is right and proper will forbid the notion that you can abide in the hotel until to-morrow. I pledge my reputation that it will immensely facilitate the legal steps necessary to secure the annulment of the marriage if you dissever yourself from your so-called husband at the earliest moment after you have discovered his tort."

Hermione was not the type of woman who faints in an emergency, though gladly now would she have found in unconsciousness a respite from the bitter pain that was rending her innermost fiber.

"I think—I understand," she said brokenly. "Will you please go?"

"But will you not come with me, Hermione?" said her father. "I give you my word of honor there will be no recriminations."

"I must be alone—to-night," she cried, flaring into a passionate vehemence. "Marcelle and I will return to my apartment. You know where it is. Come there in the morning, at any hour you choose, but go now, this instant, or I shall refuse to leave the hotel, no matter what the consequences."

Her voice rose almost to a scream, and Schmidt, a profound student of human nature, realized that any extra pressure would be fatal. He had succeeded. This girl would keep her promise, of that he was well assured, but if her high-strung temperament was subjected to undue force she would put her back against the wall and defy law and convention alike.

"Come," he said to the Earl, and, with a courteous bow to Hermione, he literally pulled her father from the room.

Hermione did not weep. She was done with tears, sick with vain regret, yet braced to unfaltering purpose. The instant the door was closed she picked up the telephone, and the wretched Krantz was soon in evidence to verify the lawyer's words.

Marcelle was crying as though she had lost a lover or some dear relative; when Hermione bade her prepare for their departure, she gave no heed, but wailed her sorrow aloud.

"I d-don't believe them, miladi," she sobbed. "Mr. Curtis—will wring the lawyer-man's neck—to-morrow.... I know he will.... Did Mr. Curtis kill poor Mr. Hunter? If not, why should he tie that

Frenchman?... And wouldn't he t-tie twenty Frenchmen if he w-wanted to m-marry you!"

Hermione stooped and fondled the girl's shoulders, for Marcelle had collapsed to her knees on the hearth-rug while her mistress was using the telephone.

"You have been my very good friend, Marcelle," she said, and the misery in her voice subjugated the maid's louder grief. "Don't fail me now, there's a dear! I want to write a letter, and there can be no question whatever that you and I must get away before Mr. Curtis returns. Don't fret, or lose faith in Providence. A great man once wrote: 'God's in Heaven, and all's well with the world.' You and I must try to believe that, and place utmost trust in its promise.... There, now! Hurry, and I shall join you in a few minutes. We shall send for our baggage in the morning, and so avoid attracting attention in the hotel to-night."

Brave as she was, when left alone in the room she pressed her hands to her face in sheer abandonment of agony. But the storm passed, and she sat down to write.

CHAPTER XIV

THREE O'CLOCK IN THE MORNING

Evans, the police captain of the 23rd Precinct, had a fairly long story to hear from McCulloch. The roundsman did not spare himself in the recital. He pleaded guilty to three errors of judgment. In the first instance, he would have done well had he taken the advice given by Devar during the halt at 42nd Street, and arrested the supposed "Anatole" then and there; secondly, he might have secured corroborative evidence of the cleansing of parts of the automobile — evidence now destroyed by the waters of the Hudson; and, thirdly, he should have asked Brodie to intercept the fugitive long before it became possible to plunge the car into the river.

"All I can say is, I sized up the situation and acted accordingly," he commented ruefully. "It did look like a good plan to give him rope enough" — here he checked his utterance, and glanced at the disconsolate prisoner — "but he fairly got the better of me when I went aboard that barge. I ought to have left one of these gentlemen to watch the quay. My excuse is that the barge seemed to offer the only probable hiding-place, and there was always the chance that he had gone into the river with the car."

"Anyhow, you got him," observed Evans sympathetically, for McCulloch was a valued and trustworthy officer.

"Well, he's here, but Mr. Brodie got him," whereupon Brodie tried not to look sheepish.

Steingall and Clancy arrived before the roundsman had made an end of his experiences, which he had to recount for their benefit. The two detectives had resumed their ordinary clothing. They looked tired, but quietly elated, and it was noticeable that Clancy's mercurial spirits seemed to have evaporated. Those who knew him would have augured from that fact that the chase was reaching its climax, but Curtis and Devar fancied that the little man was thoroughly

210

worn out and pining for rest. Never had they been more egregiously deceived. He resembled a hound which bays its excitement when the quarry is scented but restrains all its energies for the last desperate struggle when the flying prey is in sight.

The Frenchman sat as though in a stupor, and seemingly gave no attention to the details of the hunt, but he sprang to his feet in sheer fright when Steingall walked up to him and said sternly:

"Now, Antoine Lamotte, listen to what I have to say."

"I am betrayed, then?" snarled the man viciously, though his voice went off into a curious yelp of agony as a twinge reminded him of Brodie's vigorous aim with half a brick.

"Yes, the game is up. I know your confederates, and you will be confronted with them before daybreak.... No, I am not bluffing. That is not my way. Their names are Gregor Martiny and Ferdinand Rossi. Now are you satisfied?"

Lamotte sank back into his chair. His features were wrung with pain, but the momentary excitement vanished, and his manner grew sullen again.

"If you know so much I can tell you nothing," he growled.

"No. You can give me little or no information I do not possess already. But, unless you are more fool than knave, you can at least try to save your own miserable life."

"How?"

"By a full confession. Did you know that Martiny and Rossi meant to kill Mr. Hunter?"

"No, I swear it."

"Then why don't you take the hint I have given you? It will be too late when you are brought before a judge. Believe me, I shall waste no more breath in persuading you. It is now or never."

The Frenchman rose again, this time more slowly. He glanced around at the ring of faces, and, for a moment, his gaze dwelt contemplatively on Clancy. Perhaps he was vouchsafed some intuition that this man was to be feared, but Clancy remained unemotional as a Sioux Indian. When he spoke, it was with a certain dignity, and, oddly enough, his words, though uttered in English, savored of a literal translation from the French mint which coined them.

"Monsieur," he said, "I am a man who regards loyalty to his friends before all."

"An excellent quality, even in a criminal, if your friends are loyal to you," replied Steingall with equal seriousness of manner.

"But the woman who betrayed us—may she be eaten up with cancer!—is not my friend. Those others are."

"I have met with no woman. I have good reason to think that you have no real notion of the influences which led your Hungarian friends, as you call them, to commit a murder. But I rather respect your sentiment, so, to give you one final chance, I tell you now just how you were brought into this thing. You are a thief, and the associate of thieves, but you have never, so far as our records go, been convicted. Your real name is not Lamotte, though you have passed under it long enough in New York to establish some sort of claim to it, and you were sentenced to two years' imprisonment at Toulon eight years ago for a breach of military discipline. On your release you consorted with anarchists in Paris, and, to escape arrest as a suspect after a dynamite outrage on the Grand Boulevard, you emigrated to America. You are a clever mechanic, and, had you tried to earn an honest living, you would have succeeded, but some kink in your nature drove you to crime, mixed up with a good deal of political froth. When you heard that precious pair of fanatics,

Martiny and Rossi, plotting in Morris Siegelman's café to prevent a marriage between an English lady of great wealth and a wretched little Frenchman, so that the cause of a Hungarian party might benefit if Count Ladislas Vassilan secured the lady and the money, especially the money, you thought you saw a way towards striking a blow at the Austrian monarchy and also benefiting yourself. So you offered your services, and your more acute brain put them up to a dodge they would never have thought of. It was necessary for your purpose that you should figure as a respectable man, so you had cards printed in the name of Anatole Labergerie, and addressed letters to yourself under that same name at Morris Siegelman's restaurant. I do not know yet where you obtained the car, but I shall know to-morrow—the fact is immaterial now. What is of real importance is the method whereby you humbugged the janitor at Mr. Hunter's office by pretending that you had been sent there by Mr. Labergerie because the car was at liberty somewhat earlier than was expected, and the unfortunate journalist took it as a compliment, drove to his rooms, changed his clothes, and returned to the office, thus playing into your hands, because the car sent to his order by Mr. Labergerie was thereby prevented from picking him up at the appointed time. It was shrewd of you to guess that a busy man on the staff of a newspaper would be glad to utilize an automobile placed unexpectedly at his disposal, and fate played into your hands by the delay in issuing the duplicate marriage license, which he had promised de Courtois to obtain from the City Hall."

"Sir, I knew nothing of any marriage license."

"Probably not. You were concerned only with taking your confederates' money, and posing as the clever brain of the outfit. But I imagine, and not another word shall I say, that they overreached you a bit when they knifed Mr. Hunter."

Lamotte, to describe him by the name under which he figured in the annals of the crime, stretched out his hands in a gesture of emphatic protest.

"No matter what becomes of me," he said eagerly, "I ask you to believe that I did not even know they had killed Mr. Hunter until I saw the blood on the panel when I took them to Market Street."

"So. You have been slow to adopt the lead I offered you. But why, in God's name, did they stab the man? That could hardly have been their deliberate plan."

"It was a sort of accident. So they said. They really meant to force him into the car, and overpower him. The scheme was to bring him to Market Street and keep him there until — —"

He hesitated. He had given up hope for himself, but he stopped short of introducing other names into prominence.

"Until the *Switzerland* had reached New York, with Count Ladislas Vassilan and the English lord on board."

Then Lamotte yielded.

"You know everything," he said, with a dejected shrug. "Either you are a wizard, or Gregor and Rossi are open-mouthed fools."

Steingall smiled inscrutably, but Clancy, who had remained strangely quiet, did not relax the close attention he was giving to the Frenchman's least word or action. It was about this time that Curtis noticed the little detective's air of complete absorption, and he wondered at it, since Clancy and his chief seemed to have unfolded the whole mystery in a way that was at once admirable and bewildering.

"Then why don't you exercise your wits, man? I have been candor itself in my statement, but it is your own words which will be taken down by the police captain here, as you are charged in his presence with complicity in the murder, and they will be on record for or against you when you are brought to trial."

"You want me to admit that what you have said is true?"

214

"Just as you wish," said Steingall, half contemptuously. "I now charge you formally with taking part in the murder of Mr. Hunter. If you have anything to say, say it, and it will be written at once, and signed by you, if you choose."

He waited a moment, and then turned aside.

"Put him in the cells," he said. "I shall not trouble farther about him now."

"One moment, monsieur," exclaimed Lamotte, evidently believing that he was seriously jeopardizing his life by not taking the advice given so openly. "I admit that you are well informed, but I must add that I was ignorant of the murder till nearly half an hour after it had occurred."

"Pooh, that's no use. Make a full statement, or take the consequences." Steingall's tone was so offhanded that Lamotte was afraid he had lost a good opportunity of saving his neck.

"But what is there to tell?" he cried.

"Just what happened outside the Central Hotel and afterwards."

"I brought Mr. Hunter there, and nodded to Martiny and Rossi, who were waiting on the sidewalk, to show that he was inside the car. I remained at the wheel, and anyone can perceive that my position made it impossible to see what was going on when the door opened. Martiny was nearest to me, and I am sure he never used a knife, so it must have been Rossi. Is that correct?"

"I believe so, absolutely. What next?"

"Martiny said 'Vite, allez!' so I shoved in the clutch and made off at top speed. In Fifth Avenue I glanced over my shoulder to look at Mr. Hunter, and see whether or not he was struggling, but my friends alone were visible in the back seat, so I believed they had put him on the floor, and did not stop or look at them again until I reached De

Silva's house in Market Street. Then, to my annoyance, when I got down to help carry in Mr. Hunter, I found blood on the step and the panel, and the idiots told me what they had done. It is only fair to say that De Silva is innocent of any part in the affair. He didn't even know that we were bringing anyone to Rossi's room, and we took care that he should be out at the time we counted on arriving at Market Street."

"You didn't attack Mr. Hunter sooner because your orders were to wait until the last possible moment?"

"That is so."

Devar was unaware of any change in the manner of either of the detectives, because he was watching Lamotte's livid face with a species of fascinated horror, but Curtis, who had often been compelled to hold similar inquiries into cold-blooded crimes committed by Chinese coolies, found greater interest in observing Clancy. A subtle exultation had suddenly danced into the diminutive Franco-Irishman's expressive features when Market Street was first mentioned, and his coal-black eyes blazed in their slits at the sound of that name, De Silva.

A queer thought flitted through Curtis's mind, but he put it aside, because Steingall was speaking again.

"Well, you got rid of your friends. Then what did you do?"

"The rest was simple. I cleaned the car in a hurry with a bit of oily waste, took it to a yard which I have used at times, at an address which I beg you to permit me to forget, changed the number plate, and, at an hour which I deemed discreet, drove uptown in order to dispose of the car by leaving it deserted near the garage from which it came. The owner's house is on Riverside Drive. His name is Morris; he is absent in Chicago on business, while I learnt that his chauffeur was ill."

A gasp of uncontrollable excitement from Devar drew all eyes to him.

SCENES FROM THE PHOTO-DRAMA.

"Great Jerusalem!" he cried. "Next house to my aunt's!"

"There's a mistake somewhere," broke in Brodie. "I know Mr. Morris's car, and that isn't it."

Lamotte was positively annoyed that his word should appear to be doubted.

"Messieurs," he said grandiloquently, "I assure you on my honor that I am not misleading you."

Nor was he. The discrepancy was cleared up next day. The Morris automobile was undergoing repairs, and the motor manufacturers had supplied the gray car for use in the interim.

Steingall swept the matter aside impatiently.

"Go on," he said to the Frenchman. "You're taking a note of this?" he added, glancing at police captain Evans.

"Got it," was the laconic reply.

"There is nothing else," said Lamotte. "I noticed that I was being followed, and soon discovered that I could not shake off a more powerful car. I was armed, but did not want to get into trouble on my own account, and I knew that I would have to deal with three men. So I decided to throw the car in the river, and trust to my wits for a means of escape. I would have succeeded, too, had I been aware that there was a fourth man in the party. From where I lay hidden beneath the wharf I could only count the number of people who crossed to the barge. I was unable to see them, so I included the chauffeur among the three. I was wrong. Perhaps it is as well, because I meant to get away, and would have fought.... That is all.... Will one of you give me a cigarette?"

Devar produced a case, and in response to Steingall's nod, offered its contents to the prisoner, who took two cigarettes; nor could he be prevailed on to accept more. Despite his hang-dog looks he had an undoubted air of refinement. Degeneracy had claimed him as its own, yet some streak of a nobler heredity had struggled to exert its influence, only to fail.

Steingall put no more questions, and Lamotte relapsed into silence, smoking nonchalantly while the police captain's pen was scratching a transcript of the shorthand notes.

Curtis caught Steingall's eye, and drew him aside.

"That fellow told the truth about the actual murder, I think" he said. "My story coincides with his in every detail."

"I'm sure you are right," agreed the detective. "The odd thing is that Clancy should have spotted him from your description telephoned to headquarters. You remember Clancy was looking at a book of photographs when I brought you to the Bureau?"

"Yes."

"He had found him then. Some time since, during the anarchist troubles in Chicago, the French police sent us a lot of pictures, and this fellow's was among them."

"Why didn't he ask me if I recognized him?"

"That is not pretty Fanny's way. Clancy never does what any other man would do. He hates to have anyone verify an opinion he has once formed. Had you said the photograph resembled the man you saw outside the hotel Clancy would actually have begun to believe that he might be mistaken."

"At any rate," said Curtis, smiling, "you two seem to have made marvelous progress with the inquiry since a set of drunken stokers broke up a harmonious gathering at Morris Siegelman's."

"We have done pretty well, but this"—and Steingall glanced at Lamotte—"this goes far beyond anything we hoped for to-night, or this morning, for the new day is growing old."

Curtis was puzzled. He realized that the capture of the chauffeur was important, but it shrank into insignificance beside the connected history of events which the detective seemed to have at his fingers' ends.

"I suppose I must not ask questions," he said with a quizzical look into the extraordinary eyes which had earned the chief of the Detective Bureau the picturesque description coined by an enthusiastic reporter.

"No need," said Steingall. "Unless you are fed up with excitement, I purpose taking you and Mr. Devar down town again, just as soon as Evans has stopped slinging ink. Then you will appreciate the importance of the things said here."

Curtis remembered that fleeting impression he had garnered while watching Clancy during the Frenchman's statement, which, however, appeared only to confirm the ample history already in Steingall's possession. But again his thoughts were diverted from the matter by Steingall's next words.

"I take it you have not called at the Plaza Hotel since we came away together?" he said. "You certainly could not stop there during the rush after the missing chauffeur, and I suppose McCulloch brought you straight here after the arrest?"

"Yes. We passed the hotel on the outward journey, and I thought I saw a light in—in my wife's suite, but we returned by a different route."

He fancied that the detective was about to explain a somewhat peculiar question, but at that instant the police captain summoned Lamotte to his desk.

"I'll read what I have written," he said, "and, if it is correct, you will sign it. You need not sign unless you wish, but the statement will be given in court, and, if you attest it now, may count in your favor."

He recited an exact record of the Frenchman's words, and Lamotte took the pen and scrawled his name. Then, at a nod from Evans, the roundsman took the prisoner to a cell.

"By Jove! George, or perhaps I ought to say 'By George, Jove!' you did that well," exclaimed Clancy, speaking for the first time since he had entered the station-house, and addressing Steingall.

"I thought I was going to fail, but I stuck to my guns, and it came off," was the modest if rather cryptic reply.

"We, too, have fought with beasts at Ephegus, so let us into this," cried Devar. "What came off, and where was the risk of failure? To my mind, you had Lamotte in a double Nelson grip all the time."

"That's where you are in error, young man," said Steingall cheerfully. "Sometimes it pays to pretend a knowledge you don't possess, and this was one of the occasions. Mr. Clancy and I knew that somewhere in New York were two Hungarians named Gregor Martiny and Ferdinand Rossi. We knew that they were the men who killed Mr. Hunter, but we had no more notion where they were hiding, or how to lay hands on them, than the man in the moon."

"Great Scott. Haven't you arrested them?"

"No, sir. That is a pleasure deferred."

"Do you mean that you wanged that address out of the Frenchman?"

"That's about the size of it. I might have searched for a week for Martiny and Rossi, but no one in East Broadway would have owned up to seeing or even hearing of them."

"Still, you had their names pat?"

221

"Yes," said the detective, cutting the end off a cigar, "we had their names, and we ascertained why they killed Hunter, or would have killed any other person who tried to balk their scheme, but our information stopped there."

Steingall, usually so communicative, evidently meant to keep to himself the source of his inspiration, and, in a few minutes, Brodie was driving the four men to the Police Headquarters.

They went to the Detective Bureau, and Steingall telephoned the Clinton Street police station-house.

"You know De Silva's place in Market Street?" he said. "Well, within ten minutes have half-a-dozen men gather quietly near the door.... Two others should watch the back, and stop anyone making a bolt that way.... Yes, of course, there may be shooting. I'll turn up in a private auto, and stop off at the corner of East Broadway.... Leave the rest to Clancy and myself.... No, only two, but they're hot stuff."

He unlocked a drawer in a desk, and took out a pair of revolvers. After examining them to make sure they were fully loaded, he handed one to Clancy.

"I hope we shall not require them, Eugene, but there's no telling," he said.

"I suppose I'm not allowed to shoot anybody, so you might lend me a stick," suggested Devar.

"You and Mr. Curtis are remaining right here," said the detective.

"Oh, be a man, Steingall!" cried Devar disgustedly. "Don't play dog when there's a chance of a real row. Look how I swung things your way in Morris Siegelman's!"

"You might let us peep round the corner, at any rate," smiled Curtis.

Steingall meant to be obdurate, but yielded, and it was well that he allowed his sympathies to sway his judgment, or there might have been an early vacancy in the chief inspectorship.

At that middle hour of the night even New York's prowlers of the dark had retired to their foul rookeries. The streets were almost deserted, and the glare of gas and naphtha had vanished. The houses of the Hungarian quarter were stark and gloomy now, many woe-begone in their semi-dismantled aspect, and all sinister. When the automobile drew up noiselessly at the corner of Market Street, a broad enough thoroughfare, but broken and battered in appearance, the only visible forms were those of three or four patrolmen, who were sauntering aimlessly along the sidewalk. But there were eyes watching through unknown chinks in shutters, or peering through soiled curtains behind dirt-stained windows, and the quiet concentration of the police in one special quarter evidently did not pass unnoticed.

When the battle began, it partook of the vagaries of real warfare by opening unexpectedly.

It was ascertained afterwards that two men darted like shadows out of a passage in Market Street, and separated instantly. One came toward East Broadway, where the detectives and their companions had just alighted from the car, and the other, breaking into a run, dived into Henry Street, with two patrolmen after him. He it was who opened the fray, and the peace of the night was suddenly disrupted by the loud bark of an automatic pistol. Three shots were fired with a quick irregularity, and then came the deeper report of a service revolver.

Steingall and Clancy ran forward, and the fugitive coming their way had actually passed them, with two more patrolmen in pursuit, when Steingall saw him and turned instantly.

"Stop!" he shouted.

The man only increased his pace, and the detective, astonishingly active for one of his bulk, raced along at top speed.

"Stop or I shoot!" he cried again.

By that time the self-confessed outlaw was nearly opposite the car. He checked his pace, half turned, luckily not to the side where Curtis and the others were standing, and leveled a Browning pistol at the detective. He even hesitated an instant to take aim, but before his finger had pressed the trigger, Curtis had sprung at him. There was no time for a blow, but a well placed kick spun the would-be murderer off his feet, and the crash of the shot came an infinitesimal part of a second too late. As it was, the bullet struck a lamp higher up the street, and a line taken subsequently showed that it must have missed Steingall by only a few inches.

The miscreant reeled, and lost his balance. Then Curtis closed with him, caught his right wrist, and threw him heavily, but, such was the man's frenzied resolve not to be arrested, that he fired twice again before the deadly weapon fell from his grasp. He did no damage, but the uproar brought a motley crowd from the neighboring dwellings. Market Street, which had seemed asleep or dead, proved itself very much alive and awake, but the sight of uniformed police hurrying up from several directions restrained any undue curiosity on the part of its denizens.

The desperado on the ground was handcuffed at once, and, while a policeman was searching his pockets rapidly to ascertain if he carried another pistol, Steingall gripped Curtis by the shoulder.

"I owe you something for that," he said quietly. "I rather fancy he would have dropped me if it hadn't been for you.... Oh, I know what I am saying. I shall not forget.... Show a light here," he added to a patrolman who had run from East Broadway on hearing the shooting. "Now, Mr. Curtis, do you recognize him?"

"Yes," said Curtis—-whose experiences in New York were revealing an unsuspected side of his character, for in 56th Street, in Morris

Siegelman's, and now again in Market Street, he had proved himself what Allen Breck would have termed "a bonnie fighter" —"yes, that is the man who spoke to me in the Central Hotel. I imagine he is Martiny."

"Good! Put him in the car!"

The detective rushed off, but soon returned.

"Sorry to trouble you, but will you come this way a minute?" he said.

Curtis went with him. In Henry Street a small group was gathered in the roadway. A policeman had proved himself a better shot than Rossi, and Hunter's murder was already avenged in part.

The dead man was left to the district police, to be carried to the mortuary in an ambulance. Steingall, with his prisoner, returned to headquarters, while Clancy made a thorough search of the room the pair had occupied in De Silva's house.

The Hungarian did not deny his name nor his share in the earlier crime.

"It is fate," he said doggedly in his broken French. "When they tell me we have killed the man I know the police get us."

He would say no more. His words seemed to imply that neither he nor Rossi meant to do other than maim the journalist whom they regarded as de Courtois's dangerous helper; but he did not urge the plea. Perhaps he felt that when a Hungarian uses a knife, a trifling error in the matter of direction is pardonable.

"I shall not go home now," said Steingall, bidding farewell to his allies when Martiny had been formally identified and charged. "I must get this thing thoroughly straightened out before morning, though the inquest and police court proceedings will be mere adjournments. Good-night, Mr. Devar. Good-night, Mr. Curtis. Once more, thank you. And, by the way, if all is not well at the Plaza, 'phone me at once. Remember, won't you? Good-night!"

CHAPTER XV

WHEREIN THE PACE SLACKENS—BUT ONLY FOR A FEW HOURS

"Say, old man," muttered Devar, gazing fixedly at Brodie's broad shoulders as Broadway unrolled its even width before the car on the uptown journey, "are we the same couple of blighters who met in a bathroom gangway, 'B' Deck, near staterooms 51 and 52, on board the Cunard steamship *Lusitania*, about twenty-one hours since; or have we become dematerialized?"

Curtis knew that the boy was quivering with excitement, but it was useless to advise a slackening of the tension, so he merely said:

"Do you feel like a Mahatma?"

"If a Mahatma is a fellow with a head like a balloon, not in size, but in contents, yes. Have you ever had a real jag on you, not the big dinner, big bottle, big cigar sort of imitation, but the wild-eyed, imp-seeing, genuine rip-snorter?"

"No. Neither have you."

"I should have denied the charge before to-night. But I know now what it means. It is a brain-storm induced by rum. There are many other varieties, at least fifty-seven, and I've sampled fifty-six different sorts in nine hours. Do you realize that it is just nine hours since I walked into the Central Hotel, and the orchestra struck up? Good Lord! Nine hours! And do you remember, Curtis, I said as we came up the harbor that you would have a hell of a good time in New York? Ha, ha! likewise ho, ho! A good time! Eating, fighting, marrying, plunging neck and crop out of one frantic revel into another. Talk about delirium tremens, and its little green devils with little pink eyes—why, it's commonplace, that's what it is—a poor sort of pipe-dream compared with the reality of life in New York as seen in company with John Delancy Curtis, of Pekin."

Devar was not by any means the first person in the city who had associated the name of the capital of China with some bizarre and elusive element of fantasy in connection with the man who gave "Pekin" as his address. There was no explaining the conceit; it was just one of those whimsies which are alike plausible yet enigmatical. Had Curtis described himself as being of London, or Paris, or even of Yokohama, no sense of mystery would have attached itself to his personality. But, to the world at large, Pekin represents the unknown, and therefore the incongruous. It is the Forbidden City, the inner shrine of the East, the symbolic rallying-point of a race which occupies no common ground with the peoples of Europe or America. Had Curtis written that he hailed from Lhassa, his legal domicile would have lost its occult extravagance save to the discriminating few.

The mere mention of Pekin now brought back to Curtis's mind the last time he had written the word, and, by association of ideas, the queer way in which Steingall had twice alluded to the Plaza Hotel. He said nothing of this to Devar. He thought, and with good reason, that the sooner that young man was in bed and asleep the better it would be for his health, because a mercurial temperament was levying heavy draughts on physical powers, so he gave no hint of the nebulous doubt induced by the detective's words.

"The order of the day is bed for each of us," he said, bidding his friend farewell at the door of the hotel. "Therefore, I shall not offer you any sort of hospitality at this hour, except the kindest one of saying good-by speedily. You are coming to lunch, I think?"

"Lunch!" Devar's head wagged solemnly. Feverishly wakeful, he was really half asleep. "Don't talk to me of lunch. You haven't had breakfast yet, John D. New York will keep you busy yet awhile, or I don't size her up right.... Good old New York! Isn't she a peach? Well, so long! If you want me, 'phone. I'll pull a couch under the instrument and sleep with my clothes on. If I shove my head beneath a tap I'll be as right as rain. Home, Arthur."

Then Curtis entered the hotel, and a night-porter took him up in the elevator. When he opened the door of Suite F. its tiny lobby was in darkness, but the lights in the sitting-room were switched on. Evidently, then, neither he nor Devar was mistaken in identifying those illuminated windows when the chase led them past the hotel. But he was struck instantly by the fact that the door leading to Hermione's room was wide open, and, before he could assimilate this singular fact, he saw a note lying on a small table just where it must catch his eye on entering his own bedroom.

Curtis was no soothsayer, but he was endowed with a penetrating and usually accurate judgment, and he knew at once that Hermione had left him. Although he had only seen her handwriting when she signed the register at the clergyman's house he recognized the same free, well-formed characters in the "John Delancy Curtis, Esq." on the envelope. He paled, perhaps, and a pang of a pain crueller than bodily ill may have wrung his heart, but he hesitated not a second about opening the letter.

Then he read:

> "DEAR MR. CURTIS:—My father has been here, and with him a Mr. Otto Schmidt, a lawyer. They told me that Jean de Courtois is alive, and that you know it, and have known it throughout. Gladly would I have refused to believe them, but, sometimes, there are statements which cannot be lies—which partake of truth in their very essence—which sear their way into one's consciousness as white-hot iron scorches the flesh. Still, owing to my trust in you, I clung to the frail hope that there might be some mistake, so, when they had gone, I telephoned the Central Hotel, and a clerk there assured me that Monsieur de Courtois was in bed and asleep.

> "What am I to say? Perhaps, silence is best. Marcelle and I are returning to my apartments in 59th Street. Please do not come there. I feel now that I have been selfish and misguided. I fear it will hurt you if I ask to be permitted to bear the heavy expense you must incur with regard to the wretched affair

into which I have dragged you, though involuntarily, or, shall I put it? with the blind striving for succor of one sinking in deep waters. Yet, do me one last kindness, and let me reimburse you. That would be a small concession to my pride, because, in some respects, sorely as I am wounded, I shall regard myself as ever in your debt.

"Sincerely yours,
HERMIONE.

"P.S. This person, Schmidt, seems to be reliable. You might arrange matters with him."

Now, above and beyond every other characteristic, Curtis was fair-minded. He read the girl's letter once in order to learn what had happened and why she had gone: then he reread it critically, word for word, trying to distil from its disjointed phrases "that essence of truth" which Hermione had spoken of. Evidently, she had determined to keep her words within the bare walls of necessity. The note had a jerkiness of style that was certainly absent from her speech, and the fact argued that she was compelling herself to write with restraint. She was brimming over with reproach, grief-stricken, and miserable, and unquestionably shocked beyond measure, but she had forced the reflection: "I have no real claim on this man, nor wrong to lay at his door, and, although he has deceived me, I am under heavy obligation to him, so I must neither condemn nor reproach, but say nothing that goes beyond a temperate explanation of my action."

The signature itself was eloquent of the conflict which raged in her troubled brain while the pen was framing those formal sentences. Well-bred young ladies do not sign themselves by their Christian names, *tout court*, in notes written to young gentlemen of an evening's acquaintance. Yet, what was she to do? "Hermione Beauregard Grandison" had gone beyond recovery with the marriage ceremony, but "Hermione Curtis" was almost ludicrous, considering the text of this, the first note she had written to her "husband."

It was only one side of Curtis's self-reliant nature which analyzed, and criticised, and weighed matters with such judicial calm. There was another which brought a hard glint into his eyes, and caused a hand which gripped the molded back of a lightly-built chair to exert a force of which he was unconscious until the mahogany rail snapped.

Then he remembered Steingall, and his enigmatical inquiries, and turned to the telephone.

At sound of his voice, the detective cleared away any doubt as to the reason which inspired those vague questions.

"Lady Hermione has gone, has she?" he said sympathetically. "I thought as much. There was no use in worrying you about it sooner, but I was told that the Earl and Schmidt had visited her, and that she and the maid had left the hotel in a taxi a few minutes after the departure of the visitors. Will you take my advice?"

"What is it?"

"You ought to have said 'Yes' at once. Go to bed, and force yourself to sleep. Give no instructions to be called, but get up when you waken, and start a new day with a clear head. You'll need it."

"I'm not going to disturb the peace of Lady Hermione's apartments in 59th Street, if that is what you mean."

"Not quite. In fact, not at all. You are not that kind of a man. Did she leave any message?"

"Yes, a letter. Would you care to hear it?"

"If you have no objection."

Curtis read the note instantly, and, so delicate is the perceptiveness of the ear, he could almost follow the trend of the detective's unspoken thought by a hiss of breath or a muttered "Hum," as a name was mentioned or a reason given for some particular action.

"Like the majority of women, she conveys the most important fact in a postscript," was Steingall's dry comment when Curtis had reached the end.

"Where shall I find this man, Schmidt?" inquired Curtis.

"Are you in a hurry, then, to begin the suit for dissolution?"

"That does not account for my anxiety to meet Schmidt."

"He is a stoutly-built individual, with a large, soft neck, and eyes which would protrude most satisfactorily under pressure. Is that what you mean?"

"I want to make his acquaintance, and soon—that is all."

"Now, Mr. Curtis, don't destroy the good opinion I have formed of you. Let well enough alone. Schmidt has done you a splendid turn, and it would be foolish on your part to requite a benefactor by trying to strangle him."

"Mr. Steingall, I am tired, and very, very uncertain of myself——"

"So you don't want even to pretend that there is any humor in the situation. Yet, unless I err greatly, before many hours have passed you will agree with me that nothing more directly fortunate in your behalf could have occurred than Schmidt's interference as Lord Valletort's legal adviser. I know Schmidt, and Schmidt knows me. In this affair you would be a baby in his hands, just as he would resemble a bladder of lard in yours. My difficulty is that I really cannot give reasons, but you will appreciate the position when I say that, for the moment, the murder of Mr. Hunter has become an affair of state, and all information regarding recent developments will be withheld from the press. Do you follow?"

"Yes."

"I take it, too, that if Lady Hermione were restored to you, and it was left to the pair of you to determine whether or not the marriage entered into under such extraordinary conditions should become a real union, you would be satisfied?"

"I don't see how — —"

"You can at least take my word for it, Mr. Curtis, that the chance of such an outcome will be greatly forwarded if you go straight to bed, whereas any design you may have formed as to assaulting and battering Otto Schmidt would, if put into execution, probably defeat the more important object, or, at any rate, cripple its prospects of success."

"Do you really mean that?"

"I am almost sure of it. There is only one thing of which I am more certain at the moment."

"And that is?"

"That if it were not for your quickness of eye and hand — and foot, for that matter — I would now be laid out in a mortuary or on an hospital table. I appreciate those qualities when exercised on a person like Martiny, whose main argument is centered in an automatic pistol, but they would be singularly out of place if tested on Otto Schmidt, when backed by the laws of the United States, which, strange as it may seem, I also represent."

"If you put it that way, Steingall — —"

"I do, most emphatically. Let me be more precise. Promise me now that you will not stir out of the Plaza Hotel until I come to you."

"Is that really essential?"

"I would not ask you if it were not."

"What time may I expect you?"

"Let me see.... It is now nearly five o'clock. I hope to sleep till eight. I give you till nine. Bath and breakfast brings you to ten. Say eleven."

"I owe you a good deal, so I shall await you till noon. After that hour I reserve my freedom of action."

The detective laughed.

"Good-by," he said, and, as though in keeping with the other fantasies of the night, Curtis was sound asleep in quarter of an hour. He had acquired the faculty of sleeping under any conditions of mental or physical stress, short of illness or severe bodily pain, and he could awake at any hour previously determined on, so, a few minutes before nine o'clock he was in his bath. At a quarter-past nine he rang for a waiter and ordered breakfast.

"For one, sir?" said the man, who had not been on duty the previous evening, but had taken care to ascertain the names of the guests on his section of the floor.

"Yes, for one," said Curtis. "My wife and her maid are not breakfasting in the hotel. Will you kindly send up a batch of morning newspapers?"

It was only to be expected that the keen and bright intelligence of New York journalism should have fastened on to the murder in 27th Street as something out of the ordinary. But its methods were new to the man whose adult years had been passed far from his native city, and he was astounded now to find how the descriptive reporter, aided by the photographer, had depicted and dissected nearly every feature of the crime. On one point the press was silent—as yet. There was no mention of Lady Hermione, and, with a reticence which spoke volumes for the close relations existing between police and reporters, the Earl of Valletort and Count Vassilan were represented as merely "enquiring for" John Delancy Curtis, "the man from Pekin."

Curtis had spread the newspapers on the table, and, when a tap on the door of the sitting-room seemed to indicate the re-appearance of the waiter, he swept them up in a heap, meaning to go through them at leisure after breakfast.

"Come in," he said, turning casually.

The door opened, and Hermione entered.

It was what dramatists term "a psychological moment," and, according to Berkeley, one of the axioms of psychology is that it never transcends the limits of the individual. Most certainly, at that moment, the truth of this dictum was demonstrated in a manner which would have surprised even the doughty philosopher himself.

Curtis saw nothing, knew nothing, thought of nothing not strictly bounded by the fact that Hermione, and none other, stood there. He gazed at her spell-bound for a second or two. He neither moved nor spoke, but remained stock-still, with the newspapers gathered in his hands, while his eyes blazed into hers without any pretense of restraint.

She was rosy red, partly because of the wine-like morning air through which she had walked swiftly, but more, perhaps, because of a very real embarrassment and contriteness of spirit.

"I came," she faltered—"I am here—that is—will you ever forgive me!——"

Down went the papers, and round Hermione went Curtis's strong arms. He was a man of thew and sinew, against whom a slender girl's strength might not hope to prevail. The last thing she looked for was to be embraced at sight. It is the last thing any woman expects, and the one thing to which she is most apt to yield. And really, despite her fluttered cry of protest, there was something very comforting and dependable about that masculine hug. Hermione had never before been clasped in a man's arms. She was a highly kissable person, and women would embrace her readily, but the total absence of any milk-and-water convention about Curtis's method of showing delight at meeting her was at once bewildering and stupefying.

There must be a great deal, too, which does not leap promptly to the eye in the study of such a dry-as-dust subject as psychology, because three of its fixed principles are: "Experience is the process of becoming expert by experiment," "One finds a measure of truth in the naïve realism of Common Sense;" and "Action and Reaction are strictly correlative."

Applying these tests to the remarkable rapidity of decision and fixity of purpose displayed by Curtis in squeezing the breath out of Hermione, and gazing into her eyes until her proud head bent and sought refuge for a glowing face by hiding it on his breast, it will be noted first, that, for a man who had no experience in love-making, Curtis was quickly becoming expert; secondly, that Common Sense teaches that if one would win a wife one must also woo her; and thirdly, that a wonderfully effective way to obtain a satisfactory response from Hermione was to reveal the educational value of a hug.

At last, then—though not before Hermione's arms had gone around his neck of their own accord, and her lips had met his with a sigh of sheer content—he permitted her to speak. And of all things in the world she said that which it thrilled him to hear.

"John, dear," she murmured, "we have become husband and wife in a strange, mad way, but, perhaps it is for the best, and I shall try never to give you cause for regret."

By this time one hand was firmly braced around her waist, but the other was free to lift her chin until her swimming eyes met his.

"Hermione," he said, "I vowed last night that not all the men and laws in America would tear you from me. If we parted, it was you, and you alone, who could send me away, and I am glad, oh, so glad, that you have come back to me."

"Dearest, it sounds like a dream," she said brokenly. "Can a man and a woman truly love each other who have only met as you and I have met?"

"I think we have solved that problem for all time," he said, tilting her hat with the joyous abandon of a lover jealous even of the flowers and plaited straw which should hide any of the sweet perfections of his mistress.

"But you have plunged me into a sort of trance," she whispered. "I came here to explain——"

An ominous rattle of a laden tray at the outer door drove them apart as though a thunderbolt had fallen between them. Hermione rushed to her own room, there to consult a mirror, and readjust her hat and veil and disordered hair, but Curtis met a hurrying waiter.

"Sorry to bother you," he said, "but my wife has come in unexpectedly, and we shall want breakfast for two." He raised his voice:

"Coffee for you, Hermione, or would you prefer tea?"

"Coffee, of course," was the answer, in so calm and collected a tone that the waiter thought he must have been mistaken in his first impression.

"No trouble at all, sir," he said, with the ready civility of his class. "Unless you wish to wait, sir, I'll bring another cup and some hot plates, and order a further supply from the kitchen."

"You're a man of resource," cried Curtis cheerfully. "I leave the arrangements to you with confidence…. Come along, Hermione. Don't say you have breakfasted already."

"I won't, because I haven't," she said, reappearing with a smiling nonchalance which removed the last shred of doubt from the waiter's mind. But, for all that, she electrified Curtis with a timidly grateful glance, for she appreciated his thoughtfulness in giving her an opportunity to collect her scattered wits. There was need of some such respite; she had much to relate, she thought, before he could possibly understand the motives which led to her flight.

Barely half an hour ago Mr. Steingall had put in an appearance at her apartment. He had told her, with convincing brevity, exactly why Curtis refrained from adding to her perplexities by announcing the comparative well-being of Jean de Courtois.

"He was very kind," said Hermione, sweetly penitent, "but he made me feel rather like a worm when he said that if I were his own daughter he would thank God that I had fallen into the hands of a man like you. He said, too, that if I owed you something, he owed you more, because you had saved his life last night, so, being an impulsive creature, I hurried here to ask your forgiveness for that horrid note."

"There is no lie so difficult to combat as a half truth," said John. "That fellow, Schmidt, impressed you because he probably believed what he was saying. As for Steingall, he makes rather too much of what I did for him, but, if there was any debt on his side, he has repaid me with ample interest."

The waiter had left the room, and Hermione was free to blush without restraint, a privilege she availed herself of fully now.

"But, dear, you and I can hardly feel that we are really married," she said. "Yesterday—it was—different. I cannot remain here now. Perhaps your uncle and aunt will receive me—until——"

"It is surprising how easily one can get married if one is really bent on the act," said Curtis, discussing the point as coolly as if it were a question as to where they would lunch. "At any rate, we shall settle that difficulty to your complete satisfaction. I expect Steingall here in less than an hour. Meanwhile, we have lots to tell each other. I want you to know just what sort of husband you have drawn in the lottery."

"Do you take me on trust, then?"

"Absolutely without reservation."

Obviously, the conversation did not flag before the detective was announced. He looked tired and preoccupied when he came in, but his shrewd, pleasant face brightened with a cheery smile when he saw Hermione, who was pretending to be interested in a newspaper.

"I am glad to find that two people, at least, have taken my advice," he said. "Now, Mr. Curtis, I want you for an hour. The various official inquiries are adjourned till next week, and your presence was dispensed with. But we are going now to the office of Mr. Otto Schmidt, where we shall have the pleasure of meeting the Earl of Valletort, Count Ladislas Vassilan, and, possibly, Monsieur Jean de Courtois.... On no account, young lady," and he turned to Hermione, "must you run away again during our absence."

"I shall not," said Hermione, so emphatically that they all laughed.

CHAPTER XVI

A PARLEY

Nature was kind that morning. A flood of sunshine greeted Curtis when he turned into Fifth Avenue with the detective, as the latter had suggested that they might walk a little way before taking a taxi, there being plenty of time before the hour fixed for the meeting in Schmidt's office. It was a morning when life and good health assumed their fitting places in the forefront of those many and varied considerations which form the sum of human happiness. The world had suddenly resumed its everyday aspect of bustle and content. New York smiled at its new citizen, and the new citizen beamed appreciatively on New York.

"I cannot explain matters to you fully even yet— —" Steingall was saying, when an automobile drew up close to the curb, and a well-known voice cried joyously:

"Just in time. Where's the fire? There's bound to be a blaze when you two run in a leash."

Devar bounced out of the car, and Brodie grinned with pleasure. The chauffeur was beginning to like the excitement of acting as supernumerary on the staff of the Detective Bureau.

"Will you jump in, or shall I prowl with you down Fifth Avenue?" asked Devar, blithely ignoring Steingall's somewhat strained welcome.

"We are keeping an appointment," said Curtis. "I, for one, shall be more than pleased if the combination which proved so effective last night may remain intact this morning."

"Steingall daren't cut adrift from me," said Devar. "If you knew the truth about him, you'd find that he is deeply superstitious, and I'm a real mascot for bringing good luck. Perhaps he is not aware, John D., that I was the impresario who 'presented' you to an admiring public. Tell him that, and see if he has the nerve to say I'm not wanted."

"Come along, Mr. Devar," said the detective, apparently yielding to a sudden resolve. "I think I can make use of you—justify your presence, that is. Tell your chauffeur to wait for us at 42d Street."

Off went Brodie, jubilant at the prospect of his services being in requisition again. He had not yet learnt the application to all things mundane of Disraeli's quip that it is the unexpected which happens.

"Now, I want you two gentlemen to attend closely to what I have to say," said Steingall seriously, placing himself between them, so that his words might not reach other ears than those for which they were intended. "Mr. Hunter's murder has passed long ago out of the common class of crimes. It will be inquired into thoroughly, of course, and punishment will be dealt out impartially to those responsible for its commission. But—and this is the point I want to emphasize—neither of you know, nor am I at liberty to inform you— just what bounds the authorities may reach, or stop at. Have I made my meaning clear?"

"Yes," said Curtis.

"We're to be good little boys, and sit still, and say nothing, and do as we're told," said Devar.

"I'm not asking impossibilities," said Steingall, who had a dry humor, and seldom missed a chance of gratifying it. "I have merely laid down a proviso which must be observed, not for a day, or a week, but as long as any of us is alive. State affairs are not the property of individuals. They come first, all the time. If they don't suit our convenience, we must simply adjust ourselves to the new conditions."

"You alarm me, Steingall," cried Devar. "Have we been drawn into an international squabble? Don't tell me that Devar's canned salmon is really a deadly sort of bomb."

"I've heard more improbable things. But you would not be your father's son, Mr. Devar, if you can't keep a tight lip when statements are made in your presence which may astonish you. Mr. Curtis and you are now about to meet a very clever man, Otto Schmidt, the lawyer, and I fancy your name will help in the argument. Is your father in New York?"

"He arrives here from Chicago to-night."

"He has never met Mr. Curtis?"

"No, but he jolly soon will."

"But, if it were possible to get hold of him by telephone or telegraph to-day, he would say he had never heard of him?"

"I guess that's so. What are you driving at?"

"Schmidt must know your father. They are bound to have come together in more than one important deal."

"Well?"

"It seems to me that, if the father's evidence is not available, the son's gains a trifle more weight."

"Dash me if I can imagine where you are getting off at, Steingall."

"You regard Mr. Curtis as a friend?"

"I am proud of the fact."

"Stick to that, and you will do him good service."

"Well, that's easy."

The detective seemed to be picking his words with a good deal of care. He covered several paces in silence, and Curtis, who had reverted to his normal habit of sober gravity, took no part in the conversation. His estimate of its purport differed from Devar's. That light-hearted youngster was somewhat annoyed by the detective's implied hint that his friendship with Curtis rested on no more solid foundation than a steamer acquaintance, and would hardly bear the test of close scrutiny if it came to analysis on the score of prior knowledge, or if his testimony were sought as to Curtis's earlier career. But he had the good sense to understand that Steingall was actuated by no light motive, so he held his peace. Curtis went farther. He believed that the detective was telling Devar what to say and how to say it.

"Now that we have settled the matter of Mr. Curtis's references," said Steingall, resuming the talk as though it had not been interrupted, "I reach the next item. Both of you are aware that two men have been arrested, and one is dead, and that all three were concerned in the attack on Mr. Hunter."

"Yes," came the simultaneous answer.

"I want you to forget names, except with regard to Lamotte, the chauffeur. Martiny and Rossi, for the time being, vanish into the Ewigkeit."

"What—forever?" Curtis could not help saying.

"No, for a week or so." Steingall darted a quick glance to his questioner. "I have a stupid trick of adopting phrases from my pet authors," he said. "Does Ewigkeit mean eternity?"

"Yes."

"Well, then, I withdraw it."

"Try Niflheim."

"Or Rüdesheim," suggested Devar wickedly.

Steingall laughed. Despite his German-sounding name, he spoke French fluently, but German not at all.

"They're off the map," he said. "There, that's good American, and I'll get on with my story, or rather, with the lack of it. I cannot, of course, foretell the exact lines our discussion with Schmidt and his clients will follow, but if I have made you understand that your combined share in it is to say little, and be thoroughly non-committal in anything you may have to say, I am content."

"You are as mysterious as an astrologer," vowed Devar. "Having money to burn one day in Paris, I visited one of those jokers, and he told me I was born in Capricorn, under the sign of Aries, and I as good as told him he was a liar, because I was born in Manhattan under an ordinary roof. By Jove! that reminds me, John D., you're a whale on stars. Did you spot those two last night, low down in the west?"

"Yes."

"And what did they prognosticate?"

"That you and I would promise Mr. Steingall not to spoil any scheme he may have in mind by interfering at an inopportune moment."

"I suppose I ought to feel crushed, but I don't," said Devar.

"My dear fellow, if it hadn't been for you and your loyal championship at the right moment, I might easily have been in jail as an accomplice of the unknown scoundrels who killed Mr. Hunter."

"That's the right kind of remark," broke in the detective. "I think I'll offer each of you a post in the Bureau after this business is ended."

"Give me a pointer on one matter," said Devar. "You spoke of Schmidt's clients. Who are they?"

He whistled softly when he heard the names of Valletort and Vassilan and de Courtois.

"Up to the neck in it again!" he crowed. "Oh, it's me that is the happy youth because I blew in to New York at the right time yesterday."

Otto Schmidt's office was in Madison Square, perched high above the clatter of 23d Street. The windows of the lawyer's private sanctum commanded magnificent views of the city to south and west, and in that marvelously clear air the Statue of Liberty seemed to be little more than a mile away, while the villas of Montclair and houses on other heights in the neighboring State were distinctly visible.

Steingall and his friends were the first to arrive, and Schmidt received them with the air of armed neutrality a lawyer displays towards the opposite camp. He begged them to be seated, smiled pleasantly when Curtis asked to be allowed to admire the interesting panorama spread before his eyes, but gave Devar a contemplative look when Steingall introduced him.

"Mr. Howard Devar, son of my friend William B. Devar?" he asked.

"Yes," said Devar, feeling that this was safe ground. "My father and you put it that way since you pulled off the Saskatchewan Combine together, but I've heard him describe you differently."

Schmidt, who looked more egg-like than ever at this hour of the morning, disapproved of such flippancy.

"William B. Devar is a fair fighter," he said. "He gives and takes hard knocks with perfect good humor. But, may I inquire how you come to figure in a matter which, if I understand aright a message received from Mr. Steingall, concerns persons with whom you can have little in common?"

"It was a mere toss-up whether I or my friend, John Delancy Curtis, took the floor against the combination of noble lords who have retained you to look after their interests, or protect them, I ought to say; but fate favored him, so I am a mere bottle-holder. To push the simile a bit farther, Mr. Schmidt, I may describe Mr. Steingall as the referee and watch-holder. When he cries 'Time' someone will go to Sing-Sing."

Perhaps some attribute of the father revealed itself in the son, because Steingall, who thought at first that Devar had allowed his tongue to run away with him, fancied that the lawyer dropped his inquiries somewhat suddenly.

"The Earl of Valletort and Count Vassilan are due now," he said, glancing at a clock.

"Oh, they will be here without fail," said the detective. "Mr. Clancy, of the Bureau, is bringing de Courtois."

"Bringing him?" repeated Schmidt.

"Yes."

"Unofficially?"

"That depends wholly on de Courtois. He has to come, whether he likes it or not. Whether he will be allowed to go away again is another matter."

Schmidt's eyelids fell in thought. Probably he reflected that there are two sides to every argument, and he had heard but one. Certainly, John Delancy Curtis did not strike him as the dare-devil meddler, if not worse, he had been depicted by the fiery Earl.

"The Earl of Valletort and Count Ladislas Vassilan," announced a clerk, and Curtis took one square look at his rival. He needed no more to confirm Hermione's unfavorable opinion. The Count's appearance was not prepossessing. His nose was still swollen, and the earnest effort of a doctor to paint out two black eyes had not been wholly successful.

His lordship looked mightily displeased when he discovered the presence of Curtis and Devar, but he was a self-confident man, and regarded himself as a personage of such importance that he assumed the lead in this company at once. Moreover, it was evident that he had resolved to keep a firm rein on his temper.

"Now, Mr. Schmidt," he said brusquely, "your time and mine is valuable. Why have Count Vassilan and I been summoned here this morning by the police authorities?"

Schmidt looked at Steingall, and the detective seemed to be almost at a loss for words.

"I am—not aware—there is any particular call—for hurry," he said. "Are you, my lord, and Count Vassilan thinking of returning to Europe to-morrow?"

The Hungarian laughed, not mirthfully, but with the forced gayety of a man who had considered how to act, and meant to adopt a decided attitude.

"Certainly not," said the Earl stiffly, with uplifted eyebrows.

Steingall pursed his lips, and his forehead seamed in a reflective frown.

"I ought to explain," he said, "that I put that question as offering what appeared to me an easy way out of a situation which bristles with difficulties otherwise."

His hesitancy had suddenly been replaced by slowness of utterance, but it is reasonable to suppose that, of those present, Curtis and Schmidt alone noted the marked distinction.

"My good man," said the Earl, "you must have the strangest notion of the reason which accounts for my presence in New York. I came here to rescue my daughter from a set of designing ruffians, some of whom I knew of, and others whom I had never heard of. Why you should think that I may have it in mind to leave the country without being accompanied by Lady Hermione Grandison I cannot tell, and it is in the highest degree improbable that she will be prepared to sail to-morrow. Apart from my private arrangements, too, I mean to remain here until I have punished at least one person as he deserves."

"Jean de Courtois?" inquired Steingall.

"No, sir. That man who stands there, and whose name is given as Curtis."

The Earl nearly grew wrathful. It annoyed him to find that Curtis was not looking at him at all, but was greatly interested in Schmidt. That was another trait of Curtis's. He had learnt long ago to select the ablest among his adversaries, and watch that man's face. Mere impassivity supplied no real cloak, for Curtis, in his time, had dealt with Chinese mandarins whose countenances betrayed no more expression than a carved ivory mask.

"But it was de Courtois who meant to marry Lady Hermione?" persisted Steingall.

"That remains to be seen. The person who did marry her signed himself John Delancy Curtis."

Instantly the detective turned to Otto Schmidt.

"It will assist the inquiry if you tell us whether or not such a marriage, if it took place under the assumed conditions, that is, by use of a marriage license not intended for one of the parties, is legal," he said.

248

"I have no doubt whatever that, in the circumstances, the courts will find it to be illegal," was the answer.

"What circumstances?"

"That the lady quitted her supposed husband as soon as she discovered the fraud which had been practised on her."

Steingall weighed the point for a moment.

"I see," he nodded. "If she refused to remain with him, the marriage would be declared void. But if she elected to treat the marriage as a binding act, no matter how it was procured, and continued to live with her husband, that vital fact would affect the question of validity?"

"As you say, it would be a vital fact."

The detective was clearly impressed, but Lord Valletort swept aside these quibbles of jurisprudence.

"My daughter's actions will be revealed in detail to a judge," he said loftily. "At present I fail to see what bearing they have on the discussion, unless, indeed, you mean to arrest Curtis immediately on a charge which I am prepared to formulate."

"No, that is not why I requested your lordship and Count Vassilan to come here this morning," said Steingall, gazing anxiously at the clock. "I would prefer to await the arrival of Detective Clancy with Jean de Courtois, but, if the Frenchman refuses to come, he is within his rights, and I suppose I shall have to apply for a warrant, though, if I choose, I can arrest him merely on suspicion."

"Suspicion of what?" demanded the Earl.

"Of complicity in the murder of Mr. Hunter last night."

"The man was tied in his room at the time of the murder," cried the Hungarian hoarsely, speaking for the first time since he had entered Schmidt's office. He was obviously excited, and excitement is a powerful foe of good resolutions, with which the moral pavement is littered in Hungary and elsewhere.

"That does not affect the charge of complicity," said Steingall thoughtfully. "A man may be an accomplice, though the actual crime is committed at a time and place when he is far distant. It is possible for an accomplice to be in Paris, or on the high seas, while a victim is falling under an assassin's knife in New York. A man, or a number of men, can even be what I may term unconscious accomplices, in the sense that their actions and instructions have brought about a crime, though their intent may have stopped short of actual violence. I assure you, my lord, the arm of the law reaches far when life is taken, and the death of a popular and prominent journalist like Mr. Hunter will be inquired into most searchingly."

The detective spoke so impressively that Lord Valletort eyed him with a species of misgiving, while Count Vassilan, whose knowledge of English was excellent, had broken out into a perspiration.

A smooth, mellifluous voice suddenly intervened. Otto Schmidt thought fit to assume a role for which Lord Valletort was manifestly ill equipped.

"We seem to be dealing with two items which, though related, by accident, as it were, yet differ widely. The Earl of Valletort is interested only in his daughter's marriage, Mr. Steingall."

The detective wheeled round on him.

"Precisely, Mr. Schmidt, but it happens, unfortunately, that the marriage of Lady Hermione and Mr. Curtis was the direct outcome of the murder of Mr. Hunter. More than that, Mr. Hunter met his death because of the plot and counter-plot attending the preliminary arrangements for her ladyship's marriage. The two events, so far apart in their nature, thus become indissolubly connected."

"And is that why we are to have the pleasure of seeing Monsieur de Courtois?"

"Yes."

"Perhaps, before he comes, you will be good enough to give us some idea, informally of course, as to the statement,—or, shall I say revelation?—he may make."

"It is asking a good deal of a police official," said Steingall, smiling pleasantly, "but if I am assured that the discussion will really be regarded as informal, I am ready to speak quite openly."

"It is a characteristic of yours, Mr. Steingall, which has often commanded the admiration of the New York bar," said Schmidt.

"Then," said the detective, "I must begin by telling you that Mr. Clancy and I were in Morris Siegelman's saloon in East Broadway shortly after midnight last night."

A curious click issued from the throat of that distinguished Hungarian magnate, Count Ladislas Vassilan, and everyone present noticed it except the chief of the Detective Bureau. He, it would appear, was busy marshaling his thoughts.

"For all practical purposes, our inquiry began there," he continued. "We intercepted a note written by a certain gentleman, and intended to be conveyed to a Pole named Peter Balusky. He, and a Hungarian, Franz Viviadi, together with a French chauffeur, whose real name is Lamotte, but who has been passing recently as Anatole Labergerie, are now under arrest. Mr. Curtis has recognized Lamotte as the driver of the automobile out of which Mr. Hunter stepped to meet his death, and Lamotte himself has confessed his share in the crime. The precise connection of Balusky and Viviadi with it remains yet to be determined. They undoubtedly visited the Central Hotel last night. They undoubtedly were the paid agents of some person or persons interested in preventing the marriage of Lady Hermione Grandison. They undoubtedly received letters and wireless messages which seem to implicate others, far removed from them in social position, in the plot, or undertaking, that her ladyship's marriage should not take place. As a lawyer, Mr. Schmidt, you will see that I cannot possibly enter into full details, but I think I have said sufficient to prove my main contention, which is, you will remember, that it will be difficult, very difficult, to dissociate the two incidents—I mean the marriage and the murder."

During quite an appreciable time there was no sound in the spacious apartment other than the heavy breathing of Count Ladislas Vassilan. He had openly and candidly abandoned all pretense. He was now nothing more nor less than a burly, well-fed, well-dressed evil-doer quaking with fear.

"Difficult, you say, Mr. Steingall?" repeated the lawyer, selecting, as was his way, the word which supplied the key to a whole sentence.

"Very difficult," corrected the detective.

"But not impossible?"

"I would not care to hazard a reasoned opinion, but it seems to me that, in certain conditions, the District Attorney might elect to confine the inquiry to its main issues, which are, of course, the causes of the crime, and the conviction of the persons actually engaged in it."

"Why did you want to bring Jean de Courtois here?"

"Because he is the connecting link between the one set of circumstances and the other."

"Is he coming, do you think?"

Steingall looked at the clock, and showed a disappointment which he did not try to conceal.

"I fear not," he said. "I told Clancy only to try and persuade him to come. The Frenchman is pretending to be ill, but he is not ill, only frightened."

"Frightened of what?"

"Of the consequences of his own acts. In a sense, Mr. Hunter was his ally, but only from a journalist's standpoint, which centered in the sensation which would be provided by the projected marriage."

Schmidt's eyelids had fallen and risen regularly during the past few minutes. They dropped now for a longer period than usual. As for Lord Valletort and his would-be son-in-law, they were profoundly and unfeignedly ill at ease. Even a British Earl cannot afford to play fast and loose with the law, and it did seem most convincingly clear that they had brought themselves within measurable reach of the law by the tactics they had employed prior to their arrival in New York.

Oddly enough, their own possible connection with the murder of the journalist was a good deal more patent to them than to Curtis and Devar, who were vastly better posted in the evidence affecting them. Still more curiously, not a word had been said about Martiny or Rossi.

"Let us suppose," said Schmidt, when his eyes had opened again, "that Lady Hermione elects to return to Europe at once with her father, the Earl——"

Steingall shook his head with a weary smile, and the lawyer's voice ceased suddenly.

"Out of the question, Mr. Schmidt, out of the question. I am sure of it. Why, little more than half an hour ago I found her with Mr. Curtis in their apartments at the Plaza Hotel——"

"Ridiculous!" shrieked Lord Valletort in a shrill falsetto. "My daughter passed the night in her apartment in 59th Street. I myself saw her go there."

"Probably. Your lordship would know the facts if you watched her departure from the Plaza Hotel. But a woman has the inalienable privilege of changing her mind, and Lady Hermione has returned to her husband. In fact, I am given to understand that she and Mr. Curtis are arranging a new marriage, not because the earlier ceremony is illegal, or can be upset, but in deference to certain natural scruples which such a charming young lady would be bound to entertain.... There can be no manner of doubt as to the correctness of what I am saying," and the detective's tone grew emphatic in view of the Earl's pish-tush gestures. "You have a telephone there, Mr. Schmidt. Ring up the Plaza, and speak to the lady yourself."

The lawyer did nothing of the sort. He eyed Curtis in his contemplative way, being aware that the quiet man standing near a window had favored him with his exclusive attention during the proceedings.

But Lord Valletort was moved now to stormy protest. He was convulsed with passion, and seemed to be careless what the outcome might be so long as he lashed Curtis with venom.

"You are the only person in this infernal city whose actions are consistent," he roared at him. "It is quite evident that you have ascertained by some means that my daughter is exceedingly wealthy, and you have managed to delude her into the belief that your conduct is altruistic and above reproach. But you make a great mistake if you believe that I can be set aside as an incompetent fool. I shall go straight from this office to that of the District Attorney, and lay the whole of the facts before him. I——"

"Does your lordship wish to dispense with my services?" broke in Schmidt, speaking without flurry or heat. The angry Earl choked, but remained silent, and the lawyer kept on in the same even tone:

"May I suggest, Mr. Steingall, that you and Mr. Curtis and Mr. Devar should step into another room while I have a brief consultation with Lord Valletort and Count Vassilan?"

"I cannot become a party to any arrangement— —" began Steingall, but Otto Schmidt bowed him and his companions out suavely. Those two understood each other fully, no matter what divergencies of opinion might exist elsewhere.

When the door had closed on the three men in a smaller room, Devar was about to say something, but Steingall checked him with a warning hand. Walking to a window, he stood there, with his back turned on his companions, and stared out into the square beneath. Once they fancied they saw him nod his head in a species of signal, but they might have been in error. At any rate, their thoughts were soon distracted by the entrance of the stout lawyer.

"On some occasions, the fewest words are the most satisfactory," he said, "so I wish to inform you, Mr. Steingall, that Lord Valletort and Count Vassilan intend to sail for Europe by to-morrow's steamer. They have empowered me to offer to pay the passage money to France of the music-teacher, Jean de Courtois, though not by the same vessel as that in which they purpose traveling. As for you, Mr. Curtis, the Earl withdraws all threats, and leaves you to settle your dispute with the authorities as you may think fit. May I add that if you choose to consult me I shall be glad to act for you. I would not say this if it was merely a professional matter, but there are circumstances— Certainly, I shall be here at eleven o'clock on Monday. Till then, sir, I wish you good-day. Good-day, Mr. Devar. Remember me to your father. By, by, Mr. Steingall. You and I will meet at Philippi."

Once the three were in Madison Square, Devar could not be restrained.

"Steingall," he said, "if you don't tell me how you managed it, I'll sit down right here on the sidewalk and blubber like a child."

"You were present. You heard every word," said the detective blandly.

"Yes, I know you scared them stiff. But who, in Heaven's name, are Peter Balusky and Franz Viviadi? Where, did you find 'em? Did they drop from the skies, or come up from— Well, where *did* you get 'em?"

"Clancy and I bagged them quite easily after Mr. Curtis and you left Siegelman's café. All we had to do was wait till Vassilan quit. They were hanging about all the time, but afraid to meet him…. Now, you must ask me no more questions. I am going to Clancy. He is keeping an eye on Jean de Courtois."

"Did you ever intend to have the Frenchman brought to Schmidt's office?"

"Of course I did. What a question! Good-by. There's your car. I'm off," and the detective swung himself into a passing streetcar.

"Do you know," said Devar thoughtfully, "I am beginning to believe that Steingall says a lot of things he really doesn't mean. I haven't quite made up my mind yet as to whether or not he hasn't run an awful bluff on the noble lord and the most noble count. And the weird thing is that Schmidt didn't call it. Did it strike you, Curtis, that— —"

Then he looked at his friend, whose silent indifference to what he was saying could no longer pass unnoticed.

"What is it, old man?" he asked, with ready solicitude. "Are you feeling the strain, or what?"

"It is nothing," said Curtis. "A run in the car will soon clear my head. Perhaps you and I might arrange for a long week-end, far away from New York."

A second time did Devar look at his friend, but, being really a good-natured and sympathetic person, he repressed the imminent cry of amazement. Somehow, he realized the one spear-thrust which had pierced Curtis's armor. It was hateful that such a man should be told he had married Hermione for her money. It was hateful to think that this might be said of him in the years to come. It was even possible that she herself might come to believe it of him, and John Delancy Curtis's knight-errant soul shrank and cringed under the thought, even while the memory of Hermione's first kiss of love was still hot on his lips.

CHAPTER XVII

WHEREIN JOHN AND HERMIONE BECOME
ORDINARY MEMBERS OF SOCIETY

But the phase passed like a disturbing dream. Hermione herself laughed the notion to scorn: and a ready opportunity for such effective exorcism of an evil spirit was supplied by Devar's tact.

When the two young men reached the hotel Devar insisted that Curtis should take Hermione for an hour's run in the park.

"Here's the car, and it's a fine morning, and you've got the girl. What more do you want?" he cried. "If Uncle Horace and Aunt Louisa show up before your return I'll take care of 'em. Now, who helps her ladyship to put on her hat and fur coat—you or I?" That duty, however, was discharged by a smiling and voluble maid named Marcelle Leroux.

So it befell that when Brodie piloted his charges into Central Park through Scholar's Gate, Curtis behaved like a man deeply in love but gravely ill at ease, and Hermione, also in love, but afire with the divine flame of womanly faith, and therefore serenely blind to any possible obstacle which should thrust itself between her and the beloved, saw instantly that something was wrong. Curtis was just the type of man who would torture himself unnecessarily about a consideration which certainly would not have rendered his inamorata less desirable in the eyes of the average wooer. He knew that he had waited all his life to meet Hermione—to meet her, and none other—and the thought that, having found her, having snatched her, as it were, from the sacrificial altar of a false god, he should now lose her, was inflicting exquisite agony.

Happily, this girl-wife of his was adorably feminine, and she decided without inquiry that she was the cause of his melancholy.

"Tell me, John," she said suddenly. "I am brave. I can bear it."

The unexpected words stirred him from his disconsolate mood.

"Bear what, dear one?" he asked, looking at her with the wistful eyes of Tantalus gazing at the luscious fruits which the wrathful winds wafted ever from his parched lips.

"You know that you have made a mistake, and have brought me out here to—to——"

"Ah, dear Heaven!" he sighed; "if I had but the strength of will to adopt that subterfuge it might prove easier for you. But one thing I cannot do, Hermione. I refuse to set you free by means of a lie. I love you, and will love you till life itself has sped."

The trouble was not so bad, then. She nestled closer.

"What is it, John dear?" she cooed, quite confident of her ability to slay dragons so long as he talked in that strain.

He trembled a little, so overpowering was the bitter-sweet sense of her nearness.

"It is rather horrible that you and I should have to discuss dollars and cents," he said, speaking with the slow distinctness of a man pronouncing his own death-sentence, "but your father taunted me with the fact that you are very wealthy. Is that true?"

"Of course it is."

She affected to treat the matter seriously. It was rather delicious to find her lover distressing himself about money, if that was all.

"What is your income?" he demanded curtly.

"I am quite rich. I am worth about half a million dollars a year."

He groaned, and shrank away from her.

"Why did you not tell me that sooner?" he said, almost with a scowl.

"Why should I? Does it matter? Isn't it rather nice to have plenty of money?"

"Good God! It is hard to—to——" His hands covered his face in sheer agony.

"John, don't be stupid. Why alarm me in that way? Wealth doesn't bring happiness—far from it. But didn't you and I—discover each other—before—before——"

"But I know, now," he said brokenly, "and it is a mad absurdity to think that a woman of your place in the world should marry a poor engineer. Do you realize that you receive every fortnight more than I earn in twelve months? King Cophetua marrying a beggar-maid sounds excellent in romance, but who ever heard of a queen wedding a pauper?"

"You are describing yourself rather lamely, John."

"Hermione, don't drive me beyond endurance. I can't bear it, I tell you."

She caught his right hand, and imprisoned it lovingly in hers. Her left hand went around his neck, and she drew him closer.

"John," she whispered, and the fragrance of her was intoxicating, "you must not break my poor heart after taking it by storm. I want you, and shall keep you if I were ten times as rich and you were in rags. What joy has money brought hitherto in my short life? It killed my mother, and has alienated me from my father. It has driven me to the verge of a folly I now shudder at. It has caused death and suffering to men whom I have never seen. It has separated a man and a woman who love each other even as you and I love. If I were a poor girl, working for a living in office or shop, I should know what laughter meant, and cheerfulness, and the bright careless hours when the heart is light and the world goes well. You have brought these things to me, dear, and you must not take them away now. I forbid it. I deny you that wrongful act with my very soul.... John, do you wish to see me in tears on this—our first day—together?"

Brodie summed up the remainder of the situation with unconscious accuracy in a subsequent disquisition delivered to an admiring circle in the servants' hall at Mrs. Morgan Apjohn's house.

"Spooning is a right and proper thing in the right and proper place," he said, "but Central Park on a fine morning is not the locality. I was jogging along comfortably when I saw some guys in Columbus Plaza rubbering around at the car, and grinning like clowns at a circus, so I just opened up the engine a bit, and let her rip, except when a mounted cop cocked his eye at me. But, bless you, them two inside didn't care if it snowed. When I brought 'em back to the hotel, Mr. Curtis sez to me: 'We've enjoyed that ride thoroughly, Brodie, but I had a notion that Central Park was larger.' Dash me, I took 'em over nine miles of roadway, and they thought I had gone in at 59th Street and come out at Eighth Avenue."

Devar, too, appreciated the success of his maneuver when he saw Hermione's sparkling eyes and Curtis's complacent air.

"Have you got a sister, Lady Hermione?" he asked *à propos* to nothing which she or any other person had said.

"No," she answered, without the semblance of a blush.

"I was only wondering," he said. "If you had, you might have cabled for her. I'd just love to take her round the Park in that car."

But the rest of that day, not to mention many successive days, was devoted to other matters than love-making. Shoals of interviewers descended on Curtis and Hermione, on Devar, on Uncle Horace and Aunt Louisa, on Brodie, even on Mrs. Morgan Apjohn when it was discovered that she came to lunch, and on "Vancouver" Devar when he arrived at the Central Station that evening. Steingall's orders were imperative, however. Not a syllable was to be uttered about the one topic concerning which the press was hungering for information, because the shooting affray in Market Street had now become known, and the gray car had been dragged out of the Hudson, and the reporters were agog for the news which was withheld at headquarters. It was then that the magic word, *sub judice*, proved very useful. Even in outspoken America, witnesses do not retail their evidence to all and sundry when men's lives are at stake, and it was quickly determined to charge all five prisoners under one and the same indictment.

Yet, for reasons never understood by the public, Balusky and Viviadi were discharged, and Jean de Courtois was deported. Martiny was sentenced to capital punishment, and Lamotte received a long term of imprisonment. But these eventualities came long after Curtis and Hermione had been remarried in strict privacy, and in the presence of a small but select circle of friends, an occasion which supplied Aunt Louisa with fresh oceans of talk for the delectation of society in Bloomington, Indiana.

At the wedding breakfast, Steingall made a speech.

"Once," he said, "when the present happy event did not seem to be quite so easy of attainment as it looks to all of us now, my friend Mr. Curtis, playing upon a weakness of mine in the matter of literary allusions, suggested that I should substitute Niflheim for Ewigkeit as a simile. I didn't know what Niflheim meant, but I have ascertained since that it is a Scandinavian word describing a region of cold and darkness, a place, therefore, where people might easily get lost. Well, it might have suited certain conditions I had then in my mind, but Mr. Curtis will never go to Scandinavian mythology when he wants to describe New York. To my thinking, it will figure in his mind as more akin to Elysium."

Clancy led the applause with sardonic appreciation, whereupon his chief allowed a severe eye to dwell on him, though his glance traveled instantly to the egg-shell dome of Otto Schmidt, whose aid had been invaluable in stilling certain qualms in the breast of authority.

"My singularly boisterous and most esteemed friend, Mr. Clancy," he continued, "seems to be delighted by the success of that trope. I might gladden your hearts with some which he has coined, because the bride and bridegroom owe more, far more, to him than they imagine at this moment. I remember——"

A loud "No, no!" from Clancy indicated that revelations were imminent.

"Well," said Steingall, "I forget just what he said on one memorable night when four semi-intoxicated stokers held up a downtown saloon, but I do wish to assure you of this—if it were not for Clancy's genius as a detective, and his splendid qualities of heart and mind as a man, this wedding might never have taken place, or, if that is putting a strain on your imagination, let me say that its principals would have encountered difficulties which are now, happily, the dim ghosts of what might have been."

Curtis took an opportunity later to ask Steingall what those cryptic words meant, and the Chief of the Bureau set at rest a doubt which had long perplexed him.

"It was Clancy who prompted the idea of mixing up the two branches of the inquiry," he said. "Under that wizened skin of his he has a heart of gold. 'Why shouldn't those two young people be made happy?' he said. 'I haven't seen the girl,' nor had he, then, 'but I like Curtis, and she won't get a better husband if she searches the island of Manhattan.' So we allowed Lord Valletort and the Count to believe that it was their set of hirelings who killed poor Hunter, whereas Balusky and Viviadi only tied up de Courtois, and were quaking with fear when they heard of the murder, because they assumed he had been killed by some other scoundrels, and that they would be held responsible. It was they who gave us the names of Rossi and Martiny as the likely pair, and the bluff I threw with Lamotte came off."

"For whom were Rossi and Martiny acting? You have never told me," said Curtis.

"Don't ask, sir. But I don't mind giving you a sort of hint. You know, better than I do probably, that Hungary is seething with revolutionary parties, which are more bitter against each other than against the common enemy, Austria. Now, two of these organizations were keen to have Count Vassilan married to Lady Hermione, one because of a patriotic desire to draw her money into the war-chest, the other because they suspected him, and rightly, as a mere tool in the hands of Austria, and they believed, again with justice I think, that when he was married it would be Paris and the gay life for him rather than a throne which might be shattered by Austrian bullets. The Earl of Valletort has degenerated into little better than a company-promoter, and he had made his own compact with Vassilan. Add to these certain facts one other—Elizabeth Zapolya, whom Lady Hermione knows, married an attaché in the Austrian Embassy in Paris last week. Tell her that. She will be interested. For the rest, you must deduce your own theories."

Curtis remained silent for a moment. Then he seized Steingall's hand and wrung it warmly.

"Hermione and I have been wondering what we can do to show our sense of gratitude to you and Mr. Clancy," he said.

"Nothing, sir," broke in the detective. "It was all in the way of business, so to speak."

"Yes, and our recognition of your services will take shape in that direction," said Curtis. "Why, man, if it were not for you I might have been charged with murder, and if it were not for Clancy and you, Hermione might now be in Paris with her good-for-nothing father.... I'll talk this over with Schmidt."

"Schmidt is a good fellow, but he doesn't know everything, even though he may be a mighty fine guesser," said Steingall.

"I'll tell him just as much as is good for any lawyer," laughed Curtis. "He is acting for my wife and myself now in the matter of providing for Hunter's relatives. We look forward to meeting Clancy and you when we return from the West."

"Is that where you are going for the honeymoon?" asked the detective, with the amiable grin which invariably accompanies the question.

"Yes. We debated the point during a whole day, but some enterprising agent settled it for us by exhibiting a catchy sign—'Why not see America?' And we both cried 'Why not?' Mr. Devar senior, who has what you call a pull in such matters, has secured us the use of a railway president's car for the trip, and a whole lot of friends join us at Chicago. Can you come, too?"

Steingall shook his head.

"No, sir," he said ruefully. "I can't get away from headquarters. I have too much on hand. As for Clancy, he'll be carried out before he quits."

So, for two people at least, a wonderful night merged into a more wonderful month, and the dawn of a new year found them on the threshold of a happy, and therefore, quite wonderful life.

THE END